A COLD BLOODED BUSINESS

In 1991 Dana Stabenow, born in Alaska and raised on a 75-foot fishing trawler, was offered a three-book deal for the first of her Kate Shugak mysteries. In 1992, the first in the series, *A Cold Day for Murder*, received an Edgar Award from the Crime Writers of America.

DANA STABENOW

THE KATE SHUGAK SERIES

DANA STABENOW

A COLD BLOODED BUSINESS

HEAD
of ZEUS

This edition first published in the UK in 2013 by Head of Zeus Ltd

9 7 5 3 1 2 4 6 8

A CIP catalogue record for this book is available from
the British Library.

ISBN (Paperback) 9781908800442

Printed and bound by CPI Group (UK) Ltd,
Croydon, CR0 4YY

Head of Zeus Ltd
Clerkenwell House
45-47 Clerkenwell Green
London EC1R 0HT

www.headofzeus.com

for Tony Kinderknecht
the last of the original Slopers
I left out the story about Milo's pigs
because no one can tell it like he can

CHAPTER 1

"HI, JOHN. HERE SHE is."

The man on the couch met Mutt's yellow eyes and his ruddy face lost color. "Jesus H. Christ on a crutch."

Jack grinned. He was a big man and it was a big grin. "Not her." He jerked his thumb over his shoulder. "Her."

Her five-foot self barely visible behind Jack's six-foot-two mass, Kate closed the door and dumped her duffel on the floor.

The man on the couch wasn't looking at anything but Mutt. "What the hell is this, that's a goddam wolf, Morgan!"

Jack gave his stock answer. "Nah. Only half. Mutt, John King." Kate stepped around Jack. "Kate Shugak, John King. John's the CEO of the Alaskan division of RPetCo, the operator for the western half of the Prudhoe Bay field." A second man standing next to the couch received a perfunctory wave of the hand. "Lou Childress, RPetCo's security chief. You know who Kate is, gentlemen."

King glowered from Kate to Mutt and back again. He wasn't accustomed to being thrown off balance and he didn't like it. "About goddam time," he said curtly. Mutt lifted a lip at his tone, but King ignored her, if anyone on two legs can truly ignore the weighty gaze of a 140-pound half husky, half wolf, and concentrated on the woman.

She gave an impression of height, possibly because she held

her spine so straight, possibly because her gaze was so level and direct. Her shoulders were squared, her waist narrow and her hair reached it in a straight, black fall. Her face was broad with high cheekbones, her mouth full-lipped and wide. Held straight and unsmiling, it made her look aloof, even severe. A hint of epicanthic fold between brow and lash slanted over clear hazel eyes that went oddly with the rest of her coloring. Their expression was cool and measuring, containing a speculation devoid of curiosity. Her skin was a rich, golden brown, smooth and unlined, and the only warm thing about her. It looked younger than the thirty-two years Jim Chopin had told him she was.

Her eyes looked older. A lot older.

Jack repeated, "Kate Shugak, John King."

She was shrugging out of her jacket. King let his eyes wander down to the open collar of her shirt and he saw the scar, a knotted cord of paler flesh pulling at that otherwise smooth, perfect skin. He knew the story, of course. Chopper Jim's briefing had been concise but thorough, the direct result of RPetCo buying every Alaska state trooper's raffle ticket that came their way, and encouraging a similar habit in RPetCo's 1,500 statewide employees and 3,000 contractors.

She stood, hands at her sides, waiting impassively. "How do," he said shortly, and held out a hand.

They shook without speaking as she looked him over with the same frankness he had her. He was six inches taller than she was and had the same general build as a fireplug with a square face and fair, freckled skin that flushed easily. He had no discernible neck and thick, straight blond hair that fell in his eyes and over his collar. His glasses were wire-rimmed and thick-lensed and magnified the baleful glare that appeared to be his natural expression. The result would have a daunting effect on anyone across a negotiating table or on the carpet in front of him. She wondered if that was why he wore them. His frayed, faded jeans were rolled up twice at the cuffs over mustard-yellow cowboy boots, and his plaid shirt strained to contain his barrel-shaped chest.

Kate sat opposite him and Jack went into the kitchen. He opened the refrigerator and gazed inside as if it might hold the ultimate answer to the mystery of the universe. "Want a refill on that beer, John? Kate? You thirsty?"

"You got any Diet 7UP?"

"Nope. Pepsi, root beer, Coors, that's it."

"A glass of ice water then."

John King gave a snort clearly audible to Jack two rooms away. "I'll have another beer myself."

"So will I," Childress said immediately, and sat down next to John King. He was easier to pigeonhole than King, but the ability to do it gave Kate no pleasure. Brush cut, knife-sharp creases in his tailored slacks, black loafers shined so brightly she could see her reflection in them from ten paces. His tie was squared away in the best military fashion, his shirt a breastplate of starch, his expression D.I.-certified hostile. Retired military, had to be, and probably, God help her, Marine. She looked for flaws in the government-issue facade and found only one. Seated, an incipient potbelly that she was ready to bet Childress fought every meal of his life spilled over a tightly clinched, gleaming leather belt. For the rest, he was a paragon of God and country; tight-lipped and a tighter ass. Already she was bored.

He looked her over, too, but he was so annoyed that she'd beaten him to it that his perusal was less effective. She waited, dispassionate, until he looked up to meet her eyes. "Childress."

His nod was curt. "Shugak." He slapped shut a manila file

folder and tossed it into the eelskin briefcase open on the coffee table. "John, I want to go on record one more time as being against this. My department can resolve this thing internally."

"Your objection is noted," John King growled.

Kate propped her feet on the coffee table and said nothing.

The silence in the living room reached into the kitchen, where Jack dropped ice cubes into a glass, filled it and a large bowl with water, grabbed the beer bottles by their necks and juggled everything into the living room. Kate was seated on the loveseat across from John King, both of them working at not being the first to blink, while Childress practiced scowling and from one side Mutt observed the staring match with all the bored disinterest of a professional witnessing an amateur event. Jack bit back a smile and set the bowl down next to her and handed the glass of water to Kate. John King drank half his beer in one long swallow as Jack eased gratefully into an easy chair and put the footrest up. The chair gave a protesting groan but held.

John King burped, and gave the bottle a look of disgust. "Might's well be drinking sody pop." He drained it with another gulp and set the empty bottle down with a snap. Childress set his, barely tasted, next to King's. King transferred his look of disgust to Kate. "What's your fee?"

It was more of an attack than an inquiry. Keeping her tone mild, Kate replied, "Seven hundred fifty a day, plus expenses."

King snorted. Childress did, too, but it was an action unsuited to his high, thin, aristocratic nose. For King it was more natural, an all-purpose expression denoting disbelief, contempt and ridicule at will, singly or all together. "You get four hundred a day, when you're working, which Chopper Jim says ain't all that often."

Her expression didn't change. "For Royal Petroleum Company, majority partner in the Prudhoe Bay oil field and producer of fourteen percent of the nation's oil supply, my price is seven-fifty a day. Plus expenses."

He snorted again. So did Childress, who said, "You won't have any expenses. We provide food, lodging and arctic gear, and you ride to work on our own charter. All you have to do is investigate."

The last word was something between a sneer and a snarl, and Kate examined him thoughtfully. Jack watched Lou Childress try not to squirm beneath that cool survey, and had to give him an A for effort.

Kate let the silence get uncomfortable before breaking it. "What's the job?"

Again, King's question was more of a bark than a question. "What do you know about Prudhoe Bay?"

She linked her hands behind her head and leaned back. "It's a super-giant oil formation producing a million and a half barrels of oil per day, the largest oil field in North America. It sits on the edge of the Arctic Ocean 600 miles north of Anchorage, 250 miles north of the Arctic Circle, 100 miles north of the Brooks Range and 1,300 miles south of the geographic North Pole. It runs about 125,000 square acres in size, with, lately, around 4,000-plus employees. There are two operating owners, Royal Petroleum Company, aka RPetCo, and American Exploration, aka Amerex. You've been taking the oil out since, oh, since when, since 1976 or thereabouts. The field should have begun to decline in 1986 but due to new recovery techniques and the exploitation of several smaller fields in the vicinity, this decline has been delayed."

"First oil into OCC in Valdez was July 28, 1977," King corrected her, but he couldn't hide his surprise.

One corner of her mouth drew up. "I'm an Alaska Native, King. I was born and raised and I live in the Bush. We've got a new school in my village, with a brand-new gymnasium tacked on, and a brand-new power plant to keep the lights on during the Class C state championships. I'm well aware they were paid for with state taxes on Prudhoe Bay crude." She also had clear and distinct memories of what it was like trying to dribble a basketball outside at twenty below, but she saw no reason to say so.

"Taxes increased eleven times in twelve years by the Alaska state legislature," he said immediately.

Kate declined to debate the average I.Q. in Juneau. "What's the job?"

He pushed his jaw out. "One thing I gotta know up front before this goes any further. How do you feel about the oil business in Alaska?"

She knew instantly what he was getting at. "Don't you mean, how do I feel about the oil business in Alaska after the *RPetCo Anchorage* spill?" The answer was obvious on his face, and she said, "I think I'm more interested in why RPetCo hired a known drunk to steer a day's production of Prudhoe crude through the Valdez Narrows in a Very Large Crude Carrier, when two states had already yanked his license to drive a car. And I'm definitely interested in the fact that he's still working for RPetCo." Her smile was slight and humorless. "Training new tanker crews."

Childress stirred but King beat him to it. "He ain't working for RPetCo, he's working for the seamen's union. We don't got nothing to do with that."

Out of the loop, Jack thought, and wondered if John King knew George Bush from his wildcatting days in Texas. He took a sip of beer, savoring it all the way down.

"And he *was* acquitted," John King added. Kate said nothing, and he was driven to fill the sudden vacuum. "Well? I know your homestead's close to the Gulf of Alaska. You gotta have friends, relatives, who were affected by the spill." Still Kate didn't answer, and goaded, John King declared, "I gotta tell you, I'm of half a mind to do like Lou says, let his department take care of this. I don't like the idea of sending a broad in on a job like this, let alone a Native broad. But Morgan says you're the best investigator he ever had in the D.A.'s office. Chopper Jim backs him up. Shit, even the fucking FBI says you're good."

"An unimpeachable source of information," Kate murmured. "Look at all they've done for Leonard Peltier."

"Okay." King's voice rose. "I just don't want you busting my chops after the fact with whatever dirt you dish up on my people down the line, just because you think you've got an axe to grind because you're a Native or a woman or because you think all the oil companies ought to have their asses kicked back Outside where they belong. I want this kept quiet. I got enough problems already without broadcasting the fact that half my people are putting their paychecks up their noses." He realized what he'd said too late and his mouth snapped shut with an audible click.

Jack studied his beer bottle thoughtfully. John King had all the social skills of a blast furnace.

Kate took a long swallow of water and set the glass down carefully on the coffee table. "My fee is seven-fifty a day." She looked at Childress. "Plus expenses." She looked back at King. "Your checks don't bounce, that buys you a fair amount of discretion." For the third and last time, she said, "What's the job?"

As he met that unblinking hazel stare, John King remembered

7

something Gamble, the federal agent, had said. *She's about as friendly as a double-bladed axe, but if she says she'll do a job, the job gets done. It'll cost you,* he'd added, *but it'll get done.*

At that moment John King would have sold his soul for a done job. He made up his mind. "Somebody's dealing drugs on my dime," he said bluntly. Childress gave an involuntary sound of distress. "Shut up, Lou. There've been half a dozen overdoses in the last three months." When her expression didn't change, he added, "And one death."

Kate's eyes widened. "You didn't tell me there had been a death," she told Jack.

He held his bottle to the light and inspected it for flaws. "Didn't know when I talked to you Friday at Bobby's that there'd been one."

"When did it happen?"

John King looked at Childress. "Saturday night," Childress said reluctantly, still scowling. "His body was found Sunday morning, floating facedown in the pool."

That got Kate's attention, but not in quite the way John King would have liked. "'In the *pool*'?" She looked at John King with an incredulity that wasn't entirely feigned. "You've got a swimming pool on the North Slope?"

"It doubles as a fire water reservoir," he growled.

"Of course it does," she agreed with a cordiality that set his teeth on edge. "Cocaine?" He nodded curtly. "What, was it pure and he couldn't handle it? Or is somebody cutting it with Borax?"

He shrugged impatient shoulders. "I don't know and I don't care."

"Any indications the death was not accidental?"

Childress went into orbit. "Jesus Christ, John! I've had about enough of this crap! She's never even been on the Slope and now she's got crazed murderers running around the Base Camp bumping people off! I told you this could get out of hand! I—"

"Show her what you got, Lou."

"John!"

"Show her, goddammit!"

The security man's jaw clenched and his lips tightened into a thin line. After a long, tense moment he produced a small manila envelope and emptied it out on the coffee table.

Kate leaned forward to pick one of the items up. It was a creased square of waxed paper, folded into a tiny homemade envelope. She raised an eyebrow at Jack and he nodded. "That's how they're packaging the hits."

"The stewards swept up those last weekend in the common rooms of the Base Camp," John King told her, "and Christ knows that can't be even a fraction of the total." A sudden weariness assailed him, and he rubbed his hands over his face. "It hasn't been this bad since construction." He dropped his hands and glared at her accusingly. "I want it stopped."

"What's the problem? Jack was telling me on the way here that Anchorage International was rated in the top ten for best airport security in the nation last year. Sic them on it."

"We have," John King said grimly. "It's still getting through."

"Then go at it from the other end, set up a checkpoint at Prudhoe. It's your oil field, you ought to be able to exert some kind of control over what comes in."

King snorted and Childress took over. "Deadhorse," the security chief said with awful sarcasm, "is a public airport. It has three commercial carriers flying in, besides the RPetCo and Amerex charters. Not to mention the jets of every corporation flush enough to float a rubbernecker for their board. Not to mention government amphibs bringing up U.S. senators and congressmen to go fishing in the Arctic National Wildlife Refuge. Not to mention one hundred fifty trucks up the haul road every month. Not to mention the six Native villages within snowmobile or outboard or Super Cub range."

He stopped, looking at John King, who was glowering at Kate, who was smart enough not to take it personally. "Drugs are coming into the Base Camp and the Western Operating Area, Shugak. *My* Base Camp and *my* Western Operating Area. Somebody's importing that shit wholesale and retailing it to *my* people and I want it stopped. I want it stopped fast, and I want it stopped now, before some asshole who should know better gets higher than a kite and bumps into the wrong valve in Skid 14 and sends a fucking production center into fucking orbit and shuts the whole fucking line down!" He was shouting before he came to the end of his sentence, his face mottled purple with rage.

She reached for her water, sipped and rolled the glass back and forth between her palms. "All right."

Breathing heavily, he stared at her. "All right?" he said, unconsciously mimicking her calm tone.

She raised her eyes from her glass and met his. "All right, I'll do it."

It was nearly impossible to get John King off the attack once he'd begun a charge. "You sure you can handle it?" he shot at her.

"Yes."

"You'll be working a week on, a week off." He gave Jack an unfriendly look. "I wanted you up straight through until you caught the fuckers, but Morgan says that'd jeopardize your cover. You'll be hired on through UCo, can you—"

"UCo?" Kate said sharply. "Who's them? I thought I was

10

going up for RPetCo."

John King shook his head. "All our roustabouts are contract hires nowadays. Saves on paying benefits. Universal Oilfield Service Company's our main contractor, and if I'm right and I usually am"—his glare dared her to contradict him—"if I'm right, the drugs are coming in in some contract hire's toolbox and going out into the field the same way." His fists clenched and his face reddened. "I want you to go through UCo like crap through a goose. It's gotta be them. Those fucking contractors are about as loyal to the brand as Billy the Kid."

Kate wondered how much of that was the truth and how much wishful thinking, but she held her peace.

"You'll be hired on as a roustabout, which ain't a goddam Elvis movie. A roustabout does every dirty job that comes along, from signing out tools to running parts to driving bus to wellhead cleanup to picking up garbage. You seem in good shape." He looked her over critically, and this time it was a look devoid of that congenital speculation of when and how he'd get her into the sack intrinsic in any first meeting between any human male and any female who rejoiced in a functioning pulse. "But I'm here to tell you, lady, that you'd better *be* fit if you're gonna be outside at forty below in a fifteen-knot wind, humping a drill bit off the back of a pickup truck. Can you drive a pickup truck?" Jack rolled his eyes. Kate nodded. "A flatbed?" She nodded. "A bus?" She nodded again, lying this time. At this point if he'd asked her if she could launch a Saturn V rocket her answer would have been the same.

"Roustabouts' regular rotation day is Tuesday, which means you fly to Prudhoe Tuesday morning and back to Anchorage the following Tuesday afternoon. That means you leave here day after tomorrow. Got a problem with that?"

11

"No."

"It's one woman to five men in the Base Camp. The rest of the time you'll be out in the field where the ratio's more like ten to one and some of the guys working construction been up there since Christmas and you're gonna look like a stocking stuffer to them. Think you can handle that?"

As he spoke, John King looked at Jack Morgan, a shaggy, dark-haired, amiable giant who was the chief investigator for the Anchorage D.A. He didn't look like he could muster up enough energy to get out of his own way, but his reputation as an investigator was rock solid, even if he did look more like Paul Bunyan than Sam Spade. King looked from Morgan to Shugak and remembered something else Gamble had said. *There's something going on there. I don't know what it is, and I don't think they do, either, but don't get between them. It could be hazardous to your health.* King set his jaw. He wasn't going to take back a by-God word.

It wasn't necessary. Morgan looked even more imperturbable than Shugak, possibly even more so than that damn dog. Maybe it was a family trait. "Well?" he demanded. "You think you can handle it?"

Kate wondered if she should tell King about her last job, on a crabber in the middle of the Bering Sea, all her crewmates male, including her bunkie, three of them with murder, not seduction, on their minds. She nodded instead. It was easier.

"You better be sure, Shugak. You better be awful goddam sure. I want that fucking dope off my Slope." He subjected her to another long glare, which she endured without flinching. He transferred the glare to Jack. "You sure you can't send up one of your own?"

Without heat, Jack said, "What I said before still goes. We don't have the personnel available to work the caseload in town and mount a full-scale investigation on the Slope at the same time. When Kate turns up some solid evidence, then we can move in officially. But not before."

Kate could almost hear the wheels in John King's head turn to the last ratchet, engage and lock. "All right. I still don't like it, Shugak, but you're the best I can come up with. Lou's got the address. Be there at eight tomorrow morning for orientation." Childress passed a slip of paper across the coffee table, holding it by the tips of his fingers, looking as if he wanted to hold his nose. "One more thing," King said. "Can you pass a drug screen?"

For the first time Kate lost some of her composure. "I beg your pardon?"

Her voice was a rasping growl of sound and King's eyes dropped once again to the white, twisted scar that ran across her throat literally from ear to ear. The tense set of his shoulders eased for the first time in months. Someone who had survived an attack that vicious, and had disposed so speedily and efficiently of her attacker, wasn't likely to keel over the first time a horny Sloper made a heavy-handed pass. She might just do, at that. "You'll have to pass a drug screen. And you'll be required to sign a loyalty oath."

Jack had the rare pleasure of seeing Kate Shugak at a complete loss for words. The pleasure was fleeting. She got her jaw back up into working order and inquired in a tone of lethal sweetness, "Am I going to work on the North Slope or am I joining the American Nazi Party?"

Childress flushed a dark red. "It's standard procedure for all prospective employees to sign a loyalty oath."

Kate looked at Jack. "I drove fifty miles on a snow machine and spent eight hours on a train that stopped for moose every two feet so I could pee in a bottle, pledge allegiance to the

13

corporate flag and freeze my ass off on the edge of the Arctic Ocean?"

"Now, Kate," Jack began soothingly.

Kate opened her mouth to melt his ears off.

"A thousand a day," John King said.

"What?" Childress said.

Startled out of her composure for the second time, Kate gaped at King.

"Plus expenses, of course," he added. "Should run you"—he looked at her consideringly—"oh, say, around two-fifty a day?"

"What!" Childress said.

• • •

Jack closed the door behind King and Childress and leaned against it with crossed arms. "Way-ull. Ah giss now you air in thuh erl bidness."

"And Ah cain't even spell it," she replied, but her Southern accent wasn't as good as his. "What really pisses me off is how sure he was I'd say yes."

"Ah, that's just because you've never sold out before."

"Doesn't take long, does it?" she said with a small, rueful smile.

He grinned. "You hungry?" She shook her head, kicked off her Nikes and crossed her stockinged feet on the coffee table. Jack stretched out next to her, sober now. "You mean it when you said you could handle this job?"

She shrugged, and this time he pushed harder. "What would your grandmother say?"

"I don't plan on telling her." She shifted smoothly from defense to offense. "If you were so sure I wouldn't take a job working for an oil company, why did you haul me all the way into town?"

He kissed her. It took a while. When he let her come up for air, she said, "Oh."

He was more than ready to haul her into the bedroom but she wasn't ready to go, and one of Jack Morgan's many talents was an acute ability to read Kate Shugak sign. Still, there was no harm in some friendly persuasion. He slid an arm around her shoulders and pulled her against him. She felt good. He'd missed her. He wondered if she'd missed him, but that way madness lay and he dispatched the thought before it was fully formed. "How's the homestead?"

"Soggy during the day, frozen at night. Breakup SOP."

"Like town." His hand wandered. "Is the creek clear yet?"

Kate shook her head. "It's jammed with ice all the way back up to Twisted Lake."

"Going to flood?"

"I wouldn't be surprised." She grabbed his hand and looked at his watch. "What time is it?"

"Want to know where the leaders are?" Jack used the remote to turn on the television. "I see Mandy and Chick aren't making the run this year."

"Half the team's down with some kind of virus. Look, there. Turn it up."

The cheery twinkie in seed pearls and big hair and shiny earrings the size of manhole covers ran down the Iditarod leaders so quickly it was hard to make sense of the names and cut immediately to another twinkie via satellite reporting local color from Kaltag. This twinkie was enveloped in an oversize parka with the hood pulled so far forward that all that could be seen of his face was a frostbitten nose and a microphone. The picture cut to footage of a barfing dog being loaded onto a Cessna 206 and a few grave words from a gloomy veterinarian, followed by an interview with the Alaskan head of the SPCA, who unburdened himself of an unequivocal and comprehensive denunciation of the sport of dog mushing in general, the race to Nome in particular, all fifty mushers individually and collectively, the Iditarod Trail Committee, the race sponsors and, last but not least, ABC's *Wide World of Sports*.

He paused for breath and Jack turned off the set. "Next stop Shaktoolik, about time for a storm. Who does Mandy say looks good for this year?"

"She says it's DeeDee's turn but that Martin may have other ideas."

Greatly daring, Jack said, "About time for the guys to win a few back-to-back." Kate refused the lure, and he re-baited the hook and cast again. "Besides, the only reason them girl mushers win all the time is because they don't weigh as much as the guys do and they can go faster with fewer dogs."

"Is that so?" Kate said, fascinated with this new insight into the art of dog mushing. "And here I always thought it was because they trained better teams and ran better races."

Jack was betrayed into a laugh.

"Something else I've always wondered," Kate pursued, "why is it that when Rick Swenson mushes into a blizzard to win the Iditarod he's fearless and heroic, but when Libby Riddles does the same thing she's reckless and foolhardy?"

Jack surrendered unconditionally. "Just lucky, I guess." He let his hand slip again. "Did I tell you Michael Armstrong asked me to fly for him this year?"

"Is that right? You could have been a member of the Iditarod Air Force?" He nodded, and she said, "Well? What the hell are you doing sitting here?"

16

He pointed at the TV screen. "Did that look like fun to you? When they're sick them dogs run from both ends. No, thanks. The Cessna'd never smell the same again." They sat quietly for a few moments. After a bit Kate let her head rest on Jack's shoulder. Encouraged, he said in a low voice, "I know how torn up you were over that damn spill. If you think you can't handle this, I can find someone else."

He couldn't see her face, and she didn't answer at first. Eventually she stirred and said, "We knew the spill was going to happen."

He looked down at the top of her head. "Who's we?"

"The people who live on the Gulf. The Cordova Aquatic Marketing Association, the Cordova District Fishermen United, the Lower Cook Inlet Fishermen's League. Locals. They're fishermen. They know the Narrows. They know the Mother of Storms. They knew it was just a matter of time. They spent a lot of their own money lobbying for the pipeline to go overland through Canada."

Jack kept silent, knowing she wasn't finished.

"I wrote a letter to the governor after the spill, did I tell you?"

"No."

"I told him we ought to kick RPetCo out of the state as an example to other oil companies. Thou Canst Not Shit in Our Nest and Get Away With It. I suggested that with all the lawyers running around Juneau surely to God there had to be some kind of provision in the leases requiring the oil companies to maintain at least minimal environmental standards on pain of revocation of their lease agreements, and that RPetCo had as surely violated that provision, and let us boot them out forthwith."

"You get any answer back?"

"No. So I went down to the offices of the Division of Oil and Gas and looked up the leases, and of course, it's not that simple."

"It never is."

"No. The lessors have to post bonds, but some of the bonds for the smaller contractors are as low as ten grand. The highest one I found was for a million, and that one was for a drill site on the Slope. Some of the leases even say that restoration of the site shall be 'at the discretion of the commissioner.' "

"The commissioner of the Department of Oil and Gas?"

"Yeah."

"Who is a political appointee."

"Yeah."

There was another silence, which Jack broke. "So you would kick RPetCo out of the state if you could."

"Yeah."

"But you can't."

"Nope."

"So you'll work for them instead."

"For a thousand a day."

"Plus expenses."

Kate stretched. "You heard him. Won't be any."

"I guess you'll just have to make up some to justify that two-fifty allowance, then."

"I guess." He felt good against her side, warm and hard. "Besides, given the restricted access and the restricted employee roster, I can't imagine this job is going to take very long. I'll probably be up and back in forty-eight hours."

"You think King really thinks it's a UCo employee?"

"No, and neither does he, or he'd have Childress handling it. Tell me about the DB."

Jack tucked her head back into his shoulder. "Chuck Cass, thirty-four, production operator, worked for RPetCo since 1980, they brought him up to Prudhoe in 1987 from their Lima plant."

"Lima, Peru?"

"Lima, Ohio."

"Oh. Did he drown?"

"Yeah. But the coroner says he was ready to fly. He was probably on takeoff when he fell into the pool. Childress—"

"He sure is on the prod."

Jack grunted. "Sloper syndrome."

"What's that?"

"Childress makes too much money. He's afraid King's going to take some of it back if you find the dealer before he does." He paused. As security chief Childress was in a perfect position to spot the weak links in the security chain between Slope and town. And Kate was right, he had been on the prod. It might only have been the territorial imperative; it could as easily have been apprehension, even fear.

Kate moved restlessly against him and he said, "Anyway, Childress says a guard found traces of a couple lines of coke on one of the benches in the sauna. They figure he tooted up there and—"

She raised her head. "Wait a minute. A *sauna*?"

Deadpan beneath that incredulous gaze, he said, "Certainly a sauna. It's right off the pool. No well-dressed oil field should be without one."

"A sauna?" she repeated, unable to keep the amazement out of her voice. "A banya, an honest-to-God sweat on the North Slope?"

"Yup."

She considered. "This job might not be so bad after all."

"Can't you think about anything except work?" he complained. "I was hoping to adjourn this encounter to the bedroom and discuss how long it's been since I've seen you. Possibly over a snifter or two of brandy."

She stretched her arms over her head, pulling her shirt tight in interesting places. "Real women drink Diet 7UP." He was just lovesick enough to climb back in the Blazer and slip and slide on up to Carr's for a case of the carbonated beverage of her choice. She was just grateful enough to bestow a suitable reward.

CHAPTER 2

KATE PRESENTED HERSELF AT Anchorage International Airport Tuesday morning after a whirlwind Monday spent getting everything but an RPetCo-certified, Grade A stamp on her forehead, only to be turned away at the RPetCo ticket counter. The flight had been canceled due to bad weather at Prudhoe. "'Bad weather' in March means blizzard," she heard someone say gloomily. "Who cares?" someone else replied. "Let's head for La Mex. I got a three-for-one coupon for margaritas."

Wednesday morning Kate called the airport first, to be assured the flight would take off as scheduled. The whole experience felt anticlimactic as she accepted her boarding pass and walked down to the gate, where the plane was already loading. At one minute past nine, the nose gear lifted off Runway 18, northbound. The rest of the passengers dozed; Kate, keyed up and restless, rooted through the seat pocket in front of her and found a brochure published by RPetCo's Department of Public and Government Affairs.

The North Slope, she read, stretched across northern Alaska for six hundred miles, from the Chukchi Sea to the Canadian border. A hundred-mile slide north from the Brooks Range to the Arctic Ocean, the Slope was one enormous delta for the hundreds of rivers and streams that rose in the Brooks and flowed into the Beaufort Sea. Eighteen inches of delicate, spongy tundra insulated two thousand feet of permafrost, five thousand feet below which was the oil formation. Seven inches of annual precipitation froze the tundra into a barren, inhospitable desert for ten months out of the year, and then in June and July relented to melt into a soggy garden of arctic poppies and northern primroses and Siberian asters, where trumpeter swans and Canadian honkers and snow geese and green-spectacled eider ducks fed and bred with equal abandon.

There followed a series of pictures in glorious living color of said wildlife frolicking through various ponds and streams. Lest visions of Thanksgiving dinner begin to dance in the head of the reader, the brochure hastened to add that firearms were not allowed within the boundaries of the oil field. For all intents and purposes, the text intoned sternly, Prudhoe Bay was a wildlife refuge. There was a picture of John King standing in the middle of the tundra, with a drilling rig rearing its derrick discreetly in the distant background, and a caribou cow and calf grazing between them, a perfect example of industry and environment coexisting in harmony. The caption read, "'We're all environmentalists here,' says John King, Chief Executive Officer for Royal Petroleum Corporation."

Uh-huh, Kate thought, and turned the page.

Here was matter more necessary to her immediate needs, a physical description of the area in which she was to concentrate her investigation. Prudhoe Bay proper was less than a mile across, barely a dimple in the great expanse of coastline, bordered by the Kuparuk River on the west and by the Sagavanirktok River on the east, bisected by the smaller Putuligayak River. The only measurable topography other than the rivers were the pingoes, sixty-foot circular mounds in the tundra created by frost heaves, and the hundreds of shallow, elongated lakes scattered by a lavish hand from horizon to horizon. Kate turned back to the page with the picture of John King on it and found examples of both in the background. The lake looked more like a puddle and the pingo little more than an anthill.

She turned the page and was offered the short course in Prudhoe Bay history. A British explorer had mapped the area in 1910 and noted in his log the existence of shallow black puddles formed by oil seeps. In 1944 the United States Navy began drilling exploratory wells in Naval Petroleum Reserve Number 4. The first substantial paydirt in the form of the Sadlerochit supergiant oil formation was discovered by Royal Petroleum Company in April 1968, followed by a free-for-all lease sale in September that netted the state of Alaska nearly a billion dollars. What Kate remembered most about the lease sale was the fact that the Alaska state legislature had every dime of the proceeds spent in less than two years, a feat of pork barrel legerdemain that had elected officials gawking in admiration from the Yukon to the Potomac. It was that feat that eventually resulted in the creation in 1976 of the Alaska Permanent Fund, sort of a savings account for the state endowed by taxes on Prudhoe Bay crude. Half the interest generated by the Fund was divided among each and every Alaskan citizen in a yearly payment.

Last year the PFD had been over $800, considerably more than Judas's thirty pieces of silver.

Pity the poor Alaskan, Kate thought. Caught between the Scylla of the Alaska Permanent Fund dividend and the Charybdis of the *RPetCo Anchorage* spill. There was a picture in the brochure of a Very Large Crude Carrier negotiating the Valdez Narrows on a calm and cloudless day, a day very much like the one four years before when the *RPetCo Anchorage* had run aground on Bligh Reef and spilled half a day's production of Prudhoe crude eight hundred miles across the Gulf of Alaska.

Kate had taken the ferry from Cordova to Whittier the previous summer; during the entire ten-hour trip she had seen two sea gulls and three mountain goats on a cliff on the way into the Whittier harbor. That day, too, had been a day like the day of the spill, and on days like that on previous ferry trips she could expect to see rafts of sea otters, pods of killer whales, lone eagles soaring high, arctic terns swarming low, schools of silver salmon smacking their way toward shore and the cold, clear streams that had seen their first days and now would see their last.

That day, she saw two sea gulls and three goats.

She took a deep breath. The job, she reminded herself firmly, she was on a job, a job for which she would be very well paid. Her breath released on a long sigh, and she went back to her history lesson.

When construction of the pipeline was complete and the Prudhoe Bay field fully delineated and the bookkeepers done adding up all the numbers, the fourteen minority owners took a back seat to the two majority owners, RPetCo and Amerex, who would operate the field in tandem. Prudhoe Bay now consisted of a Base Camp for each operator; six Production Centers, three on a side; the field's power station, which ran off natural gas produced from the field; a compression plant that reinjected produced natural gas back into the formation until such time as a gas line would be built; Pump Station One, the first of twelve pump stations to push oil down the TransAlaska Pipeline to Valdez; and a collection of service camps dotting the field between. A gravel road called the Backbone connected the main facilities with the haul road that paralleled the pipeline, and access roads shot off in every direction to well pads and flow lines and old drilling sites and mud pits and God knew where else.

A lot of room to run and hide, should the need arise. She wondered how one lone investigator was supposed to cover that much territory, and for the first time began to doubt her ability to get this particular job done.

The brochure deteriorated at that point into a lengthy discussion of the Permo-Triassic period, faulted subsurface sandstone structures, and the difference between porosity and permeability and how the absence of either would have rendered the Sadlerochit reservoir, the largest oil field on the North American continent, unrecoverable. The slightly horrified tone of the text conveyed the impression that this outcome was utterly unthinkable.

Yawning, Kate closed the brochure and looked out the window. Anchorage in March looked a lot better from thirty thousand feet up, but you could say that about the whole state, except for Denali, which looked the same at any time of the year, all 20,320 dazzling, blue-white, sharp-edged feet of her. The Alaska Range receded, succeeded by the rolling, thickly forested and rivered landscape of the Interior, itself to be replaced by the Brooks Range.

It was the first time she'd seen the Brooks Range. A wrinkled fold of Mesozoic skin over spare Paleozoic bones (the brochure's description and, Kate had to admit, not a bad one), it rippled as far east and as far west as she could see. She stared down at it, cheek pressed to the plastic window. During this mountain range's formation the dinosaurs had evolved and roamed the earth, masters of all they surveyed, only to lay down their collective lives for, 70 million years later, RPetCo's bottom line, the state of Alaska's legislative budget, Niniltna Public School's gymnasium and the gas tank on Jack's Blazer.

She leaned back and replaced the brochure in the seat pocket. Nothing in this world put the significance of human life on earth in perspective better or faster than a geologic timetable.

Moments later they began their descent, landing under a sky as white as the ground. The 727 rolled out to a stop on the apron, the rear airstairs dropped and she followed the rest of the passengers to the bus parked at the foot of the stairs. A jumbled mass of buildings passed in review as they left the airport. The fog hung close to the tundra, causing the windows on the bus to weep long, rolling tears of condensation that collected along the sills and dripped on the shoulders of the passengers. The little lakes visible at the fog's edge were frozen hard. The fog, the snow flurries, the white, icy surface of the road and the endless length of frozen tundra melded into each other and distorted the horizon. It was disconcerting to have to remind oneself which way was up.

It didn't look anything at all like the pictures in the brochure. It looked like a Sahara of snow. Kate didn't realize she had said the words out loud until she caught the sideways glance of the tiny blonde sitting next to her. "Robert Lowell," she added.

"Uh-huh," the blonde said, who looked like a scowling Madonna with more clothes on. She also looked vaguely familiar, but Kate couldn't place her immediately. She hoped she hadn't arrested her at some point in the past. Across the aisle and up two rows sat a brunette with glossy hair and languishing brown eyes. Beside Kate they were the only two women on the bus. The rest of the passengers and the driver were men, and everyone was enveloped in the same dark blue, company-issue parkas that turned them all the approximate size of gorillas.

Next to her the blonde stirred. "Dale Triplett, production operator. First time up?"

"Yes," Kate said. "Kate Shugak. New hire."

"Hey, Dale," someone yelled from the back of the bus, "how'd Xaviera do in the time trials?"

"I don't know," Dale yelled back over her shoulder, "call me this afternoon. Which department?" she asked Kate.

"Uh, field transportation? I was hired as a roustabout."

"Ah." The blonde nodded as if that explained everything. She eyed Kate curiously. "Where are you from, originally?"

"Niniltna."

The blonde smiled suddenly and her whole face changed. "I've been there. I'm from Cordova myself."

"No kidding!"

"No kidding."

"What did you say you did?"

"Production operator."

Like Chuck Cass. In the trade this was what was known as a lead. "Production operator," Kate said with well-feigned interest. "Did you have to go to school for that?"

"No, but I did. I got my degree in mechanical engineering from the University of Alaska in Fairbanks in 1981."

For a split second Kate debated what to say next, and decided on the truth as being easier and inevitable. The brochure on the plane had made mention of how RPetCo made a point of local hire to stay on the good side of Alaskan legislators, and it was even odds she'd be running into people she knew all over the Slope. "Me, too," she said. "I mean I went to UAF, too. Class of '83."

"What in?"

"Sociology," Kate lied.

"Another useless liberal arts degree that'll never get you a

27

job. Well, well. A sister Nanook. Welcome to the asshole of the world."

"Thanks. I think." And a mouth like Madonna, too.

The bus left the Backbone to lurch around a corner onto an access road that led through a chain-link fence. The fence surrounded a mammoth collection of two-story prefabricated metal buildings set twelve feet above the gravel pad on steel pilings, all connected with arctic walkways suspended above the ground. A sign next to the double door read:

Production Center Three

Royal Petroleum Company

Prudhoe Bay, Alaska

Dale and half a dozen others got up and collected their gear. "This is where I get off. Meet you for dinner?"

A native guide, just what she needed. "Okay."

The bus doors closed behind Dale and the bus lurched back onto the gravel road. Another ten minutes and the driver drew up to the Base Camp's front door with an air of visible relief.

The Base Camp was similar in construction to the production center; boxy three-story buildings elevated on twelve-foot pilings, connected by elevated, enclosed walkways. Unlike the production center, these modules were sheathed in a copper-colored metal that gave off a warm glow in the half-light.

A security guard seated behind a glass partition examined her badge and waved her inside after the rest of the busload had passed through. Up the stairs from security was a U-shaped counter beneath a sign that said simply FRONT DESK. Behind the counter Kate saw the brunette from the bus through an office window. She was speaking in animated fashion to a man seated behind a desk who replied in monosyllables while staring fixedly at the brunette's chest.

Following the instructions of the front desk clerk, Kate fumbled her way down a hallway, found a corridor that led onto another corridor that hung an immediate right into a third corridor she thought was a dead end but in which, after some investigation, she discovered a door into a stairwell. None of the corridors had flat walls or ceilings; all the doors were set back at various distances from the hallway; the ceiling went up and down and back up again every few feet; and all surfaces were covered in bright primary colors: blue, red, yellow, green, orange. Kate felt like a rat in a Technicolor maze, and was thankful for the neutral, napless carpeting beneath her feet. She descended the stairs, opened the door at the bottom and discovered yet another corridor with offices opening off either side and a hum of industry throughout. She paused in the doorway as a female voice full of grit and gravel announced over the loudspeaker, "Attention, sports fans, three days to race day, three days to race day and counting, all racers must be registered by seven P.M. this evening, seven P.M. this evening, or they will be disqualified from participating. Odds on Xaviera have gone up to five-to-one. Thank you, and start your engines."

Kate found the door marked TRANSPORTATION SUPERVISOR and went in.

The man behind the desk waved her inside and went on talking on the phone. "Four sets of studded tires is the best I can do I'm afraid." He listened. "Make it three cases of hard hats and you have a deal. No, three. Very well, I'll send Dave over with the tires have the hats ready." He laughed. "Yes I am and so are you I won't call the unit owners if you won't." He hung up and looked across at Kate. "I imagine you would be Katherine Shugak?"

"Kate," she said. "You're English."

"British actually." He rose to his feet and offered her two fingers. "Harris Perry Ms. Shugak I'm your new supervisor welcome to Prudhoe Bay."

Perry didn't look English or British or even European for that matter; he looked as if mañana should be his middle name. His face was dark, his features swarthy and he bore a distinct resemblance to a Mexican bandido Kate had seen once in a Clint Eastwood movie on Bobby's VCR, a resemblance enhanced by the full black mustache that curved in an upside-down U over his mouth. His teeth gleamed beneath it in a practiced smile. "Flight up satisfactory I hope?"

"Sure. Wasn't it supposed to be?"

He shrugged with a nonchalance Kate found peculiar in someone occupying the hot seat behind a door marked TRANSPORTATION. "You never can tell did you receive your room assignment?"

Mutely, she held up a key dangling from a green plastic tag.

"What's the number 786 let's see now OCX outside room good you'll get some sleep and Ralph is your alternate so you might even get some closet space." He chuckled. She didn't know what he was talking about and she was having a hard time keeping up with his rapid speech anyway so she remained silent. "You can pick up your baggage down by Security this evening and get someone to show you your room." He picked up the phone and punched in a number. "Toni I've got a live one for you new hire Katherine Shugak I'll bring her right up." He hung up. "Please follow me."

He came out from behind the desk, giving Kate time enough to notice that his jeans were ironed, a knife-edge crease running down the front of each leg. In keeping with what appeared to be the North Slope uniform he also wore a Pendleton shirt in a subdued red and black check. It fit so well she suspected he'd had it tailored. She followed him back out into the corridor and down more hallways, through a dimly lit garage filled with trucks covered with mud beneath which the yellow and green RPetCo colors were barely visible, and suddenly found herself passing rapidly in front of the front desk with no very clear recollection of how she'd got there.

Perry skidded to a halt in front of an open door and Kate almost trod on his heels. "This is it let me know if you have any problems." He turned on his heel and marched off briskly.

Resisting an impulse to toss a salute at his retreating back, Kate poked a cautious nose in the open door. Cramped and windowless, the office was barely large enough to hold a desk, two chairs, a bookcase and a credenza. It was further cramped by the piggyback plant hanging like a parasol from one corner of the ceiling, the fig tree flourishing from another and the philodendron growing down the side of the bookcase on its way out the door. The bookcase was jammed with back issues of *Petroleum Intelligence Weekly* and *Business Week* and *Forbes* and plastic cups filled with water and green cuttings. Very little wall showed through the eight-by-ten black-and-white glossies of geese and polar bears and great snowy owls tacked floor to ceiling.

On one corner of the desktop sat two wire baskets. One was labeled WAY OUT. The other was labeled DEEPER IN.

Kate was staring at those signs with a growing sense of apprehension when the slender brunette from the bus, now seated behind the desk, became aware of Kate's presence. She bounced immediately to her feet and grabbed Kate's hand to sling her into a chair. The brunette beamed at her and said,

31

"You must be new hire Katherine Shugak guess what!"

Kate paused halfway out of her new parka. "What? And it's Kate."

"I just bought a partnership in a pistachio farm!"

There followed a short silence. "You bought a what in a what?"

"Do you know what pistachios cost per pound think of the money I'm going to make and if we lose I can write it off you need an accountant you will don't worry I've got a great one you just say the word." The phone rang and the brunette grabbed it and spoke without pause. "What no I can't no not now I've got someone in my office call me tonight good-bye."

She hung up the phone and drew breath, only to be interrupted when a man built like a pit bull barged into the office, banging the door off the bookcase with a resounding crash that reverberated up through the soles of Kate's boots. The philodendron cowered. Short and squat with shoulders so muscular that his arms bowed out from his torso, he had iron-gray hair and a personality to match. "What the fuck are you doing about the seventeenth of April?"

Evidently everyone on the Slope spoke without punctuation. "Cale Yarborough Katherine Prudhoe Bay field manager just call him God," the brunette said. "This is Katherine Shugak roustabout new hire what about April I don't go on vacation until May."

"What's your vacation got to do with anything the Federal Energy Regulatory Committee and the Exxon president and CEO are coming up on the seventeenth both groups on the same day who did this Francine?"

The brunette stifled herself and gave a one-word answer. "Probably."

"Call that bitch and tell her to fix it I don't care how she does it just tell her to do it or I'll have her ass nice to meet you too Shugak." The door slammed behind him.

Kate waited until the footsteps in the hall died away before inquiring timidly, "Um, exactly who are you?"

The brunette looked absolutely astounded. "Didn't I introduce myself oh for dumb oh my gawd Katherine I'm so sorry I'm Toni Hartzler public relations representative for RPetCo North Slope assigned B Shift like you."

She had to pause for breath again and Kate seized the opportunity. "Why am I here? And it's Kate."

Toni had delicate features, pale, perfect skin, dreamy brown eyes and a raucous, braying laugh that would have sounded more likely coming from a donkey. Before she could speak the phone rang. "Hello yes no not now call me tonight we'll set something up then."

She hung up and the door banged open again and again bounced off the bookcase. This time it was a short blond man with sleeked-back hair, dressed in the same uniform as the security guard at the Base Camp's main entrance. "Where is he I know he's in here Hartzler your fucking alternate kidnapped him where is he?"

"Katherine Shugak meet Glen Lefevre our local Hitler and with littler charm I don't have the faintest idea of what in the world you're talking about Glen," Toni said mildly. "Bob's at lunch or on his way out to the airport I don't know which he had a tour this morning."

"Don't give me that shit!" the guard yelled, his red face going redder. "I saw Kinderknecht spying last night when Deputy Dawg was doing his practice laps where is he?"

The grit and gravel female voice came over the loudspeaker. "Attention, sports fans, attention. The Security Department has announced an all-points-bulletin for Deputy Dawg, kidnapped from Security this morning sometime between nine and ten A.M. Victim description as follows: height four inches, length six and a half inches, weight ten and a half ounces, complexion green with brown spots. Has been known to bite. Anyone with any information leading to the rescue of Deputy Dawg and the apprehension of the turtlenappers dial 4911. There is a reward on offer of one Tundra Traveler's Certificate, guaranteed point-free with no supervisor advisory call. Glen Lefevre, call your office immediately."

The guard snatched up the phone and dialed an extension. "What WHAT I'll be right there!" He threw down the phone and shook a fist in Toni's face. "I know Kinderknecht had a hand in this Hartzler this ain't the end of this!"

The door slammed shut behind him, only to slam open again immediately. The philodendron was having a bad day. "The Federal Energy Regulatory Committee says that eating a lunch at RPetCo's Base Camp free of charge constitutes taking a bribe," Cale Yarborough barked. "They insist on paying."

"Paying who?" Toni asked with polite interest. "And how much?"

"Find out goddammit do I have to do every goddam thing around this goddam place myself?" The question was obviously rhetorical because he slammed out again without waiting for a reply.

Toni frowned, marring her perfect brow with a furrow of concentration. After a moment it smoothed out again. She picked up the phone and dialed, and winked at Kate while waiting for an answer. "Francine?" she said, her voice smooth and syrupy and now entirely without haste. "The Federal Energy Regulatory Committee says there ain't no such thing as a free lunch. They insist on paying for theirs when they come up."

Kate could clearly hear the exasperated voice coming over the receiver from where she sat. "Oh, for God's sake. How much is lunch on the Slope and how are they going to pay, cash or check? Do we ask for two pieces of identification? Do we accept out-of-state checks? And what the hell are we supposed to do with the money once we have it?"

"Find out," Toni suggested sweetly. "Do I have to do every goddam thing around this goddam place myself?" She hung up with a flourish and grinned at Kate. "Another challenge faced another crisis met another problem solved delegation is the life's blood of any young executive in the oil business, remember that Katherine and you'll do fine."

Kate's ear must have finally caught up with Toni's voice because she thought she might actually have detected a comma in that last phrase. The phone rang and Toni snatched it up. "Yes yes yes no not now have a little patience call me tonight."

Then again, maybe not.

Toni hung up and the door slammed open and a Fury erupted into the middle of the room. Nobody knocked in this place.

The Fury had a face like Carly Simon and an accent like LB J. She was dressed in a white, three-quarter-length jacket that made her look like she was about to produce a syringe and draw blood. "There it is!" she yelped, pointing at the Benjamin fig tree. "I knew that lying sack of shit took it!" She saw Kate, mouth open, and said furiously, "And just who the hell are you?"

Kate tried an ingratiating smile. "Um—Kate Shugak?"

"Well?" the Fury demanded. "Is you or ain't you?"

Toni intervened. "Katherine Shugak, new hire roustabout, Ann McCord head steward what's the problem Ann?"

The Fury rounded on her ferociously. "The problem is that

goddam alternate of yours stole that fig tree for the second time this month! I ain't got enough to do training Hump to eat Deputy Dawg's lunch without chasing after my damn plants?" She leveled a finger and commanded, "Y'all tell that prick if he steals one more plant outa the lounge he's dead meat! The same goes double for y'all!" She bent over the planter tub and, cursing loudly, shoved it out the door. She poked her head back in and said politely, "Nice to meet y'all, Katherine. Welcome to the Prudhoe Hilton. Toni?"

"Yes, Ann?" Toni said meekly.

Ann looked from Toni to Kate and back again. "Never mind."

Toni smiled. "Call me later."

The door slammed shut and naturally banged open again immediately. By now both Kate and the philodendron were used to it and barely flinched.

The man caught the door on its backswing. He wore insulated bib overalls, heavy boots and carried a parka. He had a thin face with sharp features and intense dark eyes. Those eyes widened when they saw Kate, but before either of them could speak Toni had risen to her feet and come around her desk, hand outstretched. "Otto. How nice to see you again."

He took her hand automatically, shaking it with his eyes still fixed on Kate, his expression hard to read. It wasn't male speculation of female availability, nor, Kate decided, was it the instinctive withdrawal of one race from another, she'd seen that too many times not to spot it on sight.

"Otto Leckerd, meet Katherine Shugak. Katherine's our newest roustabout. Katherine, this is Prudhoe Bay's resident archaeologist."

"It's Kate, actually, not Katherine," Kate said, patiently for her. So that was it. She hadn't seen that look since college and Anthropology 101, no wonder she hadn't recognized it for what it was.

"Shugak." He affirmed her judgment with his first words. "You're Aleut." It wasn't a question, but she nodded. Before she could dodge back out of the way he raised a long-fingered hand tipped with grimy fingernails and turned her head to examine her profile. "Classic. With those cheekbones and that forehead you'd have to be from the Aleutians. With a name like Shugak, maybe Kodiak?"

Being viewed as a specimen by a potential collector was not a new experience and never a pleasant one. Kate removed her chin from Leckerd's grasp. "Actually, my family comes from the Kanuyaq River and Prince William Sound."

"World War II relocation," he said instantly, and it galled her no end that he was right. Still, she was interested. "What's an archaeologist doing in Prudhoe Bay?"

"The Eskimos used to have a summer hunting camp on Tode Point. It turns out it used to be a place the local tribes met for kivgiq, a—"

"A dance celebration," Kate said, "yes, I know. Interesting. I'd like to see it while I'm up here, if I may?"

An odd expression Kate couldn't quite define flickered across Leckerd's face. He hesitated, exchanging a glance with Hartzler, who said smoothly, "Oh, I don't see why not, Otto, do you? It really is the most interesting place, I'm sure you'll enjoy it."

Beneath her dewy-eyed gaze and dimpled smile Otto Leckerd forgot Kate's existence. They shook hands but to Kate's inquisitive eyes the prolonged gesture seemed more of a caress than a greeting. When she saw Toni's thumb brush Otto's wrist, and saw Otto come to attention like a setter on point, all alert and aquiver, she was sure of it.

"Did your people make it up all right?" Toni asked him, turning the question from prosaic to intimate with the twist of a vowel.

He nodded dumbly without releasing her hand. To Kate's critical eye he looked perilously close to drooling.

With a husky little chuckle Toni disentangled herself. "Where are they, in the lounge?" She had to repeat the question. "Is your crew in the lounge, Otto?"

Otto shook himself like a setter coming out of the water. "Yeah, they're in the lounge."

Toni beamed at him. "How nice. Shall we pick them up and get some lunch?" She tucked a companionable hand into his arm and they strolled into the corridor, Kate a forgotten third bringing up the rear. "I have a tour this afternoon, would your people like to come along? I don't believe any of them have been to the Slope before, have they?"

The corridor opened onto the first floor of the main module for the Base Camp, and Kate was surprised at how open it was. To the right was a game room filled with pool tables and shuffleboard and lined with booths upholstered in red. There was a long, rectangular window on the back wall of the game room and through it Kate saw a large body of water. The pool, she guessed, the site of Chuck Cass's last lap.

To the left was a lounge dotted with low modular furniture, cubical tables and brass lamps. A large shelf lined with books stood in a far corner. Between the two rooms and directly in front of them was an atrium with, if Kate's eyes did not deceive her, real birch trees growing behind glass and extending up through a hole in the ceiling into the next floor. Behind that was an open double door, through which came a hum of voices and the clink of dishes and the enticing aroma of a deep-fat fryer.

In the lounge four people rose to their feet and Otto introduced them around. "Chris Heller, Kevin Woolley, Rebecca Bean, Karen Clark. This is Toni Hartzler, our lifeline to RPetCo. Oh, and Kate Shugak." Four pairs of bright, inquisitive eyes focused on Kate. "I'm sorry, what was it you do up here?"

"Besides be Aleut," one of them said, and looked to Leckerd for approval, and got it.

"Let's get some lunch, shall we?" Toni said briskly.

"Wait a minute," Kate said. "Mind telling me why I'm here?"

Toni looked at her, puzzled. "Hams gave me to understand you were my new driver."

"And you do what?" Kate inquired.

"I'm the flack." At Kate's bewildered look, Toni elaborated. "The North Slope public relations representative." Kate still looked blank. "The tour guide."

"Oh."

"And you're my new driver. You'll be driving the bus for me on tours."

Kate remembered the bus ride from the airport and experienced a sinking feeling in the pit of her stomach. "Oh."

Something in her voice gave warning. Toni raised one perfectly groomed eyebrow. "You do know how to drive a bus, don't you?"

Kate took a breath and held it. "Let's put it this way." She met Toni's eyes. "I will by tonight."

Toni's feet slowed naturally to a halt as they joined the lunch line, and Kate broke off eye contact when she nearly ran into the person in front of her, a burly man who was staring at the salad bar with a pensive expression on his square, seamed face. She followed his gaze, to encounter the unwinking stare of a small green turtle peering out of a large bowl of romaine lettuce in the center of the serving table.

They regarded each other in silence for a moment. The man stirred and reached a hand forward to move a leaf to one side, disclosing a gold, five-pointed badge painted on the turtle's shell. "Deputy Dawg, I presume," he said, giving a small, courteous bow. "Pardon me." He employed the salad tongs to transfer romaine to his plate, careful not to disturb Deputy Dawg's comfy little nest, and moved on to the three varieties of salad dressing at the end of the counter.

Kate, agape, stared from the turtle to the receding back of the man to Toni, who shrugged with elaborate unconcern. "He's a photographer for *National Geographic!*" She handed Kate a plate. Kate took it automatically. "Take some salad if you're going to, you're holding up the line."

CHAPTER 3

THEY LEFT IMMEDIATELY AFTER lunch, archaeologists in tow, but they did not go directly to the airport. On their way out of the Base Camp, Cale Yarborough charged down the front staircase three steps at a time bellowing, "Hartzler goddammit the line's back at Crazy-horse I want those broads off the Slope by sundown take care of it!"

He crashed back up the stairs without waiting for a reply. Toni looked at the security guard seated behind the window before the front door, who shrugged in reply. "Don't look mean at me. I volunteered to escort them off the field. So did the safety supervisor. So did the production supervisor. So did the communications supervisor, the transportation supervisor, the—"

"Okay okay I get it," Toni said. "Dammit it's not like I don't have anything else to do." She held the door for Kate. "I guess we're tossing you in at the deep end today Kate hold your breath."

Kate walked through the door with the distinct feeling of a lamb being led to the slaughter.

To her relief, the big blue fifty-six-passenger bus proved easier to handle than she had feared, although she soon learned to treat the soft shoulders of the Backbone with respect, and to swing very wide for turns. The weather was a uniform dirty white, ground, clouds and fog, and she knew a

41

steadily growing gratitude for the fluorescent markers on four-foot sticks planted every ten feel at the side of the road. There were moments when the next marker was all she could see. She would have driven right by the turnoff to Crazyhorse if Toni hadn't caught her in time. Thank God. The last thing she wanted to do was try to back it up.

Crazyhorse Camp was a collection of Atco trailers arranged in wings off a main corridor, and looked as if it hadn't been cleaned since its arrival on the Slope. Kate picked her way distastefully around a spill of popcorn, most of which had been ground into the cigarette-scarred carpet whose brown color was not improved by either. She followed Toni down the hall and into a corridor and up some stairs. A line of men had formed at the bottom of those stairs, wound up both flights and extended down the hall. One of them caught sight of Toni and groaned. "Oh, shit, guys, it's Hartzler."

There was a chorus of boos and whistles and catcalls. Toni beamed at one and all and put a little extra sashay into her walk as she and Kate proceeded down the second-story main hallway. The line of men (Kate, counting heads, estimated at least a hundred) had widened to three deep by the time they came to a stop in front of a door. The man closest to that door saw Toni and swore loud, long and with a facility Kate was forced to admire. When he ran out of breath he said bitterly, "Goddammit, Hartzler, why do you always get here just when I get to the goddam door?"

"What's the matter, Bill, your subscription to *Playboy* run out?" Toni asked innocently.

The man swore again and stamped off. Everyone else stayed put, staring at Toni out of hangdog faces that reminded Kate of nothing so much as a bunch of hungry bloodhounds. They made her feel slightly guilty, though as yet she had no idea why.

Ignoring them all, Toni knocked on the door. There was no answer. She knocked again. "Belle? It's Toni Hartzler. Come on, I know you're in there, open up."

After a moment the door cracked. A large, round blue eye peered out. It encountered Toni and paused. There was a long sigh, and the door opened farther, to expose a six-foot platinum blonde in a minuscule leather cowboy vest, a minuscule, pleated leather skirt and matching cowboy boots. A tiny cowboy hat perched precariously on top of all that platinum hair, and there was a tiny toy pistol strapped to her waist in a tiny leather holster and a five-pointed star pinned to the vest over her left breast. There was a lot more breast than there was vest. Kate sternly repressed what she assured herself was merely a momentary feeling of inadequacy that would soon pass, and wondered if they were real.

"Well, shoot?" the cowgirl said in a breathy blond voice. She spoke Deep Southrun, ending every sentence with a question mark. Her foot gave a petulant stomp, the front of the vest bounced, and the next man in line sighed like he was in love. "We was just selling a few lil' ol' magazine subscriptions? What could it hurt?"

"It is a pain, Belle," Toni agreed sympathetically, "but you know Yarborough. He's got this thing about selling printed matter of any kind on his side of the Slope."

Belle pouted. Her lips were very full and very wide and very red, and the man in line sighed again. "How's a girl s'posed to make any kind of a decent livin' if the field manager keeps kickin' her outa her place of bidness?" She really said it, Kate noticed, "bidness." And then she smiled, and the man in line sighed a third time. "I noticed how tense he was the last time I was up? Now there's a man I could do something for, if he'd just give me the chance?" She bit her thumb reflectively, and this time a collective sigh went up from as far back as the stairwell. "Maybe a gift subscription to *Masseuse?*" She lowered her voice and said confidentially, "Y'all tell him I said so, you hear?"

"You could do a lot for me right now," someone called from behind them, and Toni turned and gave the assembled crowd a wide, sweet smile. "Gentlemen, Ms. Starr has closed up shop for the day. Good-bye."

"Come on, Jane?" Belle called over her shoulder. "Time to hit the trail?" She opened the door and beckoned them in.

A gentleman was just rising from the bed, buckling his jeans. "Why, Bob," Toni cooed. "I haven't seen you in ages. Where've you been keeping yourself?"

"Up yours, Hartzler," he snarled.

"Oh, goodness me, did I knock a moment too soon?" Toni wondered aloud. Belle and Jane both giggled as he snarled again and shouldered Kate aside on his way out.

Belle, her back to them, bent over to drag a suitcase from beneath the bed, and Kate looked up at the ceiling and hoped she wasn't blushing. Scarves were removed from over lamps, implements and ointments from the bedside table, and in a remarkably short time they were ready; almost, Kate thought, as if they were used to the drill.

"Oh, Kate can carry that other suitcase for you, Belle," she heard Toni say generously, and found herself lugging a bag weighing approximately three hundred pounds down the hall behind Toni, Belle and Jane. "How many subscriptions did you sell this time up?"

Belle pouted again. "We were going for a new record, weren't we, Jane? Twenty thousand in two days?"

"We would have made it, too," Jane chimed in, "in another four hours."

"I'm impressed," Toni said.

So was Kate. A mathematical calculation presented itself to her fertile brain. She stopped it before it arrived at a solution. Some things it was better to not know.

The archaeologists were impressed, too, at Belle in her little cowgirl suit and Jane in her very little leopardskin sheath and shark-tooth necklace. When they got to the airport, the pipeliners standing in line on their way south were equally impressed. "Praise the Lord!" one man was heard to shout, and Toni, bidding Belle and Jane a fond farewell, observed that the two might make their goal after all, and before they reached Anchorage, too. "Push *Ms.* magazine as hard as you can," Kate heard her tell Belle. "These yahoos could stand to have their consciousnesses raised a tad."

"I'll try, honey." They hugged, and Toni waved them out onto the tarmac and up the airstairs of the waiting jet.

Toni's official tour, arriving on a special charter, kept them kicking their heels at the airport and eventually arrived ninety minutes late. It consisted of one United States senator from Illinois and his entourage, including various representatives of the environmental militia and the superintendent of the Arctic National Wildlife Refuge. They were all on their first orientation tour of the North Slope, in spite of the fact that the Honorable Levi Poulsboro sat on the Senate Energy Committee, and to a man they were determined not to be impressed. Two of them, one tall and a Sierra Club commando, one short and a member of the Wilderness Society, both aggressively determined to find fault, occupied the two front seats on the bus and cross-examined Toni all the way across the field. As Kate listened, admiration for the other woman grew. The difference between a straight and a crooked hole, the flow status of the wells on H Pad, the intricacies of tertiary recovery techniques, current manpower status in the Western Operating Area, all these were grist for Toni's mill. The two men were stumped, but only temporarily. "What about slickem?" the tall one said. "That stuff they put in the pipeline to make the oil flow faster?"

"Slickem," Toni said, her brow wrinkling, and Kate, who had by now abandoned any pretense of impartiality, feared they had her. But no. Toni's brow cleared. "Slickem, of course. I was just reading about that in *Petroleum Intelligence Weekly*. It's a long-chain polymer, I believe, sort of a gooey plastic. It's injected into the pipeline at Pumps One and Four, Four being the station just this side of the Brooks Range where the oil might need a little extra oomph to get over the hump." She smiled. The two men didn't smile back. "Yes. Well. Slickem reduces the turbulent flow of the oil in the line, and causes it to expend its energy more profitably in getting down to Valdez." She smiled again. With difficulty, Kate repressed a cheer.

The two men scowled in unison. The short one said accusingly, "Well, *we* heard that it greased the inside of the line and made the oil flow smoother that way."

Toni's fund of smiles was bottomless. "I don't believe that's the case, sir, but we'll be going to Pump One later this afternoon and we can check then."

A half-dozen caribou, looking moth-eaten from their long winter spent beneath the Central Power Station, climbed up on the Backbone and proceeded to cross to the other side. Kate muttered a prayer and pumped the brakes gently. The front bumper came to a stop inches from the oblivious caribou, which didn't even look around at the big bus sliding to a halt on their left, just kept on going across the road and down onto the snow- and ice-covered tundra on the other side. Kate took a surreptitious breath, her foot off the brake, and goosed the gas. The bus creaked and groaned and started forward again.

The senator spoke for the first time. "Where's the corral?"

Kate saw Toni at an unprecedented loss for an answer. "I beg your pardon?"

"Well, I assume you put the caribou away when you're done with them," the Honorable Levi Poulsboro said sternly. "Is there a corral somewhere you keep them in?"

Kate took her eyes off the road long enough to see if he was serious. He was. She turned back and in the mirror saw the expression on one of the archaeologists' faces, Chris Heller, a thin young man with large, very expressive brown eyes, and had to look hastily away, catching her underlip between her teeth and biting hard. She heard Toni say, with no discernible trace of hysteria, "Prudhoe Bay is a wildlife habitat as well as an oil field, Senator. Some caribou drop off from the central Arctic herd during its migration every fall and winter here. They like the shelter the modules give them. They like the pads in the summertime, too. When they're on the pads, they're up off the tundra and in the wind; it keeps the mosquitoes away."

"The pads," the Sierra Club commando said, "that reminds me." He waved a hand in a gesture that appeared to encompass the entire North Slope, Canadian border to Chukchi Sea. "When's the rest of this going to be graveled in?"

"The rest of what?" Toni said, puzzled.

He waved his hand again. "The field. When are you going to gravel in the rest of the field?"

This time Kate didn't dare look in the mirror, and instead concentrated fiercely on the foggy road in front of her. Toni, still with that astounding self-control, said, "Sir, the Prudhoe

Bay field measures approximately twelve miles north to south, and twenty-five miles east to west. That comes to approximately three hundred square miles all told. With one mile of gravel road costing upward of a quarter of a million dollars, I don't think we can look forward to graveling in the rest of the field anytime soon."

"I see," the Honorable Levi Poulsboro said with a grave nod. "You'll probably have to wait until the price per barrel of oil goes up some more."

"Probably," Toni agreed.

Quite a bit more, Kate thought.

The tour took all afternoon, beginning with the Base Camp and including the pool and the weight room and the track ("Eleven times around makes a mile," Toni told them) and the movie theater, upholstered from floor to ceiling in red plush, and moving on to cover the entire western side of the Prudhoe Bay field in exhaustive detail. The operations module housed Production Control, where three operators sat in a darkened room surrounded by an enormous, U-shaped counter. Their faces eerily backlit by the green reflection from the computer screens, the controllers spoke in low voices over headsets and tapped out rapid commands on keyboards, looking for all the world as if they were on the bridge of a spaceship headed for Iapetus, except that this computer didn't talk back.

Next door was the Communications Center and although the room was about the same size as Production Control the contrast was immediate—bright lights and constant noise and perpetual motion. This room looked like the bridge of a spaceship, too, only in this case the *Enterprise,* on Red Alert under Romulan attack. A bank of radios monitored traffic on three channels amid bursts of static, two switchboards rang nonstop, five telex machines chittered out yards of yellow tape, a fax machine spewed out page after page, its twin sucking up reams going in the other direction. A tall man with disappearing red hair, bright, inquisitive blue eyes and a wickedly attractive grin rolled rapidly in a wheeled armchair from switchboard to radio to telex to fax with never a wasted move, except the occasional collision with his coworker. She was a short, pudgy woman with small, penetrating eyes that saw everything whether you wanted them to or not and a tenor squeal of a voice, the grit and gravel voice Kate had heard calling race odds over the public address system. "Meet Warren Rice and Sue Jordan, communications operators extraordinaire," Toni announced. "You can run but you can't hide from a communications operator."

The redhead caught sight of Kate and rolled his chair over to halt in front of her. Ignoring the honorable senator from the great state of Illinois waiting for adulation next to her, he said in a deep, mellow voice that made her toes curl up just a little inside her steel-toed, RPetCo-issue safety boots, "You don't have to run from me, babe. I promise I don't bite." He grinned. "Hard."

Everyone has a weak spot, and Kate's was a deep, mellow male voice; fortuitously at that very moment an alarm whooped like the dive siren on a submarine, an entire wall of ominous yellow telltale lights went off like a pinball machine and Toni hustled them out the door. "False alarm," she said airily, to the deep disappointment of the two pit bulls, who would have rejoiced to see the roof blow off during their visit just to confirm all their deepest suspicions about oil production in the Alaskan Arctic. "Probably dumping Halon in some skid. Happens all the time, especially in the spring when the snow melts and gets down into the roof detectors."

In that case Kate didn't see why they couldn't go back and

get to know the redhead better, but Toni had her in the bus and behind the wheel before she could muster up the presence of mind to say so.

In the field they climbed up on a rig floor and watched the roughnecks change out a bit and go back into the hole, ninety feet of drill pipe at a time. Personally Kate could have spent the rest of the day there, watching the roughnecks throw the chain and manhandle those enormous tongs, but Toni dragged them back down to ground level and over to a very dull row of metal shacks surrounding equally dull, more or less vertical arrangements of pipe and valves. "Christmas trees," Toni called them, although anything less like a Christmas tree Kate had yet to see. These were allegedly the first point at which the oil came up out of the ground after the well was drilled.

They stopped at Production Center Three and the two pit bulls attacked Dale Triplett before they were all the way in the door. "We were wondering about this slickem stuff," the tall one said.

"Oh, sure, slickem," Dale said. "It's kind of neat stuff, actually. It's a long-chain polymer, kind of a gooey plastic. It's injected into the line at Pump One and"—she looked at Toni—"Pump Two? Anyway, it kind of gums up the oil, not much, just enough to slow the turbulent flow so it doesn't ball up inside the line, and instead uses its energy to push itself down the pipeline to Valdez. The crude is under such tremendous pressure when it enters the line that it can snarl around in there instead of getting on its way."

The tall man looked at the short one, who said accusingly, "Well, *we* heard it greased the inside of the line and made the oil go faster that way."

"Really?" Dale raised her eyebrows. "Well, you heard wrong."

"*This* way, please, gentlemen," Toni interjected smoothly, and marched them down cramped, dimly lit corridors over what felt like miles of metal grating, through what seemed like hundreds of boxy modules; from the eerie silence of Skid 4 where the oil came into the complex from the wellheads, to the deafening clamor of Skid 14 where the process of depressurization and drying out began. Except for the fluorescent yellow signs reading "Danger! So_2O_4 may be present! When alarm sounds vacate premises at once!" and the ubiquitous, bright yellow Scott Air Paks mounted every ten feet, there wasn't much to look at except pipe of every diameter going in every direction, all too often making unexpected, ninety-degree jogs to go off in others. For the first time in her life Kate had to duck to avoid banging her head, a lesson it took three painful whacks to learn. The scream of natural gas going through those pipes at six hundred pounds per square inch made her ears ring for an hour afterward in spite of the foam earplugs Toni had handed round at the beginning of their trek.

"There are six production centers in the Prudhoe Bay field," Toni shouted. "One, Two and Three on the RPetCo, or Western Operating Area side, and Four, Five and Six on the Amerex, or Eastern Operating Area side. Each one is designed to process 300,000 barrels of oil per day. During that process, each one can produce up to 4,800,000 cubic feet of natural gas and 30,000 barrels of water. The oil has to be degassed, dry, and no more than 154 degrees Fahrenheit before we send it over to Pump One—bottom hole temperature is 220. Kate, get the door for us, would you?"

Kate, hopelessly lost in a maze of pipe and frame and grating that seemed to go on forever, now discovered to her horror that she was lost inside the skid in which they were currently standing, too. It was possibly the single most humiliating moment of her life. Kate Shugak had never been lost before. Not ever. Put her down anywhere inside 20 million acres of Park at any time of the year and she could have found her way home blindfolded, but this metal maze was something totally beyond her experience. Dazed from the din, squinting in the dim light, head hurting from three different welts, she looked back at Toni and spread her hands helplessly.

"It's okay," Toni shouted, "it takes a while to find your way around." She reached past Kate and thumped a previously invisible bar and a previously invisible door opened. They stumbled through it in a body, grateful to leave the clamor of Skid 14 behind them.

The Honorable Levi Poulsboro was first out the production center door. The air was cold and refreshing. Kate paused for a moment, eyes closed, sucking it deep into lungs that felt starved of oxygen.

"Oh, look! How cute! Here, puppy, come here, come on," she heard someone exclaim, followed by Toni's voice, jolted out of its usual calm. "Sir, don't do that! Don't touch them! Don't!"

Kate's eyes popped open and she pushed through the crowd and found the group confronting a half-dozen little arctic foxes, no more than kits really. The Honorable Levi Poulsboro bent over to pet the lead one, the biggest and the brashest of the litter. Toni was just moving forward to prevent contact when the kit nipped at the outstretched senatorial hand and leapt smartly back.

There was a loud, disbelieving bellow. "Ouch! Goddammit! Why, that little son of a bitch!"

Toni shoved her way to his side, Kate right behind her. Toni grabbed his hand and Kate peered around to see blood welling from a small wound. "God damn it," Toni said, spacing the words through her teeth. "Everybody stay put, don't move, don't talk." She turned and approached the kits. They were almost but not quite tame, and held their ground, eyeing the brunette's approach warily.

She moved slowly, no hint of threat in her stance. The instant she was within reach her arm lashed out, exactly like a snake striking, and caught the big kit by the scruff of the neck. Before anyone had a chance to protest, she had wrung that neck in a quick, sharp twist. A high-pitched, panicked whine was cut off before it really got started. A second later, the body hung limp from her hands. The rest of the kits scattered like marbles and vanished into holes dug in the snow beneath the Production Center's foundations.

There was a moment of instantaneous shock before exclamations of horror resounded from the tour group. Kate herself was momentarily startled into immobility. Toni was more efficient at fox killing than Mutt. "Oh, poor little fox!" "How could you?" "How awful!" "It was just a little bite, he was just scared, you didn't have to kill him!"

"Shut up," Kate said curtly, regaining her tongue. She retrieved the pup's body and stowed the corpse beneath her seat on the bus. Outside she could hear Toni talking, a note of steel underlying the brunette's professionally syrupy voice. "Senator, ladies and gentlemen, please. There is an epidemic of rabies rampant across the Slope. When someone gets bitten, we have to kill the animal involved and send the body to Fairbanks for testing." That brought silence. "If the tests are positive, if that pup was rabid, you, Senator, will have to undergo a series of rabies shots."

"Which involve a very large needle and very painful abdominal injections," Kate said, raising her voice so it would be heard by everyone in the group.

"That's right." Toni moved to the attack. "None of you were supposed to come up here without proper orientation as to how you interact with wildlife on the North Slope. Did you not know, Senator, that you were not supposed to approach the animals you encountered during your visit?"

One quiet voice, not the senator's, admitted, "We knew. They told us."

"Then you know who's at fault for that fox's death. Now then. We've got a pump station to tour. Get on the bus, please."

As they pulled off the Production Center's gravel pad, a dark shape shot up over the snow berm on the right. It passed directly in front of the bus's front bumper, and in a purely instinctive reaction Kate slammed on the brakes with both feet.

The bus plunged violently three times, like a recalcitrant horse, and stalled. The shape scooted across the road, skidded down the snow berm on the left and vanished into the fog. Kate sat where she was, gripping the steering wheel tightly in both hands and trying not to shake, her burgeoning confidence in her ability to drive this monster withered on the vine.

"What's the problem?" Toni inquired from the seat behind her.

Kate swiveled and stared. "What's the problem? Didn't you see that snow machine?"

"So what?"

"Toni, I almost hit it."

"Nah." Toni shook her head. "That was Cindy Sovalik. She doesn't run into buses."

Kate asked what seemed like a logical question. "What's she doing out here on a snow machine in the first place?"

Only apparently it wasn't. "She's on her way home, of

course," Toni said impatiently.

"Home?"

"Yes. To Ichelik. It's a village thirty miles east of the Sagavanirktok. It's her home. She commutes back and forth to work from there."

"Commutes?"

"Uh-huh."

"On a snow machine?"

"During the winter, yes. Anything wrong with that?"

Kate looked out at the blowing snow and fog, through which she could see maybe two feet, and said, "What could possibly be wrong with that? I suppose during the summer she drives a four-wheeler?"

"Yes."

Kate restarted the bus. "Did I see a rifle on her shoulder?"

"Probably."

"I thought no one was allowed to have firearms in the field."

"No one is, except for the field manager and Cindy. Polar bears do wander ashore from the ice pack now and then, you know. They must have mentioned something about it during orientation."

A voice from the back of the bus added, "Right after they told us about not interacting with the wildlife."

Kate looked in the mirror to see Chris Heller's outthrust jaw and indignant eye, and restarted the bus. The drive to Pump One was accomplished in record time in a cold silence that rivaled the temperature outside. Kate heard the Sierra Club commando pounce on the pump operator who greeted them at the door, the Wilderness Society's representative close behind. "Slickem?" the operator drawled. "Well now, slickem. That'd be a long-chain polymer, kind of a gooey plastic, reduces the turbulent flow of the oil in the line so that it'll expend its energy getting down to Valdez instead of tying itself in knots north of the Brooks Range."

The short man said, "Well, *we* heard it greased the inside of the line to make the oil go down faster that way."

The operator stared for one incredulous moment, and then threw back his head and laughed. He laughed loud, and he laughed long, and when he was done laughing neither the tall man nor the short man had anything more to say.

The pump station wasn't as noisy as the Production Center had been and everyone walked and talked a lot slower and softer. They paid their respects to the three enormous pumps that hied the oil on its way, genuflected before the three Rolls-Royce generators that powered the pumps and from this shrine were ushered outside to make their curtsy to the line itself.

It looked pretty much the same as it did five hundred miles to the south where it crossed the western border of the Park, Kate decided, a silver snake four feet in diameter, except that this one appeared to be shedding its skin. Large strips of the thin metal outer layer had peeled away, big chunks of the second, foamlike layer were gouged out seemingly at random and a green plastic subderma hung in strips like velvet from a caribou rack, leaving the darker, slowly oxidizing layer of steel pipe exposed to the elements and Kate's astounded gaze.

Upon inquiry, the pump station operator shifted uncomfortably from one foot to another and sent Toni an agonized glance, who said smoothly, "Yes, well, insulation restoration and repair is a priority in next year's budget, have I shown you the cutout where you can feel the heat of the oil flowing down the line?"

She slid down the side of the gravel pad and crunched

across the snow to a spot thirty feet farther on. On any other day the two pit bulls would have sunk their teeth into the insulation story, but the station operator's laughter rang in their ears and they followed Toni mutely. The rest of the group, who had already learned everything they ever wanted to know about oil production in the frozen north and were still shaken by the fox pup's death, straggled behind in less than enthusiastic pursuit.

Kate, following more slowly in the rear, cast a casual upwards glance and halted in her tracks.

It appeared that two-inch silver duct tape was a primary means of interim insulation maintenance. Strips of it wound around the pipeline, binding the peeling layers of insulation to the line with the grim determination for which duct tape is known as an all-purpose utility fix-all in the Arctic.

Kate stood there, staring up, hands in her pockets, trying to estimate how many sixty-yard rolls of duct tape it would take to wrap around a forty-eight-inch diameter, eight-hundred-mile-long pipeline. At three dollars a roll at McKay's Hardware, and with the current price of a barrel of oil at nineteen dollars and falling fast, she was worried RPetCo and Amerex might not be able to afford it. Then she remembered that over half the pipeline was buried, and heaved a sigh of relief. The ingenuity and foresight of the pipeline's designers had not failed her after all.

"Kate?" Toni said, coming up behind her. "Did you want to take a look at this?"

Kate turned to meet Toni's inquiring brown eyes. "Okay," she said, "I give up. What's the deal with the turtles?"

• • •

"It's not their fault," Toni said back at the airport, watching the honorable senator from the great state of Illinois and entourage file up the airstairs into their plane. "Every government employee, before he or she is allowed to move up the civic ladder, is required to pass a course entitled 'How to Be a Prick in Ten Easy Lessons.'" One of the group turned at the bottom of the airstairs and waved enthusiastically. Toni gave a wide and seraphic smile and waved enthusiastically back. "Good-bye, all you little pricks and prickettes, good-bye. Click your heels, close your eyes and say three times, 'There's no place like Washington, D.C.' Thank God."

The archaeologists burst into slightly hysterical laughter. Kate decided that if she discovered Toni Hartzler was dealing dope on the Slope, Kate might have to cover up the evidence.

She negotiated safe passage back to the Base Camp and nosed the bus up to the bull rail with no small sense of triumph. Plugging the bus into the headbolt heater on the rail, she collected the pup's body from beneath the driver's seat and followed Toni into camp. They were met at the front door by none other than Cale Yarborough. "What the hell is this I hear about the fox pups on H Pad!" he bellowed, at a decibel level John King might have envied.

Kate tried to pretend she wasn't holding the body of the fox in question by the scruff of the neck and waited for Yarborough to ring the charges over Toni's hapless head for allowing a United States senator to be bitten by a fox on his, Cale's, shift.

"I'm sorry, Cale, it was—" Toni began.

Cale snatched the body from Kate's hands and cradled it in his arms and stroked its dead little head. "Poor little pup," he crooned, "poor little thing." He damned both women with an impartial glare. "At least tell me he took a good-size chunk out of the Honorable Levi Poulsboro. At least tell me that!"

"Sorry, Cale," Toni said meekly, "he only got in a little nip."

Yarborough held forth colorfully for ten minutes on the cranial capacity of the average United States senator. Ending with a blanket curse on all their offspring for generations to come, he stamped off, still cradling the stiffening body of the pup protectively in his arms. Kate followed Toni into her office. The phone was ringing and it kept ringing for the next forty-five minutes, one call after another demanding to know if the horrible news was true. Toni assured one and all it was and at the first breathing space unplugged the phone. Her beeper whined almost immediately. She turned it off.

"Is it always like this when a fox gets killed?" Kate said.

"Hey," Toni replied with an airy wave of her hand, "those pups were the adopted children of most of the west side of the field. The production operators go out every shift change to check and make sure one of them hasn't wandered into the flare pit by mistake. Belly dumpers getting paid by the yard have been known to detour through the pad just to pay their respects. I myself have been requested to put the PR van at the disposal of various departmental delegations who want to go out and take pictures to send to relatives Outside. They're so little and round and fuzzy and cute, you see. There isn't a lot that's little and round and fuzzy and cute on the Slope, and these are the first ones to den in so close to the Base Camp."

"Why's Yarborough so pissed?" Kate said plaintively.

"He drives out there himself, two or three times a week, with bologna sandwiches." Toni grinned at Kate, feet up on her desk and hands linked behind her head. "He hates bologna. I've heard him say so."

"But," Kate said feebly, "but they told us in orientation we weren't supposed to feed the wildlife."

"We're not," Toni said.

"It makes the wildlife dependent on us, they told us. Makes them forget how to hunt their own food."

"It does." Toni looked at her watch. "It's seven o'clock, end of shift. Didn't you say you were meeting Dale for dinner?"

Dumbly, Kate followed her down the hall to the dining room, to find Dale already in line.

Tonight, the serving line was presided over by a swarthy man with a luxuriant mustache clad in an immaculate white jacket that buttoned down one side and a towering chef's hat that tilted rakishly over one bushy black eyebrow. "Kate Shugak, Gideon Trocchiano," Dale introduced them.

Gideon beamed at Kate. "Rare, medium or well done?"

"I beg your pardon?" Kate stared past him at the immense grill, where rows of New York steaks sizzled merrily.

"How do you like your steak?" Gideon repeated.

"Steak?"

His smile faded a bit. "Yes. It's Tuesday."

"So?" Kate said warily.

"So Tuesday and Thursday are steak nights," Dale said impatiently, "how do you want yours cooked?"

Lunch had been rushed and nothing out of the ordinary: a choice of cold fried chicken, make-your-own sandwiches and a small salad bar. Dinner evidently was going to be different. For dinner, there was not only steak. There was deep-fried halibut in case she didn't like steak. There were steak fries, long and thick and perfectly browned and with the peel still on, a sight that nearly made Kate moan with delight. There were green beans sauteed in bacon and onions. There was a salad bar as big as the first floor of Kate's cabin, heaped with lettuce and tomatoes and mushrooms and green peppers and sprouts and a bunch of other vegetables Kate couldn't have identified at gunpoint, and no turtles (she checked). There was a cart piled high with desserts, apple pie and lemon meringue pie and cherry pie and chocolate pudding and pound cake, all of which Dale turned up her nose at, saying they could make hot fudge sundaes in the break room after dinner, if Kate wanted.

"If I want?" Kate said. "If?"

Holiest of holies, there was a dispenser armed with two spouts that gave forth an inexhaustible supply of fresh milk. Kate filled four glasses; by then her tray was heavier than Belle's bag. She staggered from the serving line into the dining room with the growing conviction that working for an oil company had its advantages.

The first person she saw in the dining room was Jerry McIsaac.

CHAPTER 4

HE LOOKED UP FROM a table groaning beneath the weight of an equally well-laden tray and saw her at the same time. He surged to his feet. "Kate? Kate! What the hell are you doing here?"

"Jerry!" She put her tray down on his table and returned his hug with extra.

With a final thump on her shoulders he pulled back to look at her. "How long has it been, two, three years?"

"Too long," she said, sitting. "What are you doing up here?"

"The same thing I did in Anchorage, for a lot more money. Anyway, I asked you first." He eyed her. "You aren't—working, are you?"

She smiled at him, a vague, unfocussed smile that should have warned him.

She remembered the first time she had seen Jerry McIsaac. It had been in an apartment in Mountain View where a baby-sitter had arrived to find the parents had already left. Her charge, an eighteen-month-old boy, had been beaten unconscious in his crib and the baby-sitter, a frightened fourteen-year-old who couldn't stop shaking, had nonetheless retained the presence of mind to dial 911. Jerry, lead paramedic on call out of the Airport Heights fire station that evening, had been first on the scene, two minutes from the time the call came in. Even so, he was too late. The baby was pronounced DOA at the hospital.

He was looking at her with a quizzical expression; she said, "I was remembering Petey Washington."

Jerry was a tall, plump, rubicund man with big blue eyes and a wide-open smile that faded at her words. Like her, his memory was good, far too good. He cut a bite of steak and chewed it thoughtfully. "Yeah." He swallowed. "Your first call, wasn't it?"

She nodded. Arrested on duty at Fort Richardson, both parents had worked hard at blaming the other for their son's death, but Kate's meticulous recording of the detail of the bruising found on the child's body and the physical evidence surrounding the scene, plus patient, painstaking interviews with neighbors above and below stairs had resulted in time for both. Hard time. In fact—she made a quick mental count—Petey Washington's father shouldn't be eligible for parole for at least five more years.

None of it had brought Petey Washington back from the dead, though.

Their eyes met. "First time's always the worst," he said.

Her smile was involuntary and fleeting and more than a little sad. He had said that to her that awful night in Mountain View. He had said it to her while he was holding her head, as she vomited up the remains of the Lucky Wishbone jumbo cheeseburger and fries she'd had for dinner. Jerry was intimately acquainted with her previous job, as well as with the circumstances surrounding her departure. Jack had kept her more recent activities from public notice, and she was fairly certain in this instance that Jack would qualify Jerry as "the public." "Yeah," she said, and busied herself with her food.

She could feel his eyes on her bent head. "So what brings you up to the frozen north?"

"Work. I got myself hired on as a roustabout. Just came up this morning." She gestured at her laden tray and met his eyes with a twinkle in her own. "I may never leave."

He laughed and, it seemed to her, relaxed a little. "I know. It does sort of give new meaning to the horn of plenty, doesn't it?"

Dale sat down between them. "Hi, Jerry. You two know each other?"

Kate filled her mouth with steak to avoid a reply. It was perfectly done, a moist, steaming pink on the inside and a thin crust of black on the outside.

"Yeah, we both used to work in town," Jerry said easily, and Kate thanked him with a glance. Swallowing, reluctantly, she wiped her mouth and said, "Why'd you quit?"

His wide shoulders moved in a small shrug. "Burnout."

"Bad?"

He grimaced. "Bad enough for me to make the move up here."

"Here is better?" Kate asked, thinking of the drug overdoses, Chuck Cass's death.

"Up here only grown-ups get hurt, and usually they're only hurting themselves."

Kate saw his point.

"Anyway, I went back to school and got my physician's assistant degree—"

"Congratulations."

"Thanks, and Lil Rogstad—remember her?—was already up here and put in a good word for me, and the rest is history."

"Lil's here, too?"

"Yeah, she's my better half on this shift."

"Hi."

Toni's voice sounded next to Kate, and a note in it made her swivel around to look. The other woman's eyes were fixed on Jerry's face with what could only be described as a languishing expression in them. A half smile curled her mouth. "Looks like old home week. Mind if I join you?"

The table shook and slopped Kate's milks into her tray as Jerry leapt to his feet. "Hi."

"Hi. Didn't I already say that?" she asked Kate.

"At least once," Dale said, tucking into her salad.

Jerry pulled out a chair and Toni settled into it gradually, taking her time, snuggling back into it like a kitten curling up on a pillow. "You can sit down now," she told Jerry softly.

His face flushed. Dale giggled. Kate hid a grin. Toni looked from Kate to Jerry. "You two know each other?"

Before either of them could answer a beeper went off. A rustle went over the dining room as all 145 people in it checked their pockets. Over the tinny speaker on Jerry's beeper Sue Jordan's gravelly voice said, "Jerry, medical emergency, call the operator, call the operator immediately." The last word was barely out before the same voice came over the loudspeaker. "Jerry McIsaac, call the operator immediately, Jerry McIsaac, call the operator immediately."

Jerry cursed fluently. "You can run but you can't hide." He went to a wall phone, dialed zero and listened. When he came back to the table he said, "Sorry, gotta go, got an emergency at CC2." He paused, tray in hand, and looked at Kate. "You up on your skills?"

Her fork stopped in midair. "I'm still rated in CPR, and I remember all the pressure points."

He grinned. "Good enough. Want to come with?" She looked down at her steak and back up at him mutely. He

65

grinned again. "Plenty more where that came from. The night shift'll be happy to cook some up for us when we get back."

"In that case, you bet."

Toni pouted, almost as well as Belle. "Abandoned, deserted, forlorn, bereft." Dale sat up straight in her chair, a little indignant. Toni ignored her and sent a dazzling smile over to the next table. Four burly men trampled each other in her direction, one of them actually overturning his chair.

Kate was appalled when Jerry dumped all that food in the trash before setting his tray in the dishwasher's window. She herself managed to gulp down a glass and a half of milk before her tray was ripped ruthlessly from her hands. "What's going on?" she asked, trotting behind Jerry as they crossed the arctic walkway to the fire/safety module. "I assume we're going on some kind of a run?"

"You assume correctly. Drug overdose at Arctic Construction." Kate's ears grew points. "He's locked himself in his room and won't come out. He says he has a knife and that he'll kill anybody who tries to come in after him. He's already cut one guy, his roommate, and Lil's got *him* under sedation in her ambulance." The walkway ended in a large, two-story garage with offices to the sides. The garage contained one ambulance, space for another, a ladder truck and a water truck parked on the first floor. Jerry crashed down the steps two at a time, the metal staircase shaking beneath his weight, and ducked into his office long enough to grab one parka for himself and chuck another at Kate. The garage door was rolling up and Jerry was backing the ambulance out of the fire station before Kate gathered her wits together enough to break into a gallop and tumble in through the passenger side door. She felt as if the William Tell Overture should be playing somewhere in the background.

Construction Camp Two had been built by RPetCo to house construction crews for the length of their contract. It was twelve miles west of the Base Camp on the Backbone and the snow had begun to fall, with attendant winds bellowing encouragement, so it was a sweating, swearing forty-five minutes before Jerry could pull onto the gravel pad that housed the camp. A yellow grader, sounding a loud and indignant beep, materialized out of the gale like something out of *Aliens* and backed around the ambulance, leaving great mounds of snow curling in its wake. The operator, peering grimly through the windshield, dropped the enormous steel blade with a muffled crunch inches from their front bumper and started another pass. Jerry parked at the camp's bull rail, next to the other ambulance, and they waded through drifts up to their thighs, ducking their heads against the wind that blew icy trickles up their noses and down their necks. Jerry inhaled the wrong way and sneezed violently as they shoved through the front door. Kate dug a handful of snow out of her collar and stamped her boots. "Hey, Lil," she said to the dark-haired woman bending over a gurney. "Long time no see."

"Kate! What the hell are you doing here?" She looked past Kate to Jerry. "The other guy's still in his room. Sam'll show you." She bent back over her patient.

"Nice to see you, too," Kate said mildly.

"Come on," the security guard standing to one side said, and double-timed it down a hallway, Jerry and Kate on his heels. They turned a corner and found another six guards and one man not in uniform standing outside a closed door.

"Kate, this is the camp supervisor, Tom Parry. Tom. Kate, she's riding with me for the evening. He in there?" Jerry said, gesturing toward the door.

"No," the camp supervisor, a dark, tense man with an

unshaven Neanderthal jaw, said with asperity, "we're having a hall party. Of course he's in there, you silly bastard."

Jerry gave him a long look and the other man shut up. "What's he on, anybody know?"

"Just before he passed out his roommate said he's been doing a lot of coke," one of the guards volunteered.

"Why didn't his roommate tell somebody before it went this far?" Jerry grumbled. It was recognized to be a rhetorical question and went unanswered. "Well, what's his name?"

"Martin Shugak."

"What!" Kate said.

Jerry looked at her. "You related?"

"If it's the same guy, he's my cousin."

"Good," Jerry said, "we can use it."

"Maybe," Kate said, recovering some of her poise. "We don't exactly get along."

"Hard to believe," Jerry drawled. "Where's he work, Tom?"

"He used to be a carpenter for Arctic Construction. He's been up for nineteen weeks straight, since October."

The thought of Martin behind a band saw was enough to turn every hair on Kate's head white. She struggled not to show her distress.

"Goddammit!" Jerry was furious. "I've told those friggin' construction superintendents time and again not to let their people work back-to-back shifts. Fuckers never learn." He unclenched his fists and took a deep breath. His face smoothed into its usual, good-humored mask. Kate had never seen Jerry McIsaac lose his temper with a patient, not even the time the drunken fisherman had run over Jerry's foot with a snow blower when Jerry insisted on treating the broken leg the fisherman had just given his six-year-old daughter. He signaled for silence and stepped forward to knock gently on the door.

"Martin? Martin Shugak? This is Jerry McIsaac, the medic over at the Hilton. Why don't you open up the door so we can talk?"

From behind the door came a wild stream of hysterical profanity.

Jerry winked at Kate. "Tone it down, Martin. We've got a lady present. Talk all you want, but watch the language, okay?"

There was a brief pause. The door opened a fraction. The voice, less close to cracking, said, "You really got a woman out there?"

With a sinking feeling Kate recognized his voice. It really was Martin. "It's Kate, Martin," she said when Jerry nodded at her. There was no immediate response and she added, "Remember, your cousin? From Niniltna?"

The door opened wider. Through the crack Kate could barely make out Martin's face, but she could see all too clearly the queer blank look in his brown eyes. His voice sounded high and shaky. "What the hell are you doing here?"

The question of the day. She hoped he was too out of it to draw any conclusions. "Same as you, making a buck, roustabouting for RPetCo. Listen, Martin, it really is you, isn't it? I can't see your face too well."

The door opened wider. The ring of security guards closed in behind Kate. Martin's eyes bulged. He jumped back and the door slammed shut. Another string of abuse poured out from behind it.

Jerry glared around. "Who the fuck do you assholes think you are, the A-Team? Back off!" The guards looked at him with stubborn faces. Jerry shook his head angrily and nodded at Kate to continue.

"Martin, it's Kate again. No one is going to hurt you out

69

here, I promise. Why don't you open the door?"

"I know what you're trying to do! I'm not stupid! You're talking nice to get me to come out! I'm not stupid!"

She winced at the raw sound of his voice. "Listen, Martin, nobody out here thinks you're stupid." There was no sound. Kate saw the sweat on Jerry's forehead, saw the fanatical desire for rape, pillage and plunder in the eyes of seven frustrated wannabe rent-a-cops. Her shirt was sticking to her back. "Sure is hard, Martin," she said, "talking to a door. Maybe you could open it up just a crack. Maybe I could come in." Next to her Jerry shook his head violently. She ignored him. "Martin? How about it? Just me?"

They waited. After a long time, during which Kate had nightmare visions of Martin cutting his wrists not five feet away with her powerless to stop him, her cousin spoke. That vulnerable quaver was back in his voice. "Get them goddam security guards farther back. You tell them I got a knife and I'll kill anybody who tries to mess with me!"

"They know, Martin," Kate said, straightening. "We don't want anyone to get hurt. Come on now, open the door."

The door opened abruptly and banged back against the wall. Everyone jumped. One guard took an involuntary step forward. Martin saw him and his face contorted and the eight-inch hunting knife whizzed between Jerry and Kate to stick, quivering, in the wall behind them.

For a single, paralyzed moment none of them could move. Then one guard made a low diving tackle through the door for Martin's knees, another went for his shoulders and the rest of them followed like a net dropping from the ceiling, and from then on the sequence of events became increasingly confused. Martin shrugged off the first two guards and tossed a third out the window. Fortunately the camp had only one floor, but the pilings holding the camp up off the pad still made it at least a ten-foot drop, not to mention the cuts the glass caused when she went through it. In the melee Jerry's fist caught Kate on the side of the head and he got himself kicked in the stomach for his pains. He doubled over, clutching his belly and wheezing. Kate sat next to him on the floor, holding her head, which had already taken enough abuse for one day. She caught sight of a two-inch roll of duct tape sitting innocently on top of one nightstand. The all-purpose, super-duper utility cure for every bush ailment, including holding the TransAlaska Pipeline together. She touched Jerry's arm and pointed. He realized her intent immediately and nodded. She snagged the spool of tape with one hand and they launched themselves back into the fray.

With one guard per arm and four others and the camp manager holding his legs and the seventh security guard climbing back in the window to sit on his chest, Kate and Jerry got Martin's wrists taped together. It wasn't a particularly neat job but it was an effective one, and from then on their task was relatively easy. They taped his legs together at the knee and ankle and then they let Martin lie in the middle of the floor while the Impossible Mission Force leaned up against the walls and each other, nursing their bruises and waiting for the shaking in their legs to quit. Both beds in the double room were broken, the door hung drunkenly from one hinge and snow was whirling in through the smashed window to form a small drift on the floor beneath. An interested crowd peered in from the hallway.

"Look at that little prick," Jerry said resentfully, still puffing for air. "He can't weigh a hundred and twenty pounds wringing wet."

"How you must love this job," Kate said, leaning her head

against the wall and closing her eyes.

"I'd bet my left nut he was scoring his coke with a speed chaser."

"All grown-ups, and only hurting themselves, is what I think you said."

"Bastard better not have handed any of that crap out to his friends." Jerry pushed himself to his feet and looked over at the guard who had gone out the window, now standing in a corner with blood trickling down her left temple. "You okay, Wedemeyer?"

Wedemeyer managed a weak smile, slid slowly down the wall to the floor and passed out.

"Well, shit," Jerry said, disgusted. His beeper went off again and the entire room, not excluding Martin, jumped a foot in the air. "Jerry McIsaac, call the operator, Jerry McIsaac, call the operator immediately."

Jerry leaned his forehead in one shaking hand for a moment. "It's going to be one of those nights, isn't it?" he asked the floor.

It was. There was another medical emergency, this one at Rig 63, and the operator advised the senior physician's assistant on staff to betake himself there at once. Jerry made arrangements for Martin to join his bunkie in Lil's ambulance and asked Kate, "You want me to drop you off at the Base Camp?" Kate looked at him as if he'd lost his mind. He shrugged. "It's your funeral." But as they climbed into the ambulance he gave her a sideways grin. "Just like old times, ain't it?"

"Ain't it, though?" she agreed.

They fought their way through the wind and snow across the field to H Pad. Where the access road turned off the Backbone they found a bright orange Chevy Suburban

72

encrusted with years of drilling mud, though it didn't need to look its best since it wasn't going anywhere in the immediate future. Of the four tires, only one was still on the road, and from the looks of the front axle, it would be the only tire on the road for a while. Jerry got out and checked the cab.

"Nobody inside." He climbed in and got on the radio. "RPetCo Base, this is Medic One, we've just turned off on the H Pad access road and there's a Suburban off the road here. Looks like the rig rep's. It's partially in the way of oncoming traffic, you'd better get Transportation out here."

"Medic One, RPetCo Base, we know about that, we have dispatched equipment."

Jerry raised an eyebrow. "Okay, RPetCo Base, Medic One out."

A quarter of a mile farther on they came across a forklift, painted the same bright orange, "Naborhoff orange," Jerry said when Kate asked. "They paint all their equipment that color, the same way Brinker paints all theirs Brinker blue."

"Why?"

"Keeps 'em from stealing each other's equipment. Hey, look. It's missing a fork."

"It's also in the ditch," Kate said. "Upside down."

"You noticed that, too?" Again Jerry got out to look, and again there were no discernible bodies, although it was hard to be sure someone hadn't staggered off into the howling storm. He climbed back in the ambulance and reached for the radio. "RPetCo Base, this is Medic One again, yeah, Sue, about a quarter of a mile down the access road from that Suburban is a wrecked forklift. It isn't as much of a traffic hazard as the Suburban, but you'd better notify Transportation anyway. And maybe get the rig to run a nose count? I don't see anyone at the scene, but if the driver's wandered off

73

somewhere we'd better find out."

"Yeah, Jerry, actually we know about the forklift, too, and the drivers have already been, ah, found."

This time both eyebrows went up. "Okay, RPetCo Base, Medic One out."

A half mile more and they were on the well pad. A row of well houses passed on their right, and something that Kate thought at first was another well house, but when they approached closer and the headlights picked it out of the blowing snow, it resolved itself into a jim-dandy of a helicopter, or what had been one. It was painted the same Naborhoff orange as the Suburban and the forklift and was in about the same shape. Canted heavily over on one side, one of the rotors was bent like a paper straw. The skin of the starboard pontoon had a large hole in it. The pilot's door was missing. The inside was already coated with a layer of fine, dry snow. It had missed coming down on the nearest well house by a scant twelve inches.

Jerry rubbed his chin, regarding the helicopter musingly. After a while he reached for the mike. "RPetCo Base, this is Medic One. I bet you already know about the chopper."

"Roger that, Medic One."

"Uh-huh," Jerry said. "Is it a full moon tonight, by any chance?"

"I'll check."

"Thanks, Sue, Medic One clear." He hung up the microphone and turned to Kate. "You remember McIsaac's Three Laws?"

Kate, mesmerized by the downed chopper, said woodenly, "Uh-huh."

"Okay, what's the first law? Kate? What's the first law?"

Kate roused herself from her absorption. "McIsaac's first

law is to look out for myself."

"Okay, what's the second law?"

"Second law is to look out for my partner."

"The second and most important law," he corrected himself. "And the third?"

"Third law is to look out for my patient."

He gave her shoulder a rough thump. "That's my girl. I think tonight we'll make the second law the first law, though, okay? Let's go."

Kate wasn't sure whether she wanted to or not, but she couldn't let Jerry face whatever lurked inside Rig 63 all by himself. She raised a square chin, squared heroic shoulders and marched up the stairs leading to the rig's camp. She wasn't, however, quite so foolish as to take the lead, and when Jerry opened the door she waited until he was well inside and no audible blows had been struck or shots fired before she followed.

It was quiet inside. Too quiet. A tall, big-bellied man in striped gray overalls and an orange, duck-billed Naborhoff cap glared from beneath grizzled eyebrows. The subjects of his glare were seated back to back in the center of a room Kate identified as the rig camp's dining and recreation area. There was no one else in the room except for a white-clad kitchen helper, his back to them. He was scrubbing out the serving line as if his life depended on it. From the expression on the big-bellied man, Kate thought that it might.

"Hey, Bear," Jerry said to the big-bellied man. He sounded cautious, not without cause. Rage radiated off the big-bellied man like heat.

"Jerry," Bear said through his teeth.

Still cautious, Jerry inquired, "What's going on?"

Bear looked at him. Jerry didn't back up but only because

pride wouldn't let him. Bear's gaze shifted to Kate, who received the distinct impression of being scorched. Lastly, Bear looked back at the two men in the center of the room, who weren't sitting still because they wanted to but because there were bound in place with enough rope to restrain King Kong. "Ask them," the big-bellied man replied, still between his teeth.

Jerry got a penlight out of his bag and shined it in the two men's eyes. He looked at Kate. She reached for one man's wrist. His skin was cool and clammy to the touch, his pulse rapid and erratic. He was incapable of focusing on her upraised fingers, much less counting them. He sported several bruises about his face and neck. His arms and legs looked whole, but she wondered if she should check for broken ribs. Instead, she straightened and nodded in response to the question in Jerry's eyes.

He straightened. "Coke?" The big-bellied man's red face became redder. He gave a curt nod. "On the floor?" Another nod. "And in the chopper? And the forklift? And the Suburban, too, I suppose?"

Bear nodded again, although Kate couldn't see how he managed, so rigid with wrath was he.

"Fuck 'em if they can't take a joke," one of the men mumbled inopportunely behind them.

The kitchen helper froze. In the next instant he began to sidle around the serving line. Next to Kate, Jerry sucked in an audible breath and with a show of amiable briskness inquired, "I suppose you'll be making their services available to the industry? Fine, good, I'll just call Security, get them taken off your hands." Without waiting for the other man's permission he pulled his radio out. "Security guards have been dispatched to the scene," Sue assured him, twice. Kate could tell he wanted to ask how many and how soon, but he managed to restrain himself.

They waited until the security guards showed, whiling away the interim two hours by making one-sided conversation with Bear, whom Jerry introduced as Bear Honeysett, RPetCo's rig representative on Naborhoff 63. Those two hours, two of the longest in Kate's life, were just long enough for her to decide she was glad John King hadn't hired her through a drilling contractor. She might have had to pee in a bottle in front of a witness, but at least she was alive to tell the tale. If she and Jerry had left the two roughnecks alone with Bear Honeysett, she wasn't sure they would have been.

Back in the ambulance she said, "Just so I've got the sequence of events straight—those two got higher than kites, got kicked off the rig floor and took off in the Suburban?"

"Uh-huh."

"And when they ran it off the road, they came back and took the forklift?"

"Yup."

"And when they wrecked the forklift, they came back for the *helicopter*?"

He grinned at the windshield. "Looks like."

Kate sat back in her seat. "Why are they still alive?" She wasn't talking about the damage the three separate vehicle crashes should have inflicted on the roughnecks' hapless bodies.

Neither was Jerry when he replied, "Good question."

Kate said, and it wasn't entirely part of her investigation when she did, "You people have a real problem with drugs."

The engine caught and turned over. "Oh, hell, Kate," Jerry said easily, "you know if you had your way you'd bring back Prohibition. Looks like the weather's clearing a little."

77

It was. During the next thirty minutes the snow ended and the wind died down, enough to see the commotion outside Construction Camp One as they drove by on the Backbone. "Now what's going on?" Jerry wondered when they caught sight of the crowd standing outside one of the modules.

"A block party?" Kate guessed, but in her defense it must be said that by now it was the wrong side of two o'clock in the morning and she had never been a night person.

They parked ten yards behind the crowd and, the evening's experiences beginning to have their effect, tiptoed up behind the gathering of men. Kate caught a whiff of deep-fried fat and identified the kitchen module, which indeed it proved to be, as attested to by the two enormous garbage Dumpsters flanking the double doors, as well as by the two not less enormous grizzly bears with their heads down in them.

"Oh, shit," Jerry said, backing up. He was alone. Kate stood rooted in place, staring as the crowd of men, most of them in their T-shirts and clutching cameras to their chests, shouted and whistled and stamped, trying to get the bears' heads out of the Dumpsters long enough to snap their picture. Flashbulbs were going off like firecrackers. With what Kate thought was extraordinary self-control for a grizzly bear in March, the bears ignored them until one man crept up behind one and yanked his tail.

Kate's jaw dropped.

The bear roared indignantly and swung around on his haunches, one paw raised, a perfect pose for the pipeliner's friend, who stood at the ready with a Canon Sure Shot. The flash went off six feet from the bear's face, and he roared again, all four inches of claw extended.

"You dumb son of a bitch!" someone growled. Stupefied and still gaping, Kate looked over and saw a man in a state trooper's uniform. He stepped forward, another big-bellied man with the added authority of age and uniform, and the crowd melted before him. He came to a stop in front of the two pipeliners. The bears had turned back to the Dumpsters. With magnificent indifference, the trooper didn't even look their way. Instead, he hitched up his gun belt in the menacing gesture Kate was convinced all state troopers were taught their first day in trooper school. The pipeliners, who had laughed in the bear's face and jeered at its anger, knew real danger when they saw it and snapped into an attitude of acute attention.

The trooper hitched up his gun belt a second time, and said in the slow, caustic drawl cultivated by state troopers the world over, "Just now, I was of two minds who to shoot, you or the bear." He paused long enough for that thought to register. When it did, he leaned forward, nose to nose with the tail-puller, and dropped his voice but not the drawl. "Next time, I won't have any doubt." He paused again. "Now git."

The pipeliner started backing up, treading on the toes of his camera-toting friend. "Yes sir no sir sorry sir whatever you say sir." The trooper watched them back and fill up the steps and inside the module with a merciless eye. It was the beginning of a virtual stampede.

When the door closed behind the last pipeliner, the trooper turned to the bears. "And as for you two, it's too early for you to be up! Hibernate, dammit!"

The two bears, with an I.Q. a good ten points above that of the average pipeliner, knew when they were outclassed. They extricated themselves from the Dumpsters and cantered out of camp.

Kate let out a long sigh. The trooper heard it, turned and caught sight of Jerry. "Hey, McIsaac."

Jerry drew a shaking hand across a sweating brow and walked forward on unsteady feet. "Jesus, Joe. I thought for a minute you were going to be in need of my professional services."

The trooper grinned, a white slash of teeth in the dim light. "Naw. They're just cubs, babies, yearlings. Wouldn't hurt a fly." He looked at Kate, and back at Jerry.

"Kate Shugak, Joe Graham. Kate's just hired on with RPetCo."

"Shugak," the trooper said thoughtfully, "Shugak." He met her eyes. "You a friend of Jim Chopin's?"

"We've met," Kate said reluctantly.

The trooper snapped his fingers. "Kate Shugak, from Niniltna, right? I remember now. Jim was telling me about that deal with the bootlegger a while back. Nice job."

"Thanks."

Kate's monosyllabic response was unencouraging, and the trooper, about to expand on the subject, paused. "Right," he said. "Well, nice to meet you. Jerry."

"Joe."

The trooper drove off. Jerry looked down at Kate. "What deal with the bootlegger?"

"It was a long time ago," Kate said dismissively. Jerry just looked at her, and she sighed. "A guy was selling whiskey inside tribal borders. Billy Mike asked me to stop him."

"And?"

"I did."

"Oh." Like the trooper, Jerry didn't push it.

• • •

Kate spent what was left of the night in the dispensary with Martin.

He scowled at her from his bed. His skin was flushed, his pupils large and black and bottomless. "What the fuck are you doing here?"

"Glad you know who I am now," she said dryly, and pulled up a chair.

He twisted against the wrist restraints. "Get me out of these things."

"Not a chance."

He thrashed beneath the covers, the muscles of his face and throat distended. "Cut it out, Martin," Kate said, bored. "You know the drill. So do I. Next stop, detox."

He stared at her, and relaxed. "Shit. Well, hell, it was worth a try."

She grinned at him.

"You're not here to lecture me, are you?"

"Nope." She looked him over dispassionately. "You sure are a mess, though."

"Fuck you."

"Thanks anyway, I gave at the office." He snorted a laugh. "How long you been up here? I hadn't heard."

"How could you, stuck away on the homestead like you are. You're a regular hermit, Kate."

"How long?"

He closed his eyes and let his head fall back on the pillow. "Forever. Five, six months, I think. Since October anyway."

"So you came up right after fishing."

"Uh-huh."

"How'd you get the job?"

He shifted restlessly. "Billy Mike put the word out, RPetCo wanted to do some seismic testing on Niniltna Tribal

Association grounds. He swapped permission for half a dozen jobs on the Slope."

Kate nodded. She looked down at her clasped hands. "Where did you score the dope?"

He shrugged irritably. "Where does anybody score dope?" He eyed her suspiciously. "You got any particular reason for asking?"

She batted her lashes at him. "Who, me?"

"'Who, me?'" he mimicked her. "Yeah, you. I know you, Shugak, you never do anything without a reason. What the hell are you doing here?"

She started a plausible lie but his body began to shake and sweat beaded on his brow. He swore weakly.

"I'll get Jerry," Kate said, rising.

"Kate," he called after her.

She paused at the door, looking at him over her shoulder. "What?"

The sweat was dripping off his forehead now. "It's not that I'm not glad to see you. It's just that whenever I screw up, you're always in the front row."

"Yeah, I know, Martin. I've always been lucky that way," she said, and went out.

CHAPTER 5

SHE DROVE JERRY AND Martin and Martin's roommate, both of whom Jerry had judged needful of immediate medevac, out to the airport and saw them onto the Lear jet ordered up for that purpose. It took half an hour to help load all the various boxes and bags and stretchers and patients. A security guard stood at a distance, not offering to help as Kate sweated to get a small but very heavy box over the sill.

"Careful!" Jerry leapt to help her and together they hoisted the cargo inside. Kate shoved it in with more vigor than care and Jerry said, "Careful," again.

Kate craned her neck to see in. "Martin awake?"

Jerry shook his head. "Both of them are out cold. Let's hope they stay that way."

"If they don't, if Martin doesn't, tell him I'll come see him in detox next week. He'll be thrilled."

"Okay." His face looked gray in the harsh light of the halogen lamps posted around the apron, and Kate said, "You look beat, buddy. Grab some Z's on the way home."

His smile was watered down and his salute weak. "I'll do that. Thanks, Kate."

"Wouldn't have missed it for the world. Please, don't think of asking me again anytime soon."

The strain on his face lightened and he laughed and waved as the Lear's engines began to whine.

She made it back to camp safely, floating in a kind of euphoria beyond exhaustion, and was on her way to breakfast when Toni scooped her up outside the dining room and swept her down the hallway. She was back in fast forward mode. "Come on Kate we have to get to the airport."

"We're going to the airport?" Kate was forced into a trot to keep up with Toni's long-legged strides. "I haven't had breakfast yet." I haven't even been to bed yet, she thought, blinking to clear bleary eyes.

"That's okay you probably won't get lunch either."

"What, more hookers to deport?" Kate said grumpily. She wanted a meal and a bed, in that order. She wanted time to think about what the episodes at the construction camps and the rig meant to her investigation. She wanted to slow down to a walk, but when she tried to Toni urged her back into a trot.

"I believe they prefer the term 'entrepreneur,'" the other woman said blandly. She thumped the swinging doors wide and strode into the great arctic outdoors as if she owned it. "How long have you known Jerry?"

Kate woke up enough to stare at the back of Toni's head. The brunette had twinkie hair, big, shiny, blow-dried, every perfect strand in artful place. "Oh, I don't know, six, seven years. Eight." She yawned, a jaw-cracker that wasn't entirely faked. "Don't ask me to do complicated mathematical computations this early in the morning."

"He told me you worked together in Anchorage."

"We did. Sort of."

Snow crunched beneath their feet. Toni paused next to the door of the bus and turned to look at Kate. "Jerry and I are involved."

"I noticed." Kate couldn't help herself. "There seems to be a lot of that going around."

Toni fluffed her hair and gave Kate a flirtatious look from beneath her lashes. "There's a lot of me *to* go around."

Irresistibly, Kate laughed. She held up both hands, palms out. "Okay, all right, Jerry's a big boy. It's none of my business."

Toni refrained from the obvious reply, and they got in the bus amicably if not in perfect accord.

• • •

For the rest of the week Kate was assigned to drive Toni's bus, and for every day of the rest of that week Toni made ruthless use of her services. No sooner had one tour departed than another arrived. A dignified group from Bahrain who wanted to see if oil came out of the ground any differently in the Arctic than it did in the Persian Gulf, a Texas oilman who almost wept at the sight of seven-inch tubing (the largest his East Texas fields used was one-inch), a rollicking crowd of Russians who wanted to drill for oil in Siberia and who wanted to take Toni with them when they went home, a delegation from Colombia who told hair-raising stories of local drug lords strafing drill rigs and who regarded the North Slope as a haven of peace and security, a coven of mixed media reporters, an Israeli paratrooper on maneuvers with the Alaska Air National Guard, and a lone RPetCo stockholder who was vacationing in Alaska and on impulse hopped a plane to Prudhoe, arriving Friday afternoon on MarkAir and calling the Base Camp for a look around before his plane left at seven that evening—Toni met, fed and toured them all, seraphic smile and composure unshaken. It was all Kate could do to keep up with her, to muscle the big bus around the soft-shouldered gravel roads, to not get lost in the vast, fiat expanse of arctic tundra.

That vast expanse daunted her, going on forever, horizon to horizon, with miles and miles of gravel roads heading off in every direction on the compass. "You should have been here in the beginning," one of the roughnecks told her, "when all that was up here were the rigs and if one of them moved to a new pad overnight, the next morning you didn't know where the hell you were." The local landmarks were more stationary now, and more individual. The Base Camp was easy to spot, backed up as it was by the 112-foot communications tower. It sprouted a dozen microwave shots, deep, round frames with what appeared to be white cloth stretched across their surfaces, and looked like small drums. Jungle drums, Kate thought. The bush telegraph. If the power goes out, we could pull the shots down and beat on them.

When she got them, her off hours were nothing less than decadent. Every night she regularly drove others out of the sauna by turning the thermostat up as high as it would go and ladling water on the fake coals with a lavish hand, although she had to get used to sharing it with men. At home, a sweat was segregated by sex. It felt uncomfortable wearing a suit, too, but it was still better than no sweat at all. She was unable to hide the scar on her throat, and it occasioned curious, sometimes appalled looks, and a few blunt queries, but she ignored both and after a while the questions stopped, if not the looks. Something about the scar, combined with the husky edge it gave her voice and her composure concerning both, caused the men to pull back a little, for which she was profoundly grateful. Reaction on first meeting her had varied, from those who assumed she had been hired to fulfill a quota and treated her with barely concealed contempt, to those who only saw one more woman to take a shot at and wouldn't leave her alone. Kate felt alternately like live bait in a shark pool and a test case for affirmative action. It was wearing. She consoled herself with the reminder that it was also temporary.

She didn't swim, the undeniable temptation of getting wet all over cooled by the gruesome recollection that the pool was the site of Chuck Cass's last lap. Evidently the rest of the inmates felt the same way; that first week she never saw anyone in the pool. From the markings, it was exactly five feet deep all over. She wondered how tall Cass had been.

Somewhat to her surprise there wasn't a lot of talk about Cass's death, and the few times she tried to raise it in general conversation were countered with what was the main topic on everyone's mind, the rumor of a rif, a reduction in force. A man named Bert Something, Kate gathered a communications technician, was very concerned about a balloon payment coming up on his Anchorage bowling alley. "I just can't afford to get laid off right now," he told Kate earnestly.

Thwarted, Kate tried to raise Chuck Cass with Jerry and again he turned the conversation into another channel. Out of respect, Kate desisted. Jerry never had liked discussing his failures. She discovered Cass's room number and found the room empty, the closets and drawers cleaned out and the corners denuded of so much as a hairball. "A loner," Dale Triplett said briefly, adding, "At least he wasn't like a lot of the other guys, always coming on, always groping for a feel."

"He was a good operator," she got his boss to say after thirty minutes of dancing around the subject. "The equipment he worked on ran." When Kate tried to touch delicately on the cause of his death, the man said, voice rising, "I run a clean shop." He gulped down the rest of his coffee and left the table, and left Kate with as much information as she had had to begin with, zero.

Ranking right up there on the plus side of the job with the

sauna was of course the food. Gideon had taken a fancy to Kate, and Thursday night saw to it that she received the tenderest cut of beef on the grill, as well as the most perfectly steamed fresh asparagus. Dinner Friday was lasagna, heavy on the mozzarella, and Gideon made sure that Kate received an extra-large slice and prompt seconds. Kate had always had a distressing tendency to think with her stomach and was now beginning to wonder if she'd died and gone to heaven, but it didn't distract her from noticing that the kitchen was a place where everyone in the Base Camp eventually and inevitably came, and would make a fine distribution point for retail sales of illegal substances. The serving line seemed a bit public, though, and the offices, storage rooms and freezers, a cramped maze tucked behind the kitchen, offered little privacy, either. She was glad. She'd never eaten food this good before in her life, and she rebelled at the prospect of busting the chef who cooked it over a trifle of drug dealing.

At this rate, Kate realized glumly, she was going to be incapable of fingering anyone for dealing dope on the Slope.

Friday, in between the Texas oil man and the RPetCo stockholder, she was occupied in fending off the attentions of a mechanic from Field Maintenance who appeared to have fallen deeply in love with her at first sight in the sauna the night before, in spite of the wide gold wedding band on his left hand. She had pointed this out to him and he had looked amazed and wounded. "But, Kate, all wedding licenses are revoked north of the Arctic Circle!"

"Frank," she had said gravely, "I had no idea. I beg your pardon."

"Then we're on for that drink?"

Friday morning produced a pinch on the ass as she was stretching to clean the windows of the bus. She didn't rip his arm out of its socket and jam it down his throat only because the action might draw inconvenient attention her way.

Instead, that evening over dinner she explained the matter to Dale Triplett.

At the end of her story, Dale patted her mouth with her napkin and looked around the dining room. "Sandy? Marie? Almeda? Judy? Sue? MCP alert."

Five women, pretty much the entire female population of the room at that moment, rose from their tables and made their way over to stand next to Dale, who unclipped her beeper and slapped it down in the center of the table. Five beepers slapped down next to it.

"Who?" Sue Jordan demanded.

"Frank Jensen."

There was a unanimous chorus of approval and Sue said, "It's about time. When?"

"Tonight."

"How do we get him out of his room?"

"We'll get Billy Bob to get up a pinochle game."

At nine that night, Kate handed Dale a screwdriver and inquired in a mildly curious voice, "Mind telling me what we're doing?"

Dale unfastened the screws holding a screen to the wall. "We're hiding beepers in Frank Jensen's room."

"Uh-huh," Kate said, taking the screen. Frank Jensen's room decor consisted of *Playboy* and *Penthouse* centerfolds, a plaster nude on its own three-foot pillar (Kate couldn't begin to imagine how Jensen had gotten it up to the Slope) and a wine rack, the contents of which Sue examined and sneered at. She was now maneuvering a second beeper behind the heater, Almeda was burying a third beneath socks in a drawer ("We have to make one easy," she explained), Judy a fourth between the mattress and the springs on the bed and Sandy was taping (with duct tape, naturally) a fifth to the side of the window shade facing the window.

"Then," Dale said, reaching for a beeper and secreting it in the vent, "we'll set them off." She reached for the screen and screws.

"Uh-huh," Kate said, passing up the screwdriver again.

"At about, oh, four in the morning would be about right, wouldn't you say, girls?" She finished tightening down the last screw and smiled at Kate's brightening face. "One at a time."

"Yes!" Kate said.

"But wait, there's more," Sue said.

"What more?"

Sue opened the door to the suite's anteroom. "Notice how each suite has four rooms, two bedrooms, a bathroom and a shower?"

"Yes," Kate said, fascinated, "I had noticed that."

"Notice how all the doors to the suites lock from the inside?"

Kate began to have a clue. "Yes."

"We wait until Jensen's in the shower tomorrow morning and lock his bedroom door, *and* all the suite doors on the hall."

"Are we sure he showers?" Almeda said, brow wrinkled.

"Good question. Does anybody know if he has his own truck?"

"Yes," Kate said, glad to be able to have an answer. "He followed me out to the airport today."

Sue looked pleased. "Good. One of Number Two's control techs owes me a favor. We'll get Jensen out there and make his truck disappear."

This was beginning to get out of hand, and Kate said,

"Oh, hey, guys, I—"

Sue looked at her, square chin thrust out, little eyes narrowed. "You know why men don't suck their own cocks?"

Kate, unnerved, said in a small voice, "No."

"Because they *can't*."

Kate looked around the circle of stern faces and swallowed. "Oh."

That seemed to cover the situation for the rest of them, and Sue Jordan marched into the hall attended by a train of five. Kate meekly brought up the rear, beginning to feel a little sorry for Frank Jensen.

The next day she stayed as far away from Field Maintenance as was physically possible. It was easier than she had expected because Saturday was race day, and business as usual in the Western Operating Area of the Prudhoe Bay field was suspended for the duration.

The deal with the turtles, Toni had told Kate on her first day up, was that a turtle representing each of the departments would race in the Base Camp Saturday evening. "Why?" Kate had asked, which she thought was a valid question, and Toni had replied, "Because it's there." "What does the winner get?" Kate had inquired further, and Toni had raised her face to the heavens, closed her eyes and intoned, "Glory."

No one was ever able to explain to Kate's satisfaction from whence the idea of racing turtles had sprung, let alone why race them at all, but the Slopers threw themselves into the event with passion and verve. Each department had one turtle, each turtle had two departmental trainers, and bribery and corruption was the order of the day. Saturday morning an official race judge was named, bribed, impeached, removed and replaced in the space of two hours, Saturday afternoon Deputy Dawg was kidnapped again, and Saturday evening

91

began with a junk-food junkie's dream come true set up in the dining room. Gideon had outdone himself, having scattered individual stands for hamburgers, hot dogs, pizza and tacos among the dining tables. A fifth, with by far the longest line in front of it, dispensed hot fudge sundaes piled high with real whipped cream and chopped walnuts and even the cherry on top. Kate had two. She would have had three if Dale hadn't forcibly dragged her from the room. The turtles hadn't even raced and already Kate was disposed to approve.

The race was to take place in the AstroTurf room. The AstroTurf room occupied the center section of the second floor of the main module of the Base Camp, overlooked by the windows of every inside room of the two residence floors in the module. All of them this evening were flung wide and shoulder to shoulder with spectators. Every now and then someone fell out, but no one was hurt because the room was so packed with people they never made contact with a hard surface.

A roll of green plastic tarpaulin was spread in the middle of the room and two white circles painted thereon. One was large and touched the edges of the tarp, the other small and occupied its center. The turtles would race from the outer circle to the inner one, a distance of precisely five feet. The race would be in three heats, the winner the turtle with the shortest average time.

Cheerleaders appeared, dressed in down snowsuits, bunny boots and balaclavas pulled over their faces and with mopheads for pompoms. They were unsteady on their feet, and they forgot their cheer halfway through, but Kate was charitably inclined to think their snowsuits had constricted the vascular flow to their heads, limiting brain function.

The cheerleaders retired and Production's Xaviera arrived

in a gilt sedan chair borne on the shoulders of her pit crew, followed by Control Systems' champion pulled in a chariot and escorted by a twenty-man honor guard. Kate wondered who was manning the Production Centers' control systems. Probably the same guy who had stolen Frank Jensen's truck, for which a security bulletin had been issued over the public address system that afternoon. Catering's Hump appeared in a mayonnaise jar, led by a drum majorette dressed in the most beautiful kuspuk Kate had ever seen. The knee-length parka was made of cinnamon-colored corduroy with gold cord and red fox fur edging hem, wrists and hood. The wearer was a redhead with pale redhead skin and the combination was enough to cause a momentary pause in the din, but only momentary.

"What a gorgeous kuspuk," Kate said.

Dale looked around. "Oh, yeah, one of Cindy Sovalik's. I think she makes more money making kuspuks than she does making beds."

For a moment Kate couldn't place the name, and then remembered the close encounter with the snow machine her first day up. She looked back at the redhead. Cindy Sovalik sewed better than she drove.

Projects' entry, Tom the Twertle, arrived at the head of a conga line of Twertle cheerleaders, followed by Safety's RP 1 on a miniature fire truck complete with hook, ladder, lights and siren. Deputy Dawg, rescued from kidnappers for the second time that week, rode in in Glen Lefevre's shirt pocket. Behind Kate someone hissed, "I hear Deputy Dawg's high on Absorbine Jr."

"No!"

"That's what I hear."

"Hey! Judge! Judge! Deputy Dawg's been doped!"

The first heat was delayed while race officials called in Official Race Veterinarian Jerry McIsaac to administer a breathalyzer test. Deputy Dawg passed, and Security lodged an official complaint with the officials, alleging slander, calumny and harassment. A loud yelp of electronic sound cut across the uproar, the crowd pressed forward, the noise level increased exponentially and the race was on. During the first heat, trainers inspired their champions with shouts of "Turtle soup!" and "Tortoiseshell combs! Think tortoise-shell combs!" During the second heat a motorized turtle materialized out of the crowd and, with silver antennae whipping back and forth, ran circles around the mortal turtles. During the third heat, Hump was humped.

It was no contest. Deputy Dawg won all three heats by a good five lengths. Second place was tied three ways, and officials announced a runoff between Xaviera, RP 1 and Tom, during which Deputy Dawg took off on his own and again finished first. Attempts on Security's part to claim both first and second place were thwarted. Catering's complaints of sexual harassment against their runner were ignored. During a post-race interview conducted by a reporter from the *Campfollower,* the company's in-house newsletter, Glen Lefevre attributed Deputy Dawg's resounding success entirely to his trainer, Chuck Stange, who had been drafted by Security specifically for his experience and expertise in amphibian athletics. He added that they were looking forward to more competition next year.

For a moment, for just one admittedly fleeting moment, Kate wondered who was ahead in the Iditarod. She was pretty sure she was the only person in camp that night who did.

Fascinated with this new insight into the process of getting oil out of the ground, she bore witness to the events of the evening from beginning to end. Nearly everyone attending the races stayed up all night at various parties in various rooms scattered throughout the Base Camp. Kate, in Dale's tow, attended them all, and after she'd been offered her fourth toke and her fifth line began to appreciate John King's concern. Up until now, she had seen no evidence of drug use in the Base Camp itself, but tonight it was everywhere; in Ziploc bags, cut into lines on mirrors, in the ubiquitous waxed paper envelope, on one man's knuckles when he substituted it for salt as he knocked back straight shots of tequila. Eyes were unnaturally bright, laughter was loud and raucous and Kate saw at least one incipient orgy. "Caligula would have felt right at home," she remarked finally, caught between amazement and disgust.

"What?" Dale said. She followed Kate's gaze to see a production supervisor who was old enough to know better empty an envelope of cocaine on the inside of Toni Hartzler's wrist, who made great play with her lashes as the supervisor raised her wrist to his nostrils and snorted. "Oh, hell, that's just Hartzler. That gal goes through men the way Hobo Jim goes through guitar strings."

"I meant the dope," Kate said. "It's all over. It's everywhere we've been."

"I admit," Dale said, her brow creasing, "it's not usually like this. People must have been stocking up for Race Day for the last year."

Virtually everyone was using, but Kate couldn't find anyone selling and she walked miles through the Base Camp that night, down hallways, in and out of suites, through the break room half a dozen times, around the AstroTurf room twice, looking. All she found was a dozen little waxed paper envelopes and a smeared pocket mirror. It wasn't enough, not nearly enough. I'll have to come back up at least one more week, she thought, and forgot to wonder why the realization did not annoy her.

The partiers were present in force, if groggy, when the kitchen doors opened at five-thirty A.M. Sunday morning. Gideon had put together a magnificent brunch celebrating the successful conclusion of the races, featuring tiger prawns, oysters Rockefeller and chocolate cheese torte. Along about six-thirty A.M., the public address system crackled into life. "Frank?" a feminine voice said. "Frank, are you there?"

The diners sat up and looked around themselves for a Frank. "Yeah, I'm here."

"Oh, Frank," the female voice said, "I miss you so much, I need you so much, when are you coming home?"

"As soon I can get on a plane in your direction, baby. Where are you?"

The woman's voice dropped an octave. "In bed, where else?"

"Oh, baby. What have you got on? That little pink thing with the cutouts?"

At this point a distressed yawp went up from a far corner and Frank Jensen raced out of the dining room as if his ass were on fire. A few minutes later the broadcast cut off abruptly, ending with just an echo of Sue Jordan's gravelly chuckle. The dining room was roaring with laughter. Kate looked across the table at Dale with respect and not a little awe. "Remind me never to piss you off."

Dale clucked her tongue and gave her head a mournful shake. "It's his own fault. If Frank would just learn to use the pay phone in the break room instead of the company tie line, those darn communications operators couldn't listen in on his private conversations." She anointed her oysters Rockefeller with a lavish amount of Tabasco sauce, picked up one shell with her little finger elaborately crooked and let the bivalve slide slowly onto her tongue. She swallowed. "Or tape them for broadcast at a later date and time."

Sunday, the Western Operating Area entered into a field-wide conspiracy to let the oil pump itself out of the ground, which it did anyway, while everyone slept off their excesses. The Sunday night buffet featured prime rib, and if Kate had been dead she still would have been there, plate out and salivating.

On Monday morning Kate and Toni toured the Saudis and the Russians around the field, delivering them over to the Amerex guide at Checkpoint Charlie at noon, receiving in return the head of Ducks Unlimited and his wife. He was very friendly, his wife even more so, and Toni was friendliest of all. That evening, Kate saw her being even friendlier with Gideon Trocchiano behind a cart loaded with Bismarcks and maple bars.

On Tuesday, five pounds heavier and no closer to discovering who was retailing cocaine to RPetCo's employees, Kate flew back to Anchorage. She spent most of the ninety minutes en route thinking, not without a trace of envy, of Toni Hartzler's comprehensive love life.

CHAPTER 6

THE PHONE RANG EARLY the next morning, too early. The bed in Kate's cabin loft didn't have a phone next to it. The cabin had no phone at all, or electric lights, and nothing she had experienced thus far in cohabitation with Jack had led her to believe that she might ever wish to install either. Jack had her immobilized in a comprehensive bear hug and had naturally slept through the first ring. He slept through the second, too. "Jack. The phone."

His arms tightened and he nuzzled his face into her hair. "Leave it. Machine'll pick up."

The phone rang again and stopped, and Kate heard the mutter of a voice from somewhere downstairs. By now she was wide awake. She rose early at home, but there she didn't have any incentive not to. She turned over and found one, and was served breakfast in bed for her pains. "Who was it on the phone?" she said around a mouthful of Jack's specialty, eggs scrambled with anything he found in the refrigerator that wasn't actually moving off the shelf on its own.

He filched a pillow and nudged her over so he could sit next to her. "Jane."

"What did she want at six in the morning?"

"She says something smells from under the duplex."

"Does it?"

"I wouldn't be surprised, considering who lives in it." Jack

98

picked up a piece of her toast and put it between his teeth and leaned toward her. She laughed and bit into the other end, and for a while it was the best it had ever been between them.

Later Kate watched through Jack's kitchen window, coffee mug suspended halfway to her mouth, as the owner of a Scotch terrier came to blows with a jogger who had just trodden in the terrier's morning bowel movement.

"Life in the big city," Jack said over her shoulder, his arms sliding around her waist.

She allowed herself to rest against him. He nibbled the side of her neck. It felt good, so good that she disengaged herself on the pretext of refilling her mug. "Where's it go?"

"The bike trail?"

"Yeah."

"Through the tunnel on the left, it runs all the way to Kincaid Park. Through the tunnel on the right, it goes uptown. It ends on Second Avenue, I think." He poured coffee and drank it while she told him about her week. When she recounted the extradition of Belle and Jane, he said, a delighted grin spreading across his face, "Hookers? On the Slope?"

"I believe they prefer the term 'entrepreneur,'" she replied gravely.

When he stopped laughing he gave her a shrewd look. "You're enjoying yourself."

She thought it over. "Maybe. A little. It's—" she searched for the right words, and wound up saying lamely, "it's different."

"It is that," he agreed. He drank coffee, watching her over the rim.

"What?"

"Nothing. I'm just waiting."

"Waiting for what?"

"For that great downpour of the wrath of Shugak. The Kate Shugak I know doesn't tolerate booze, drugs or mind-altering substances of any kind, in any amount, anywhere near her or hers. I'm having trouble accepting the fact that you spent Saturday night in the middle of what sounds like a user's Utopia and everybody came out alive."

She was a little taken aback. "You make me sound like Carry Nation."

"You are a little like Carry Nation at times. That was a hatchet you used to break up that bootlegger's cache a few years ago, if I'm not mistaken."

"That was Niniltna."

He raised an eyebrow. "And this is only an oil company, and only oil company employees, and so nothing to overexcite yourself about?"

"Go to hell," she said sweetly.

He laughed and drained his mug. "Why don't you walk up and meet me for lunch at the Downtown Deli? About eleven-thirty or so?"

"Sounds good."

"See you then." He swooped down for a hard, quick kiss. On his way out the door he paused and called over his shoulder, "Oh, yeah, John King called while you were in the shower. He says he'll call—"

The phone rang, and Kate picked up the receiver as Jack closed the door behind him. "Shugak?" King barked. "That you? What'd you find out?"

"Nothing," Kate told him, "except that RPetCo's racing turtles are among the finest I've ever seen."

"Did you find evidence of any drugs?"

"Well," Kate admitted, "rumor has it Deputy Dawg *was* high on Absorbine Jr., but the breathalyzer test came up clean, so there's no proof."

She allowed him to vent some of his spleen and then interrupted him without compunction or apology. "These things take time, King. I can't just walk up to someone doing a line of coke and ask him where he got it."

"Who'd you see doing coke?"

She winced away from the roar of outrage. "I won't tell you."

"God the hell damn it all, I—"

"King!" she bellowed. The shock of her harsh, torn voice ripping down the line caused him to fall silent, she was sure only temporarily. "You don't want the doers, you want the dealers. There's no point in fingering people who are only buying. I'm going to have to backtrack, and I'm new to the Slope and to Slopers. It won't happen overnight." As she spoke she remembered again the crack she had made to Jack about being up and back in forty-eight hours, and was grateful King had not heard it. "Try for a little patience, okay? In the meantime, I'd like to see the manifests for all the charter flights for the past twelve months. Oh, yeah, and the medical logs, too."

"Talk to Lou." He gave her Childress's extension. "And, Shugak—"

"I'll talk to you before I head up on Tuesday." She hung up before he could launch into another diatribe and dialed the security chief's number. "Childress," she said, "this is Kate Shugak. I want to look at the flight manifests and the medical logs for the last twelve months."

"Out of the question," he snapped back. "Those are restricted company records. You're not cleared for them, shit, you're not even a real employee."

"John King assured me I could count on you for every

101

assistance," Kate said mildly. There was a pause simmering with resentment. "The flight manifests and the medical logs. At Jack Morgan's house no later than this afternoon, please. I assume you don't want me picking them up in person."

Childress muttered a curse and there was a savage crash of receiver in cradle in Kate's ear.

There was a caribou in the freezer from last year's hunt, carrots, celery, onions and potatoes in the refrigerator and beef broth in the cupboard. "Jack, you sweet devil, you shopped for me." The ingredients for the stew went into the Crockpot on the counter. Kate, running out of domestic steam, poured herself another cup of coffee, opened the newspaper, found Doonesbury and went straight from Zonker to *The New York Times* crossword puzzle, a segue that pleased her with its linear progression.

At nine-thirty she put down her pen and stretched out a hand for the phone book. She found the number she was looking for and punched it in. It rang once. "Good morning, Downtown Detox."

"Hi, this is Kate Shugak. I'm calling about a cousin of mine, a patient there, should have been brought in last week."

"What is his name?"

"Martin Shugak. That's S-H-U-G-A-K."

"One moment." There was a rustle of paper, a silence during which Kate could hear the woman breathing, the sound of a hand muffling the receiver and a muted rumble of voices. After a moment the voice came back on. "Ma'am? Mr. Shugak checked himself out last Friday. Against all advice, I might add."

"I see." Kate was saddened but not surprised. "Did he say where he was going?"

The woman hesitated. "Did you say your name was Kate?"

"Yes."

"He left a message for you."

Kate's mouth twisted. "Is it repeatable?"

The woman laughed. "He said, quote, 'Tell her I'm going home,' unquote."

Kate's heart lifted a little. It might be a lie, but it might also be the truth. "Thanks." She hung up.

Martin. If he'd just stay home. If he'd just stay off the sauce. If, if, if.

Tilting her chair against the wall, she looked out the window. A slight breeze stirred the leafless limbs of the trees. The surface of the lagoon was a crust of rapidly rotting ice. On the other side of the lagoon was a collection of the ugliest houses she'd ever seen in her life, enormous boxes built of ninety-degree angles and finished with clapboard siding, plunked down on lots so close together the owners could probably hear their neighbors inhale.

A little red car with windows tinted so dark she couldn't see inside drove by, the thud of its stereo enough to rattle Jack's kitchen window in its frame. She closed her eyes and rested her head against the wall. On the homestead the pussy willows would just be starting to come out. The creek out back should be clearing of ice, not that its swift-running water ever completely froze over during the winter.

She felt disoriented, afflicted with a sense of wrongness, of not belonging. She was home from the Slope, and yet not home.

Images passed quickly beneath her closed eyelids. Waxed paper envelopes. Grizzly bears head down in garbage. The honorable senator from the great state of Illinois cradling his wounded hand. The expression in Jerry's eyes when she deliberately recalled Petey Washington to both their minds.

The flirtation in that up-from-under glance from Toni by the truck that morning. The broken helicopter. The swing of the chain on the rig floor, the scream of the gas in the pipes overhead in the Production Center, the trim line of wellheads in their neat little houses. A million and a half barrels of oil a day, and the people who produced it from the source never saw a drop.

Oil. Crude. Petroleum. Black gold. Dinosaur piss. Raghead blood. Fossil shit. Gasoline, Blazo, kerosene, propane, paraffin. Three-in-One, 80/87, WD-40, 10W-30. It came in all consistencies, all numbers, all essential to life as we know it. The kingdom of heaven runs on faith, the kingdoms of earth on oil. Who had said that? She couldn't remember.

When it washed ashore in Prince William Sound, the crude came in in sticky gobs, in tar balls, in what they called mousse, crude whipped to a froth in the action of the sea. It rolled into shore in large waves, in small blots, in medium-sized blobs. It infiltrated every crack, every crevice, it penetrated beneath every rock and grain of sand. In a very short while it came in entangled with spruce needles and driftwood and green glass Japanese net floats, and with the bodies of loons, grebes, cormorants, geese, ducks, cranes, gulls, murres, puffins, auks, bald eagles, seals, sea lions and sea otters.

Kate remembered the first sea otter she had seen after the spill. Somehow he had fought his way ashore, to a beach as covered with oil as he was, and when she came up to him she saw that his eyes were red and enraged and terrified, heard his labored breathing, wheezing, in and out. He was licking his fur, grooming it with his claws, frantic to rid himself of the oil that gummed the individual hairs together, that destroyed his insulation, his means of flotation. He died as she watched, painfully, taking a long time about it, but she stayed with him until it was over. The most she could do for him was bear witness.

During the rest of that long, horrible summer, she never again made the mistake of going down to the shore without her rifle.

She came to with a jerk and the chair bounced forward on its front legs, almost unseating her. Her heart was beating rapidly, high up in her throat. Next to her Mutt whined once, a short, anxious sound. She looked around to find worried yellow eyes fixed on her face.

"Want to go for a walk?" Mutt wagged an eager assent. Neither of them had spent this much time indoors since Mutt had moved in with Kate, and neither of them liked it much. Lack of outdoor exercise was answerable for a great deal, all of it bad, and beginning with hallucinations in the morning.

She closed the door of Jack's townhouse behind her, and paused for a moment on the doorstep, looking. The townhouse was one of a row of townhouses facing a street. On the other side of the street was a park, and on the other side of the park, a lagoon. Street, park and lagoon stretched east to west; the row of townhouses faced south. The eastern shore of the lagoon was bordered by Minnesota Bypass, a five-lane street with a roar of nonstop traffic coming off it.

She turned her back on it. The bike trail ran beside the lagoon; they got on it. It split almost immediately, the right fork disappearing into a tunnel burrowed into the side of a gravel embankment supporting a set of railroad tracks. She walked through the tunnel and emerged onto the headwaters of Cook Inlet. It was after ten o'clock, and the temperature had warmed enough to cause the glaze of ice underfoot to melt into a layer of slush that slopped wetly with each step. The sky was pale blue behind torn white wisps of swiftly scudding clouds. Mutt padded at her side, making an occasional foray to investigate an interesting smell, but never letting Kate out of her sight. The spring breeze ruffled her coat with a gentle hand and was soft on Kate's cheek, and stayed that way up the curve of the trail to Second Avenue, where the Coastal Trail ended and the city streets began. Beyond the alder-infested slope to their left was the Alaska Railroad station depot, the railroad yards and Anchorage's waterfront, a stretch of mud flats constantly renewed by glacial silt washed down the Knik and Matanuska rivers into Knik Arm. Kate turned right on E Street and walked up to Fourth Avenue. Half the galleries she remembered had been replaced by stores selling T-shirts appliqued with pictures of eagles on the wing against a setting sun and "Alaska—The Great Land" printed beneath. She found one with a dog sled team and musher on it and an inscription that read, "Alaska—Where Men Are Men and Women Win the Iditarod." Kate, who bought her plain white T-shirts by the dozen from Hanes's discount catalogue for six bucks each, bought one of these for sixteen dollars that she told herself was for Mandy.

A block down Fourth, in the window of a gift shop with the straightforward name of Alaska Native Arts & Crafts, an ivory otter caught her eye. Up on his hind legs in the midst of a menagerie sculpted from soapstone, antler, jade and wood, tiny paws held just so, thick tail disposed in a graceful curve, whiskers immaculately groomed, he stood just three inches high, black eyes bright with curiosity, every detail faithfully and exquisitely rendered. He was irresistible. He also looked familiar. Kate went inside, Mutt padding next to her.

The clerk, a woman of character, included both woman and wolf in a friendly, unruffled smile. "Hello. May I help you?"

Kate nodded toward the window. "The ivory otter. The one next to the soapstone bear. Is that Wilson Oozeva of Gambell?"

The woman's smile widened. "You have a good eye." She went to the window and brought back the carving. "He's good, isn't he?"

The little otter sat on the glass-topped counter between them, a soft gleam of ivory perfection. Touching one forefinger to the otter's perfectly groomed fur, running it down the thick curve of the tail, Kate said, "Yes. On his good days, one of the best."

"Do you carve yourself?"

"No."

"Ah. A collector, then."

Kate shook her head. "No."

Her chin dragged her collar open, exposing her scar, but all the woman said was, "Were you interested in buying this piece?" She smiled again. "To begin a collection, perhaps?"

Kate's first instinctive response was refusal. She had no use for knickknacks that existed solely to be dusted. But when she started to shake her head the otter caught her eye, his bright, black gaze fixed on her face, his head cocked at an inquisitive angle, and suddenly she heard John King's voice saying, *Plus expenses, of course. Should run you, oh, say, around $250 a day.* She reached out and picked him up. He looked up at her from the palm of her hand, vital, expectant, fairly quivering with life. Any minute now he was going to drop to his forepaws and scamper up her arm. "How much is he?"

'Two hundred dollars."

"Okay," Kate said. She wondered what Jack would say. Well, he was the one who had told her to find something to justify her expense account with. "And after all, we have to support the home team," she told Mutt when they were in the street again. Mutt raised a skeptical eyebrow. Kate ignored her and tucked the tiny box carefully away in the inside pocket of her jacket.

She found Cyrano's and, physically incapable of passing a bookstore, any bookstore, entered and emerged thirty minutes later with a hundred dollars' worth of books, one of them actually in hardcover. She felt a little dizzy. She'd never been in Anchorage before with this sense of having money to burn. It was unnerving to realize how easily she could seduce herself into spending it.

She wandered back up the street, determined to avoid further temptation at all costs, when through another window she caught sight of a painting so stunningly bad the vacuum it left behind in the artistic firmament sucked her in the door. It proved to be only one of an entire glorious exhibit by a single artist, presided over by a woman wearing a square-shouldered smile featuring her dentist's best and most lucrative work. The smile faded as she took in Kate's worn jeans, shabby jacket and brown skin. Her assistant, a younger edition dressed for success in the same dark suit and the same perfect porcelain smile, came forward in response to some signal Kate missed. "I'm terribly sorry, but we don't allow dogs in the gallery."

"Okay," Kate said agreeably, and nodded at Mutt, who, after a long, considering look that caused the younger woman to back up a step, shouldered through the swinging glass door and took up a position directly outside. Kate smiled. "Okay?"

The young woman's gaze moved from Mutt to Kate, falling to the open collar of her shirt. At the sight of the scar her face lost color. "Uh, certainly." A significant harrUMPH came from behind the counter. "Certainly," she said in a stronger voice, shocked gaze unable to lift itself from the scar. "My name is

Yvonne. Was there something I could help you with?"

"No, thanks, Yvonne, I just saw the picture in the window and wanted to take a closer look." She looked over Yvonne's shoulder and her eyes widened. "Oh," she breathed. "That would be by the same hand, wouldn't it?"

"Yes." Yvonne followed Kate to a red and purple monstrosity that covered most of one wall. Kate stared, enraptured. It was a sunset. Maybe. The paint appeared to have been applied with a trowel. She looked closer. Something resembling medical gauze and mirrored chips of glass and what might have been a razor blade had been incorporated into the globs of paint. In another corner a syringe with a broken needle had been glued to the canvas. Not a sunset, after all, Kate decided, but the residue of a run with Jerry McIsaac. She couldn't quite reconcile that theory with the peony in a third corner, though. A lily she could have understood, but not a peony.

"Quite an interesting technique, wouldn't you say?" Yvonne said brightly, next to her. "Carroll is one of our most promising young artists. Notice how the effrontery of line clashes with the insolence of color, and how his choice of supplementary media connect the two to make a statement."

Kate hung on every word. "I hadn't quite seen it that way," she said, adding earnestly, "And what statement would that be, exactly?"

Yvonne started to tell her and was stopped by another meaningful harrUMPH. Kate repressed a grin and stepped back, immensely relieved that she'd already justified her expense account. There were some things even RPetCo's money did not deserve to be spent on.

The door opened behind them, and Kate turned, curious to see who else had been suckered inside by the putative picture in the window.

He was an old man, dressed in dirty jeans and a red wool shirt frayed at the elbows. He had no coat. His face was dark and seamed, his black hair lank, his eyes rheumy and he needed a shave. A battered cardboard box under one arm, he stopped just inside the door, converged upon by both dress-for-success suits in the same moment. "Yes, sir, may I help you?" the older woman said. Her tone was sure she couldn't.

He held out the box. His movements were slow, made so by age or alcohol or both. "This is my work."

"We don't buy art," the older woman said.

"This is my work," the old man repeated, his voice rising.

The woman's voice raised to match his. "We don't buy art. Go down to Taheta or one of the other shops. We don't buy art."

The old man seemed bewildered by the force of her reply. "This is my work. All I want is two hundred dollars to get home."

The woman's voice rose to a shout. "We have no money to buy art! Go to Taheta!"

"All I want is to get home!"

Kate pushed between the two women. "Let me see, uncle," she said to the old man, her voice gentle.

She could smell the alcohol coming off him from where she stood, but he held himself erect. When he saw Kate, his bleary eyes widened. He spoke a phrase and she shook her head. "I'm sorry, uncle, I have no Yupik. Please, show me your work." To Yvonne's boss, she said, "Mind if we sit here for a moment?"

She did, but something in Kate's cool gaze gave her pause. "Of course not," she said finally, forcing an insincere smile. She glanced through the glass door, obviously nervous that another legitimate customer might be discouraged from entering her gallery when they saw the customers she was currently entertaining. There was only Mutt, who yawned at her through the glass door, displaying her fangs to advantage, and she retreated hurriedly behind the counter.

Kate slipped a hand beneath the old man's elbow and guided him to one of the chairs against the wall. "Sit, uncle."

"I just want to go home," he said, his voice exhausted of energy.

"I know," she said. "I know. Please, show me what you have."

The cardboard box was filled with pieces of ivory carved into animal figures. There were walruses and caribou and bears and salmon and otters. The best piece was a sleek, fat seal, with an impish, grinning human face peeking out of the fur on his back. All were old, very old, yellow in color and cracked, their edges worn smooth.

Kate replaced the little seal with a reverent hand. "Uncle," she said, looking up at him, "where did you get these?"

"They are my work." He refused to meet her eyes, but a tinge of red crept up into his cheeks, and she knew. She folded the lid of the box down and reached for her wallet. The little otter and the books had dug a big hole in her reserve of cash. She debated whether to take him over to the other gallery, and rejected the notion at once. If she could keep him from selling them, she would. "Here's forty dollars. No, uncle, keep your work. It is too good to sell. Take it home."

"I can't get home," he muttered, shoving the box back at her. "I don't have any money."

She folded his hand around the bills, and spoke slowly, holding his rheumy eyes with hers. "This is all I have right now. I'll get more, and meet you in front of the Army-Navy

Surplus store tomorrow morning. I'll give you a ride to the airport and put you on a plane. Where do you live, uncle? What is your village?"

He looked at her, dazed. "Savoonga. I just want to go home."

Savoonga, on St. Lawrence Island, at the southern entrance to the Bering Strait and closer to the Chukotsk Peninsula of Siberia than to the Seward Peninsula of Alaska. Gambell was on St. Lawrence Island, too. Instinctively she reached inside her jacket and touched the box holding the little otter.

There were restive movements from behind the counter. In a calming voice Kate repeated her words and hoped they got through. Again, he pressed the box on her, and this time she took it. She was afraid of what he'd do with it if she didn't.

They went outside together. He smiled when he saw Mutt and said something to her in Yupik. Mutt ducked her head, flattened her ears, gave her tail an ingratiating wag and even went so far as to give a small yip in salute. The old man smiled kindly at both of them in farewell. "Don't forget, uncle, tomorrow morning," Kate called. "In front of Army-Navy, about ten o'clock. All right?"

He raised a hand and shuffled off. To Mutt Kate said, "And when did you learn to speak Yupik? I thought you only spoke Aleut."

Mutt raised a superior eyebrow and didn't reply in either tongue.

Kate spent her last two dollars on a cafe mocha double tall and walked the two and a half blocks to the Downtown Deli, juggling bag, box and coffee cup and trying hard not to feel depressed. It was too early in the year for the tourists to have taken over as was their invariable habit, and Jack had already found them a table. From the expression of restrained fury on

112

his face it had not been a good morning. She slid into the booth and eyed him warily. "Hi."

The waiter, also the owner, also a former mayor of Anchorage, bustled up with two beers and set them both in front of Jack. He saw Kate and paused, pushing straight black hair out of his eyes. "Kate. Long time no see."

"How are you, Tony? I voted for you for governor, what the hell happened?"

He laughed. "I don't know. Never underestimate the call of the weird in Alaskan politics."

Kate thought of their sitting governor and agreed wholeheartedly.

"What can I get you?"

"Coffee, with cream."

"Can do."

The ex-mayor left and Kate looked across at Jack, who was finishing his first beer. "What happened this morning to turn you into the Grinch?"

He drained his bottle, burped and said one word. "Jane."

"Ah." Kate's coffee arrived and she doctored it heavily with cream and sugar. It was best to keep her blood sugar up when Jane was the subject under discussion. She ordered a Reuben (she was in Anchorage, after all, Alaska's stand-in for Sodom *and* Gomorrah, she might as well act like it). Jack ordered a roast beef-tomato-cream cheese combination that was hell on the cholesterol and made Kate wish instantly that she'd ordered it instead. "What'd she want?"

He snorted. 'This time? Only the title to the duplex."

"What?"

"You know I wanted to put it on the market last year?"

"I thought you had."

"So did I," he said grimly. "Remember I offered to split the profit with her fifty-fifty?"

"I remember," Kate said. She also remembered the reservations she'd had about the plan at the time. She offered the same opinion now she had then: none.

He nodded again, this time at an official-looking envelope lying on the table that showed signs of being wrung as if it were a substitute for someone's neck. "Today she tells me she's retained an attorney. He tells me she told him that I told her that the duplex was her retirement fund. He's filed papers and clouded the title, so now I can't sell it." He jerked a contemptuous thumb. "And she showed up at the office today to inform me that if I sign the title over to her, *and* pay her thirty thousand dollars, that she'll call him off." He glared at her. "It's not funny, Kate. Now I've got to get an attorney and defend the title to something I've owned for twenty years!"

"You never should have let her stay there rent-free after the divorce," Kate couldn't help saying.

"If it wasn't for Johnny I wouldn't have." She said nothing and he glared at her again. "Shut up, okay?"

"Okay."

"Just shut the hell up."

The sandwiches arrived. Jack's looked good but Kate's tasted like fruit of the Tree of Knowledge, and she closed her eyes in momentary ecstasy.

Around a mouthful of roast beef Jack said indistinctly, "If you say I told you so, I will kill you."

"Mmmphmmm," Kate said, more interested at that moment in pastrami.

He relaxed enough to give half a grin. "What have you been up to this morning?"

She swallowed. "Justifying my expense account."

She produced her otter, and he fingered it appreciatively.

"Nice [...]

"I th[...]

He ga[...] found m[...] Permanent[...] nodded at t[...]

She told [...]

"Ivory?" [...] scrap ivory se[...] pound Outside[...]

"This isn't sc[...]

"May I?" He [...] "Holy shit. I guess[...] time, admiring the[...] crafty expression of[...] saw the seal. "I'll say it isn't. Wha[...] on its back?"

Kate thought back [...] the stories and legends learned at Ekaterina's knee. "The Aleuts believed that animals possessed souls that could change into human form. Hunters would see these, they called them anua, in the fur or the feathers or the eyes of what they were hunting."

He held the little figurine higher to examine it more closely. "What was this for?"

Kate shrugged. "Could have been any number of things. Since it's a seal, maybe as a decoration for a harpoon, but it served more than a decorative purpose."

"How so?"

Kate took another bite of sandwich and said thickly, "Say an Eskimo hunter went seal hunting, and he used a harpoon. He would decorate the harpoon in honor of the seal, to please its anua. The anua lived on after the seal died, transferring to another, as yet unborn animal. The hunter believed the anua life."

to feed the hunter again

creasing. "I remember. Anua was
down the Chain. Where those two
te nodded. Jack looked down at the tiny
at him from the back of the ivory seal. "He
acter, doesn't he? Looks like Puck." He handed
back to her. "He dig it out of his backyard, you

"Out of his family's graveyard, more likely," Kate said, sighing. She put down the seal and picked up her otter. "Who flies to St. Lawrence nowadays?"

"I don't know. Cape Smythe Air from Nome to Gambell, probably. MarkAir from Anchorage to Nome."

"After what they did to Wien Air Alaska, you couldn't get me on a MarkAir jet at gunpoint," she said promptly.

"You're not the one doing the flying," he pointed out.

"No," she said, but she didn't sound all that certain.

He sat up. "You aren't, are you? You're not feeling like you have to personally escort him home?"

She shifted in her seat. "I don't know. I've never been to St. Lawrence Island. I'll never make this kind of money again. Maybe I should." She set the otter on the table next to the seal. The seal was the color of old ocher, lined with tiny cracks, bearing its weight of culture and tradition with a life force undimmed by the passing of the years. Next to it, the otter was the color of fresh cream, every etched line sharp and clear, the heritage of the past and a legacy for the future captured by the carver's art in a three-inch piece of ivory. "I could pay my compliments to Wilson Oozeva personally."

Jack wet his forefinger and picked up crumbs of bread, licking them off one at a time. Without looking at her he said, "He won't be there tomorrow, you know."

She looked out the window. "Maybe. Maybe not."

His voice was gentle but inexorable. "You shouldn't have given him the money. You know he headed straight for the nearest bar."

"Maybe," she said, her eyes fixed on the foot traffic passing in front of the restaurant, at Mutt waiting patiently next to the door. One man paused as if to give her an approving pat on the head, met that unblinking yellow stare, thought better of it and moved on. "Maybe not."

Her profile was obdurate, the line of her mouth stubborn. He sighed and drained his second beer. "What are you going to do with that?" He nodded at the box.

"Keep it for him."

"What if you never see him again?" She shot him an annoyed glance. He persisted. "That stuff belongs in a museum, Kate."

Kate picked up the seal again, admiring the taut spotted skin stretched smoothly over a layer of fat, its round nose, its delicately carved flippers. She remembered Olga Shapsnikoff, on a day in October of the previous year, in a town far out on the Aleutian Chain, answering Kate when Kate had said much the same thing of an ivory storyknife wielded by her daughter.

It's a beautiful thing, Auntie, Kate had said. *And valuable. It should be in a museum.*

Its spirit would die, locked up in a place where it was never touched, Olga had replied.

"Maybe," Kate said slowly.

"And maybe not," Jack said, nodding his head as if he understood everything when in fact he understood nothing at all. He was good at it; with Kate, he got plenty of practice. "What are your plans for the afternoon?"

She put the seal back in the box and forced a smile. "You've got cable. I figured I'd channel-surf. Find me an old John Wayne movie while I wait for Childress to deliver that paperwork."

He made a face. "Can't you think of anything better to do?"

She looked him over, letting her gaze linger in places. "Uh-huh, but not alone."

He told himself he was too old to blush and made a business of examining the face of his watch. "Gotta go."

"Chicken," she said softly.

"Late," he retorted. "Want the Blazer? I can get a lift home."

She looked at the box and the sack of books. "Sounds good." On the street Jack said, "By the way, I called Axenia this morning."

"Oh."

He looked at her quizzically. "Such enthusiasm. I thought you'd want to see her."

"I do," she said.

It didn't sound much like it to him. "Good. I invited her to dinner Saturday night."

Three days and two nights away. She might be ready by then. "How nice."

They walked down to the Captain Cook Hotel's parking garage and found the Blazer, and Jack kissed her good-bye with enough promise to make her look forward to five o'clock.

Back home, she rummaged through the chest freezer in Jack's garage and found Mutt a bone with a roast still attached. Jack would curse them both, but who had shot the caribou in the first place? Shot, skinned, gutted, cut and wrapped, she might add, overlooking the fact that Jack had been along on that hunt. Leaving Mutt and bone on the porch, she went inside and curled up with one of the morning's purchases, Susan Faludi's *Backlash,* not the most restful book she could have chosen after a week in male-dominated Prudhoe Bay. She turned a page and the phone rang. Kate picked it up. "Hello?"

"Hi," a young voice trembling on the verge of tears said. "Is this Kate?"

"Yes," Kate said. She sat up, book slipping from her lap. "Johnny?"

"Yes. Dad told me you were in town."

"For a little while. How are you?" There was a sniff and a gulp. "Johnny? Are you all right?" This time there was a definite sob. "Johnny, where are you?"

She heard traffic in the background, another sniff. "At the 7-Eleven."

"The one down the road from the duplex? On the corner of Lake Otis and Northern Lights?"

"Yes."

"What are you doing there? Why aren't you in school?"

"It's an in-service day, nobody's in school except teachers."

"Then why aren't you at home?" No answer except a sniffle. "Where's your mom?"

"I don't know."

Kate didn't like the sound of that. "Do you want me to come get you?"

The young voice quavered. "Would you? Please? I called Dad's office but he wasn't there. I thought he might be home."

"Wait right there, Johnny," Kate said. "Don't move. I'll be there in fifteen minutes."

She was there in ten. The thin, towheaded boy with the

tear-streaked face was waiting for her outside as she pulled up. She put the Blazer into park and swung out the door in the same motion. He was dressed in T-shirt and Technicolor jams and nothing else. "Johnny, where's your coat? And where the hell are your shoes?"

He looked at his feet, curled bare on the sidewalk in front of the store. He mumbled an answer and Kate leaned forward. "What?"

His face was pinched, his voice numb and exhausted. "She took them. When I said I was going to Dad's. She took my shoes and socks away and hid them."

He shivered, hugging himself, and Kate collected her wits and hustled him into the Blazer. They detoured on their way to Jack's by way of Fred Meyer's, where Kate bought the boy a pair of Air Jordans, not having spent any of RPetCo's money yet that afternoon. At first Johnny objected but when she explained the situation he got into the spirit of things and they went for broke on an official NFL Seahawks jacket. She bought him clean underwear and a couple of Markie Mark T-shirts while she was at it. She was eyeing a Nintendo Game Boy when she came to and took herself and the boy firmly in tow and got the hell out of there.

Back at Jack's, she made a tuna sandwich and poured out a glass of orange juice, and was pleased when Johnny showed enough spirit to make a face at the juice and ask for Coke. She gave him the same answer she had given his father. "Real women drink Diet 7UP."

He shuddered. "Yuk."

She watched him chew in silence for a few minutes. "You want to talk about it?"

He looked down at his plate. "No."

Johnny was about a foot taller than she remembered and

consequently would have approximately three thousand more exposed nerve endings per square inch. Kate wasn't so old that she couldn't remember the feeling. "Okay," she said equably, rising. "Finish your sandwich. Your dad ought to be home around five or five-thirty." She paused. "You want to call your mother? Tell her where you are?"

"No."

Kate kept her voice gentle. "She'll be worried about you."

"She won't be worried, she'll be mad. She'll know I came here."

Oh-kay, Kate thought. "Okay," she said. Johnny was warm, clothed, fed and, for the moment, safe. Let Jane worry. "Come on into the living room when you're done. We'll watch a movie."

"Kate."

His low voice stopped her at the door.

"Don't tell him."

She looked back at him, towhead bent over his sandwich, and felt a wave of weariness sweep over her. How many children had she interviewed in her time, how many broken, bleeding babies had she seen in a panic, begging her not to put their parents in jail, begging her not to hurt the monsters who had hurt them. It never changed. Sometimes she lost hope it ever would. "Okay." He looked up, relief in his face, and she said, "On one condition. I won't tell him if you will."

His face twisted. "I can't."

She kept her tone gentle, the words undemanding. "Yes, you can."

He was silent, and she turned again. "Kate." She turned back. He raised his head and met her eyes with a look in his own that shouldn't have been there for another ten years, if ever. "Thanks."

"Hey, no prob. Shugak's the name, rescue's my game," she said, keeping it light.

When he joined her in the living room she put *The Terminator* on the VCR and they settled down to watch one of two movies in which Arnold Schwarzenegger had been perfectly cast. When the first one ended they started the second, and had Sarah Connor nearly out of jail when the doorbell rang.

Johnny jumped, paled and looked at her, mute. Kate gave his shoulder a comforting squeeze and went to answer it.

To Kate's surprise, it wasn't Jane, it was Axenia, her cousin and a younger, shorter, plumper edition of herself. "Axenia," Kate said, surprised. "Why aren't you at work? And what are you doing here tonight? I thought you weren't coming to dinner until Saturday." A movement caught the corner of Kate's eye and she looked around.

Oh, joy, O rapture, O bountiful Jehovah. Axenia had brought Ekaterina with her.

"Come vid me iff you vant to liffe," commanded Arnold Schwarzenegger from the living room.

Kate took a deep breath. "Hello, Emaa," she said, and stood back, holding the door open.

Axenia beat them both to the first punch. "What are you doing here, Kate? I'm fine, I really am, I'm all grown up now and I can take care of myself. I don't need my big cousin checking up on me every five minutes to see if I—"

"Time," Kate said mildly, closing the door. "Axenia. Axenia, just hold it!" Axenia did and, if the expression on her face was anything to go by, was furious at herself for doing so. "I'm not here to check up on you. I've got a temporary job, and I'm staying with Jack while I do it. That's all."

Axenia wasn't convinced. She jerked a thumb over her

shoulder. "Then how come you sicced her on me?"

Kate looked at her. Just looked, one long, paralyzing stare out of suddenly very cold, very hard hazel eyes. When enough color had climbed into Axenia's face to satisfy her, she said in a voice no less deadly for its mildness, "If I ever hear you speak of your grandmother in that way again, in or out of her presence, I will personally kick your ass from one side of this town to the other. You show respect for your elders. Is that understood?" Axenia hung her head, her face sullen, and inexorably Kate repeated, "Is that understood?"

Axenia mumbled something Kate chose to hear as "Yes." Ekaterina, her lined face impassive, watched Kate out of calm eyes, hands in the pockets of her black cloth coat. Kate took a deep breath and got out her self-control. She even managed a smile. "Emaa. It's good to see you. Come in, sit down. I'll make some tea."

The door knocker was plied with vigor. Kate's smile felt as if it had been pasted on. "Excuse me," she said to her grandmother. Wonderful. Now she got to fight with Jane in front of emaa.

But it wasn't Jane this time either, it was Childress, carrying a large cardboard box and wearing a bad-tempered scowl. "Here," he said without preamble, shoving the box at Kate, who staggered a little beneath its weight before shoving it back. "Just remember, Shugak, you're responsible for these files. They are by God confidential and I expect them to be treated as such or I'll by God fire your ass no matter what John King says."

Ekaterina took one look at the RPetCo logo on his cap and stiffened into a short, stout pillar of outrage. If she'd been wearing skirts she would have gathered them up to keep them from any contaminating contact.

"I should be done with them by Monday," Kate told Childress. "You can come get them then."

"We can't have them out of the office over the weekend," he informed her with no little relish. "If you're working for me, you'll have to follow procedure."

"Why, those files turn into a lot of little pumpkins Friday night at five?"

Next to her, Ekaterina drew in an audible breath and in spite of herself Kate cringed inside. "You are working for him?" her grandmother demanded, an inch of frost on every syllable. "You are working for an oil company? And for *RPetCo?*"

"And what's so terrible about that?" Childress demanded pugnaciously.

"Don't yell at my grandmother!" Axenia said, bristling.

The door slammed back—really, Kate thought, proud of her detachment, Jack's house was beginning to resemble Toni Hartzler's office on the Slope—and Jack roared into the room. "What's all the shouting about? I could hear you from the car! Oh. Hello, Ekaterina."

The older woman inclined her head. "Jack."

"I'm sorry I yelled, I—"

"Hi, Dad!" Johnny made a standing jump from the living-room doorway that landed him with both legs wrapped around Jack's waist.

"Johnny? Hey, hi, kid. I thought I didn't get you until Friday afternoon, I was going to—"

Someone hammered at the door. "How delightful," Kate told Jack with an extremely sweet smile he instantly and intelligently distrusted, "it's going to be a party."

She opened the door and, finally, there stood Jane.

Once again Kate was struck by Jack's ex-wife's resemblance

to a medieval gargoyle, and an early thirteenth-century gargoyle at that, back when pre-Renaissance sculptors harbored no illusions about the material shape of evil. It wouldn't have been all that bad a face, really, Kate thought, trying to be fair, if Jane could just get the jealousy and the malice out of it.

"Hello, Jane," she said, determined to maintain at least the bare minimum of civility Ms. Manners called for in these situations.

"Kate," the tall, thin blonde spat. Her eyes were small and near-together and Kate could barely make out their cold blue color between the heavy eyeliner and the heavier mascara. There was so much of both that Kate was surprised Jane could keep her eyelids up beneath the weight. She could, though, and her gaze was first surprised and then venomous. "I might have known you'd be here."

At this point Mutt decided it was time to make her presence felt and padded forward. Kate put a restraining hand on her head. "So you might," she replied affably.

"You kidnapped my son!"

"For shame, Katya," Ekaterina said, and for a moment Kate thought she was talking about Kate's alleged kidnapping of Johnny. "For *shame*." She singed Childress with a look. "To take money from these people, how could you?"

"I guess our money's as good as anybody's," Childress snapped, bristling, "and the salmon and the herring are coming back into the Sound, our biologists say so."

Jane yanked Johnny out of his father's arms—shoeless, Kate noted, Jane made a habit of that—and propelled him toward the door. "I'm sure the judge will have something to say about your living arrangements when it's time for the hearing. Jack," she said, with what Kate felt Jane was sure was a magnificent sneer, preparatory to making a grand exit.

The effect was spoiled by her recalcitrant son and the equally recalcitrant door, which had a built-in bitch detector in the knob and stuck. Jane tugged, cursing. It sprang open unexpectedly and the leading edge caught Jane a hell of a crack across the forehead. She paused, momentarily stunned.

Nose in the air, Ekaterina swept through the open doorway as if she were wearing a long satin train and Jane was only one of many footmen. Axenia followed, looking less majestic and, Kate was glad to see, a little embarrassed. "See you Saturday," Kate said. It was as much threat as it was promise, and from the expression on Axenia's face, she knew it.

Johnny wriggled free, and coming to, Jane grabbed him.

"Don't let her take him, Jack," Kate said.

Improving on her sneer, Jane said, "I've got custody, he can't stop me."

So much for Ms. Manners. "I can." Kate separated Jane from her son, spun Jane around by her shoulders, planted a foot in Jane's derriere and pushed. Jane flew outside, arms outstretched, to fall face forward in four inches of new, wet snow that must have fallen since Kate had brought Johnny home because Kate didn't remember it being there before.

Neither did Johnny. "Hey, cool," he said, "I didn't know it was snowing. Can we go sledding, Dad?"

Jane scrambled to her feet, spit snow out of her mouth and began screaming a predictable mixture of obscenities and threats. Axenia's car door slammed, Ekaterina's car door slammed, Jane's car door slammed, and Kate kicked Jack's front door and it slammed shut for the last time with a loud, satisfying thud.

"I'll be back," Arnold Schwarzenegger intoned from the living room.

Jack looked from his still-reverberating front door to his wide-eyed son to a thin-lipped, furious Kate. "So how was your day, dear?"

Next to him, Childress observed, "For an old, fat broad that dame moves pretty fast. Now where do you want these goddam files?"

• • •

Jack was right. The next morning Kate dropped him off at work, ran a few errands and by a quarter to ten had commandeered a parking space strategically located near the Army-Navy store. She waited for four hours, plugging the meter, the box of ivory in the seat next to her, a wad of bills in her pocket from the cashing of her first Slope paycheck. The old man never showed.

CHAPTER 7

FRIDAY MORNING KATE BEGAN the Augean task of wading through the RPetCo files. The medical logs overflowed with the jargon so dear to the hearts of all medical practitioners, a translating job that was not aided by the cuneiform calligraphics equally dear, but a morning's worth of sifting, a lot of coffee and the stubborn conviction that she could in fact read English brought to light several interesting observations.

One was that there had been two previous rashes of drug-related incidents on the west side of the Prudhoe Bay field, each occurring within a twenty-four-hour period. There were other drug-related cases spread out throughout the year, but these two were the most concentrated and bore a striking similarity to the experiences of Wednesday night of the previous week. Kate read the list of injuries suffered by the A Shift physician's assistant on the first occasion with a sympathy tempered by relief she hadn't been the one on the receiving end of the pool cue.

With a tablet and a pencil she made a list of dates and names. Cross-checking the names against the employee roster she'd filched from the Slope the previous week, she placed each employee on the list in his department or, in the case of contractors, with his employer, and on his assigned shift. Finishing, she stacked the medical logs and reached for the pile of manifests.

There were a lot of them, one per flight for the last year. There were nine flights in an ordinary week, one on Mondays, Fridays and Saturdays, two on Tuesdays, Wednesdays and Thursdays. The manifests were fairly straightforward: lists of passengers in alphabetical order, varying from 63 to 102, depending on whether the 727 had been reconfigured to carry freight and passengers or passengers only. Tuesdays, Wednesdays and Thursdays it usually carried two igloos of freight on all four flights. An example of an exception was the day the plane had been delayed due to weather, Kate's first flight north. Wednesday morning the Transportation Department had been faced with changing out three shifts of employees at once instead of just one, and the plane had been reconfigured to fly all seats to accomplish this feat with the greatest dispatch. She rifled through the stack until she spotted another canceled manifest and paged forward to the next flight. As she had expected, reconfiguring the plane to all passengers appeared to be standard procedure the day after a canceled flight, unless there was a medical evacuation, in which case the medevac igloo usurped the extra seats.

By eleven her eyes were beginning to cross and she rose from the kitchen table and stretched. Mutt was on her feet immediately, eyes pleading. They took the left fork of the bike trail this time, and the left tunnel, toward Point Woronzof. Wednesday's snow had melted and the trail was down to the pavement in most places, but the sky was a leaden gray and a brisk wind nipped at Kate's ears and stung her cheeks, as if to remind one and all that though the calendar might say spring, it was only March, and not to get too cocky or the inevitable April blizzard could just as easily be two feet deep instead of one.

The sound of jets taking off increased as they neared the

end of the north-south runway of Anchorage International. It was Friday, one of RPetCo's one-flight days, Kate remembered, departing at nine A.M., returning to Anchorage at three P.M. There were benches next to the trail, and she kicked one free of a layer of ice and sat down to watch a Federal Express 747 hurtle into the air a hundred feet over her head. The roar of the engines struck her like a blow, and as she plugged her ears with her fingers Kate remembered the gas screaming through the pipes at the Production Center. It occurred to her that this might be the noisiest job she had ever taken on, on or off the Slope. The jet climbed up and outward and Kate unplugged her ears. The smell of jet fuel exhaust stung her nostrils, but the resulting quiet was a physical relief. She leaned her head against the back of the bench, tucked her hands in her pockets and closed her eyes.

When John King had made his unenthusiastic offer of employment eleven days ago, she had accepted it as a lighthearted romp through RPetCo's discretionary fund, nothing more, with the added bonus of a look at the North Slope. She'd never been farther north than Fairbanks before, and like Dutch Harbor, it was a trip beyond her wallet if it went unsubsidized by a job. She'd even toyed with the idea of demanding a bonus, depending on how fast she brought the dealer down. Jack, damn his eyes, had been right in his assessment of her initial lack of concern over what Slopers might or might not be inhaling, snorting, popping or mainlining. As far as Kate was concerned, they all had more money than God and they all thought they owned the world. If they couldn't handle it, too bad.

Something had turned that indifference around. It might have been the sight of Martin, ill and hostile in that hospital bed. It might have been the pipeliner yanking on the bear's tail—if he hadn't been on drugs he should have been. It might have been the thought of the two Naborhoff roughnecks throwing that chain up on the rig floor, higher than kites and in danger of losing more than a few fingers.

She realized, with a growing sense of annoyance, that this job had put a face on the monster. No longer could she think of the oil companies at Prudhoe Bay as monolithic corporate juggernauts getting the oil out of the ground no matter whose nest they shit in along the way. Instead there was Dale Triplett, a production operator who could tell you how many barrels of oil there were within the walls of her separation center at any given moment. There was Sue Jordan, who came into the communications center after hours to give the night operator a coffee break and stayed on until morning to handle the medevac and notification of next of kin. There was Gideon Trocchiano, convinced that a good meal could cure anything that ailed you, from homesickness to the Prudhoe Bay galloping crud, and who was determined to prove it with liberal doses of thyme, garlic and parmesan. There was Jerry McIsaac, on call 24 hours a day, 180 hours a week, hand never very far from his medical bag, self never very far from his ambulance, ready to respond at a moment's notice to any injury, no matter how slight. There was Toni Hartzler, whose supply of humor never ran out, no matter what the provocation from ignorant Outsiders.

Sure, they only worked one week of every two. Sure, they pulled down more in a year than Kate would see in her lifetime. Sure, they washed no dish nor made no bed during their week up. They still spent half their lives six hundred miles from home and family and any semblance of a normal life, and most of them never drew a breath of fresh air from the day they got off the plane at Prudhoe until the day they got on it again.

She wouldn't go so far as to say she admired them. but she'd damn well take her best shot at ridding their workplace of the drug of their choice.

Not that she was convinced she'd get any thanks for it. A jet clawed its way into the sky over her head and she plugged her ears automatically. The sheer volume of product she'd seen during the post-race celebrations Saturday night was enough to stagger anyone. The universal casual acceptance of its presence was equally staggering. If something wasn't done, and soon, someone was going to get killed. She remembered Chuck Cass. Someone already had been.

Again she thought of that delayed charter, and the events which followed, and wondered if there was a correlation or if it was all just coincidence. She didn't think so. Kate wasn't big on coincidences.

Mutt went looking for trouble and found it, stampeding a mangy-looking cow moose out of the undergrowth. To Kate's relief Mutt decided either that she wasn't that hungry or that the cow looked a bit stringy for her refined palate, and allowed the cow to escape into a clump of alders. A while later she came back with a satisfied expression on her face and a bit of rabbit fur sticking to her muzzle. "Shame on you," Kate told her. "Terrorizing these poor little citified rabbits and mooses."

Mutt uttered a short, joyful bark and bounced forward to nip at the hem of Kate's jeans. Another leap away, and she paused to look hopefully over her shoulder.

"Oh, ho, so it's going to be like that, is it?" Kate gave chase, catching Mutt's tail and giving it a brief tug before running for her life. Mutt nipped the left cheek of her behind and streaked ahead to run three times around a conveniently placed birch. She stopped, looking at Kate expectantly, ears up. Using a long patch of ice yet to melt in the shade of the birch, Kate took a long running jump and slid past Mutt and the tree, giving Mutt a smack on the butt as she skidded by.

They played tag all the way back to Earthquake Park, where Kate cried uncle, and the rest of the journey home was accomplished at a walk more befitting two grown women of their age and maturity, although once Mutt did try to trip her, and once Kate bumped Mutt into a drift of wet snow. They emerged from the tunnel flushed and out of breath, and much refreshed.

Jack came home for a late lunch and Kate drove him back to work and kept the Blazer. Instead of returning directly to Jack's and her mound of paperwork, she drove to Bean's Cafe and parked. Inside, a tattered, tired group of men sprinkled with a few women were eating lunch, their exhaustion lightening a little as the hot foot hit their bellies. Some were unkempt, some were downright dirty, most of them smelled. None of them was her old man. She described him to a woman administering a tuberculosis test to anyone who would sit still for it, but the woman, although sympathetic, had other concerns on her mind and wasn't much help. From Bean's Kate went to the Brother Francis Mission, a large building that looked exactly like what it was, a former municipal warehouse converted to a shelter for street people. Upon inquiry she was directed to a tall man with a shock of untidy gray hair and an official mien who stood listening with a patient expression to another man who looked merely officious. As Kate came up behind them she heard the officious man protest, "You're not helping here, Brother Bob, you're merely enabling these people to stay drunk."

Brother Bob murmured, "We're enabling people to stay alive," but the officious man wasn't listening, and after holding forth for another five minutes without once pausing to draw breath he marched out. As he marched Kate noticed he looked neither to the left nor to the right, probably for fear that if he saw someone warm and dry, who otherwise might be dying of exposure out on the street, that it might change his ideas, and above all else, a change of ideas was the thing most to be feared.

Kate described the old man and Brother Bob said, "Could be any one of a dozen men we see here every night," echoing the words of the woman at Bean's. "Although when it starts getting warmer, they start moving outside." He looked at her. "Is it important?"

Kate thought of the box of carvings riding around in the back seat of the Blazer, of the old man's bewildered, exhausted face when he had said, *I just want to go home.* "Yes," she said. "It's important."

He looked at her curiously. "He a relative?"

She hesitated and almost said yes, before she remembered she didn't even know the old man's name. "No," she said finally. "Not a relative. But I want to help, if I can."

"You'll have to find him first," he said, not unkindly.

"You have any idea where I should start looking?"

He looked her over, this time with a critical eye, lingering on Mutt, who met his gaze with an inquiring yellow stare. What he saw apparently satisfied him. He named half a dozen bars, and said, "If you don't find him in any of those, check the hillside above the railroad yards. A lot of our people build Visqueen tents down in the alders come spring."

Kate drove uptown and checked the bars, one after the other. It was not an uplifting experience. She dodged three fights in the first two, and they all smelled of beer and vomit and stale cigarette smoke.

The last one, the Borealis Bar on Fourth Avenue, was almost exactly like the previous five: dark and smoky, Randy Travis on the jukebox telling the world why he cheated. A bar ran down one side of the room, tables that hadn't been wiped in memory of man crowded together across a filthy floor. One couple, eyes closed, bodies pressed tightly together, swayed between two tables without moving their feet.

A group of four men sat around another table, fresh glasses newly arrived from the bar. The three older ones were cheering the fourth one, barely a boy. All were Native Alaskans, all were conspicuously drunk, and as Kate watched the cheers took an ugly edge. "You too proud to drink with us?" one of them demanded.

"No," the boy mumbled, trying with ineffective gestures to shove away the glass held under his nose. "Doanwannanymore."

"I think he thinks he's too good to drink with us," one of the others said.

"Come on, Phil," the third man said. "We'll teach him to show respect for his elders." Two of them pinned the boy's arms and tilted his head back and the third pinched his nose and poured the drink down his throat so that he had either to drink or suffocate.

Kate leapt forward instinctively. "Stop!" She slapped the glass away and heard it crash somewhere behind her. "Stop it!" She pulled the boy free and put his head between his knees. His thin shoulders heaved beneath her hands as he choked and gasped for breath. Kate was so upset she forgot herself and began to lecture. "What the hell is the matter with you? Is this the way they taught you in the village? To make someone do something they don't want to, that's bad for them? Shame on you!"

She would have been surprised and probably incredulous

if she'd known how much she sounded, and looked, like her grandmother in that moment.

The other three men were so far out of it they could only stand, weaving, and curse. "What the fuck do you think you're doing?" "S'not nanny your business." "Yeah, fuck off." "Yeah, fuck off."

"Leave my brother 'lone," one said. He managed to focus long enough to step forward and paw at her.

Mutt growled once, low down in her throat. When they didn't hear her she upped the volume. They heard her that time, looked down, dropped their hands and started backing up in a body.

Kate squatted next to the boy. His face was streaked with tears and he swiped ineffectually at the mucus running from his nose. "You okay?"

He didn't look at her. "Yes."

"You need a ride somewhere?"

"You got any money?"

She did. A lot of it, in cash, wadded in her pocket. She looked up and saw the three men standing at a distance, eyeing a Mutt who was eyeing them right back. "No," she said. "I don't have any money. Or not much. You hungry? I could buy you a burger."

He shook his head. After a moment she rose to her feet, and looked mean in the direction of the three men. Mutt looked mean, too, and they backed up another step. They were still backing up when Kate walked out the front door and back into the relatively clean air outside.

There was a McDonald's across the street and she went inside and ordered the biggest Coke they had and drank it down in one long swallow. She lowered the cup, the smell of deep-fried fat hit her nostrils and she barely made it to the bathroom in time. She retched and gagged until there wasn't an ounce of fluid left in her entire body. When she came out of the stall there was a young woman in a McDonald's uniform waiting with a mop and bucket. She gave Kate a look of disgust and disdain. "Jesus, you people."

Kate started to say, "Wait a minute, I wasn't drinking," but the other woman shouldered her aside roughly and began applying the mop to the floor with jerky, angry movements.

Sometimes there is just no cure for a situation. Kate stifled her anger, washed her face and hands in the teeth of the other woman's repugnance and left.

She and Mutt walked down E Street and up Second to the beginning of the Coastal Trail. The gutters ran free with melt-off but the sidewalks were still covered with a combination of slush and ice. Walking was tricky. It got trickier when she pushed through the alders and began slipping and sliding down the hillside. In places the snow was up to her behind, and her tennis shoes and jeans were soon wet through. She had built up enough speed to scare herself when a limb caught her cheek with a sharp sting. She yelled out a protest and grabbed instinctively for her face. Her feet still churning, she crashed into some kind of stretchy barrier that held for a second and then gave.

She tumbled forward and would have hit hard if the tangle of tree limbs and enveloping material hadn't cushioned her fall. When she got her breath back, she fought her way to her feet and the first thing she saw was Mutt, staring down at her from the lip of the little hollow with an expression of incredulous delight. "Oh, ha ha, very funny," Kate said sourly, and looked around.

She had somersaulted into a tiny clearing, sheltered from wind and, judging from the thickness of the overgrowth, pretty efficiently from rain as well, although not as well as it had been before Kate's arrival. In the clearing there was an old tin pot, battered and rusted. There were the ashes of a fire, lukewarm to the touch. There were two bottles of Thunderbird, both empty. There was a woman, curled in a fetal position on another square of plastic with a third bottle cradled in her arms. She was dressed in ragged jeans and a thin nylon jacket, long dark hair matted around her face and neck. She was a sound sleeper, considering Kate had just crashed through her roof. She kept sleeping as Kate re-stretched the square of plastic tarp and refastened it to the trees, and she was still sleeping when Kate left.

Mutt, discovering what was wanted, nosed out another three shelters in that stand of alders, all of them as luxuriously furnished and none with the residents at home. They checked out another section of hillside close to the Alaska Native Service Hospital with the same result. At five o'clock Kate gave it up, climbed laboriously back up the hillside, found the Blazer and drove home to take a very long, very hot shower.

Jack didn't say "I told you so," but he was so sympathetic and understanding the entire evening that Kate wanted to kill him anyway.

The next morning Kate invaded Costco, emerging $398.76 later, secure in the knowledge that the outhouse on her homestead was not going to run out of toilet paper until the next century, and grateful that Jack had a large garage.

That evening Axenia surprised Kate by arriving exactly on time and playing the part of the perfect guest. She complimented Jack on the dinner (which Kate had cooked), played Tetris with Johnny on his new Game Boy and generally stayed as far away from Kate as she could and still be in the same house. Kate let her. Axenia didn't mention Ekaterina's whereabouts or why she had been in Anchorage in the first place, and Kate didn't ask.

Sunday morning was spent fighting over the Sunday paper with Jack and Johnny, after which father and son went skiing at Alyeska. They invited Kate along but she could tell their hearts weren't in the invitation, and she shooed them off on their own, glad to see the backs of both of them. She was beginning to feel crowded. Johnny had the television on from the time he woke up till the time he went to bed. It was wearing. She consoled herself with the thought that it was also temporary, and curled up again with *Backlash,* trying to ignore the sound of jet engines on short finals to Elmendorf Air Force Base, the yells of children playing in the park across the street and the cars driving by with rap music booming loud enough to be heard in the fillings in her teeth.

● ● ●

At five p.m. Monday the Bobbsey Twins presented themselves on Jack's front doorstep, wearing identical scowls. "You got the files?" Childress said, a belligerent thrust to his jaw.

"No," Kate said, "I sold them to Sheila Toomey. She says there's enough in them to keep the *Anchorage Daily News* going for the next year." She stood back, holding the door open. John King stamped inside. Childress, his face brick-red, followed with a damning glare. They seated themselves in the living room. Kate perched on the arm of a chair and didn't give them a chance to start in. "Last Tuesday's charter was delayed."

John King folded his arms across his chest and eyed her over the toes of his boots. "So? It happens."

"So it came in a day late, twenty-four hours overdue."

"And?"

"And that night I personally witnessed three separate cases of drug-related behavior in widely dispersed areas across the field."

Childress muttered beneath his breath. John King said, "Keep talking."

Kate gave a slight shrug. "Could mean nothing. Could be a coincidence." She met King's bespectacled glare without flinching. "Could mean the dealer changes out on a Tuesday, and his or her customers went a little overboard when they finally got their supply."

"You got any evidence?" Childress demanded.

"Yes."

"What?"

"The same thing has happened twice before."

"What a load of crap!" he exploded. "John, let me—"

"Shit," John King said, his scowl deepening. "You sure about this, Shugak?"

"No. All I'm telling you is there is a pattern. Three times during the last twelve calendar months there have been a rash of drug-related incidents to which your North Slope medical staff have responded. Prior to each time the incidents occurred, the charter was delayed either one or two days."

Childress started to speak and Kate held up a hand. "There's something else. Toni Hartzler, Public Relations. Gideon Trocchiano, Catering." She took a breath, held it. "Jerry McIsaac, physician's assistant."

The room was still for a moment. King had flushed red up to the roots of his hair, and he growled, "What about them?"

"They all change out on Tuesday."

"So does half of Production and most of CPS," Childress snapped. "John, don't listen to this shit! There's no motive here! All three of these people are making over seventy grand a year, what possible motive could they have for selling dope?"

John King said sharply, "Hartzler's making seventy?"

Kate interrupted both of them without apology. "I'm not looking for a motive, I'm looking for opportunity." They were silenced. "I'll find out how, you can work on why after the fact. There's more. All three of these people have their own transportation, not something that comes easy on the Slope unless it's assigned to the job. And all three of them have jobs that keep them out in the field, all over the field or, as in Trocchiano's case, a job that brings the field to them. Each time the incidents occurred, Toni Hartzler, Gideon Trocchiano and Jerry McIsaac were scheduled to fly up and were late getting in due to the charter delay. And each time, the incidents occurred after they were on the ground."

"Goddammit," King muttered.

"One other thing. The odds are big against all three of them being on the same plane on the same day at the same time. Trocchiano is a contract employee in catering, whose staff works two-and-one. McIsaac is in and out on medevacs. Hartzler is up and down on tours; from what I can tell from the manifests, half the time she flies commercial, accompanying her tour group from gate to gate."

"But all three of them were all on these flights."

"Yes, except for McIsaac, who flew up on the second charter last Wednesday."

"Then why include him?"

"Because he was on the other two flights, and he did make it up on Wednesday, just not on the same plane. He has to be included."

"John," Childress said, unable to contain himself a moment longer, "this is crap. Let me sniff around UCo, put out some feelers, I can find out where it's coming from and then—"

"It's coming directly into the Base Camp," Kate said.

That silenced him, but not for long. "How do you know?"

"Because I was offered toots from wholesale amounts of it in half a dozen rooms in the Base Camp on Saturday night."

John King surged to his feet. "What! Why the hell didn't you tell me when I called you Wednesday?"

"You hired me to find the dealer. I haven't yet. Besides, King, it's not UCo and you know it."

"And just how the hell do you know that?" Childress demanded.

Still looking at John King, Kate replied, "UCo contracts out to both sides of the field. It's a given that if a UCo employee was doing the dealing the problems would be occurring on both sides of the field at once. They aren't, are they?"

Silence. A long one.

John King stirred. He removed his cowboy hat, smoothed back his hair and reseated the hat with the air of a trail driver ready to ship the herd out to Abilene in the teeth of rustlers, tornadoes and hostile Indians. He looked across at Kate, yet another hostile Indian. "You find the fucker for me, Shugak. That's all I care about. I don't give a damn if my mama's the one doing the dealing, *just find* her."

She nodded. He left.

Childress snapped his eelskin briefcase shut and paused, looking at her, his upper lip lifting as if he smelled something bad. "I don't need your help, I didn't ask for it and I don't want it." He stepped forward so she'd have to tilt her head to meet his eyes. "I'll be watching, Shugak. You fuck up one time, I'll be there and I'll have your ass off the Slope so fast you won't have time to kick your heels together three times."

Kate remembered Toni's invocation of that same spell and

142

gave an involuntary laugh. It infuriated Childress and he stamped out the door.

"So much for the drugs being brought up the haul road by contractors," Jack observed from the doorway.

"You hear all that?"

"Uh-huh." He tossed a thick manila envelope in her lap. "Present for you." She opened it up and found a report on Lou Childress inside. "He doth protest too much," Jack said when Kate looked up. "Makes me nervous."

She shook her head. "Dicks R Us, We Suspect Everybody."

"You know my methods, Watson," he replied with a modest inclination of his head.

"You read it?"

He shook his head. "Just got it today. Investigator told me Childress is maxed out on all his credit cards, though, and he just refinanced his house."

"Lot of people did that when the interest rates went down," Kate observed. "It's hard to think the head of RPetCo Security, who has to be pulling down a hundred grand a year minimum, could be dumb enough to deal drugs."

"Stranger things have happened."

"What drugs?" Johnny wanted to know. He came all the way into the room and stood next to his father. Both of them were sunburned.

"Cocaine," Jack told him. "It's a case Kate is working on. What do you want for dinner, squirt?"

"Peach pancakes," Johnny replied promptly. Jack rumpled his hair. "Hey, Dad," Johnny said, ducking away, "don't mess with the mane."

"Sorry," Jack said, hiding a grin. "No peach pancakes today, no peaches in the cupboard."

"How about McDonald's?" Johnny said hopefully.

"One Big Mac coming up," Jack said. He looked at Kate. "Sound okay to you?"

She shook her head. "I've taken a moral stand against eating at McDonald's." She saw their looks and added, "Don't ask."

The next morning Jack drove her to the airport. On the ramp he got out to get her bag out of the back. She took it and jerked her head at Johnny, riding shotgun in the front seat. "Call your attorney." He nodded. "I mean it, Jack. He doesn't want to live with her and he's old enough to choose. No judge with any brains or balls is going to force him to."

The lines in his face relaxed and he kissed her, hard. "See you next week."

She entered the swinging doors in time to see Billy Bob Nielsen, production operator at One, accosted by a Hare Krishna, equipped with carnations, copies of the Bhagavad Gita and an ingratiating smile. The smile slipped a little when the big man picked him up and set him head down in the March of Dimes wishing well, to the accompaniment of a round of applause from every passenger and worker in the terminal.

Kate paused next to Dale, who was watching with an expression of deep appreciation. The big man came up to them, dusting his hands. "Nice job, Billy Bob," Dale told him.

Billy Bob's grin split his beard from ear to ear. "The fulfillment of a life-long dream."

It didn't get him a seat next to Dale on the charter, however. Chris Heller was on the flight, and he grabbed it, settling in between Kate and Dale. "Hello," Kate said.

It took him a minute to place her. "Oh, hi. Kate Shugak, right?"

"How are things at the dig?"

He beamed. "Great, we think we're about to find a body."

"Terrific," Kate said.

"Any more asshole senators you gotta take around this time up?"

"Only if I get real lucky." She reached into a pocket and her hand closed around a small, hard object. "I'm coming out to visit Tode Point this week."

He ran a hand through his hair and grinned, displaying a deep dimple in one cheek. "I have been warned. The kids'll be ecstatic, a real-live Native American in their real-live Native American dig."

Kate noticed Dale trying to pretend she wasn't listening and introduced her. "Dale Triplett, Chris Heller. Dale's a production operator. Chris is an archaeologist."

"No kidding? An archaeologist?" Dale inspected this new life form with cautious interest. "How about that. So? Was there really a Curse of the Pharaohs?"

"Absolutely," Chris said at once. "There was an inscription on the wall outside the door where Carter and Carnarvon went in." He dropped his voice to a spectral whisper. "'They who enter this sacred tomb shall swift be visited by wings of death.'"

Dale's eyes widened. Breathlessly, she prompted, "What happened?"

"Carnarvon died of blood poisoning five months after the burial chamber was breached. Carter was fired and discredited. One witness to the opening of the tomb was murdered by his wife, another was killed by a taxi in the streets of Cairo. The Egyptian government fell five times in the five years following the discovery. And Lady Carnarvon was killed by grave robbers." He thought for a moment. "And eaten," he added.

Dale looked suitably appalled and hid behind the morning paper to ward off further gory details.

Kate gave Chris a speculative look. He dimpled. "I thought so," she said, and opened her own paper to the crossword puzzle. The first clue to meet her eyes was "boy king" in three letters. She wouldn't tell Chris and Dale what made her laugh.

Eighty-seven minutes out of Anchorage the 727 touched down at Prudhoe. Peering through the window, Kate saw a snowdrift piled higher than the bus waiting for them that hadn't been there the week before. "Guess it snowed a bit after we left," Toni observed from the next row.

Kate looked around, thinking that on this, the first day of her second week, Slopers had either slowed their speech or her ears had caught up with it. She shuddered to think it was the latter. "Where's Jerry, do you know? I didn't see him at the airport."

Toni yawned and stretched. "He had to go into the office for some medical seminar or training session or something. He'll be up tonight." The plane rolled out to a halt on the apron and there was a rustle of movement as people folded their newspapers and stood to search the overhead racks for their carryons.

When Kate emerged into the chill arctic air, Toni was waiting at the foot of the airstairs with the tour bus and a bland smile. "You recovered from last week?"

"Am I with you again this week?"

"Uh-huh."

Kate considered saying no, she wasn't recovered. Before she could decide Toni said, "Good, because today's going to be a real challenge."

Kate climbed in the bus, stowed her flight bag beneath her seat and at Toni's instruction drove to the MarkAir terminal, where Toni greeted a German film crew, which was arriving on the same plane with a separate delegation from Nippon Steel, none of whom, it evolved, spoke English. *"Ohio gozaimas"* was the extent of Toni's Japanese and she knew more or less how to ask for a room in German so that she could produce a sentence that went something like, "Good afternoon, do you have a bed with a toilet?" which everyone agreed was hilarious but didn't get them any forrader.

One of the Japanese men beamed at her and said loudly, "Bangoon! Bangoon!"

Toni arrived at what seemed to Kate to be the logical conclusion and led him to the men's room. When he came out he said again, "Bangoon! Bangoon!"

"You just went, sir." Toni pointed to the door.

The man shook his head. "Bangoon!" he cried. He began waddling across the floor in what looked like an imitation of Charlie Chaplin. "Bangoon!" There was a spontaneous burst of applause from assorted pipefitters, welders, secretaries and roughnecks standing in line at the ticket counter, and the little man beamed some more and reiterated, "Bangoon!"

"Oh!" Kate said, a light breaking. "Penguins!"

"Hai!" he said, nodding vigorously. "Bangoon!"

"He would like to see some penguins," Kate informed Toni in a sternly controlled voice.

"Penguins?"

"Penguins."

"Bangoon!"

Toni didn't miss a beat. "I'm terribly sorry, sir," she said gravely. "Penguins are found only in the southern hemisphere, in the Antarctic." The man looked blank and Toni shook her head slowly, from side to side in an exaggerated negative movement. "No bangoon. No bangoon at Prudhoe Bay, sir."

The little man looked at Kate for confirmation. She mimicked Toni's solemn head shake. "No bangoon in the Arctic, sir," she repeated when she trusted herself to speak. "Only in the Antarctic."

He was crestfallen, and as she later explained to Kate, Toni felt so guilty she rustled up four caribou wintering, in previously unmolested placidity, beneath Production Center One so the little man's trip wouldn't be a total loss. He used up three rolls of film and departed the North Slope that evening in a happy glow, after having bestowed a lacquered wooden box on Toni and a pair of equally elaborate chopsticks on Kate. His compatriots smiled and bowed a lot, and the German TV crew shot file footage in efficient, businesslike silence.

At dinner Kate found Jerry in the serving line. "Hey, Kate. How was your week off?"

"Truthfully?" she said, ladling home fries onto her plate with a lavish hand. "I'm glad to be back on the Slope."

He laughed. "Yeah, I know how that gets." He paused, looking down at her. "You and Jack still . . ."

"Yeah."

"Him and Jane still fighting?"

"Yeah."

He laughed again. "Then I really know how that gets. So you're staying with him?"

He was making a salad as he spoke, and Kate regarded his profile thoughtfully. He scooped up a wedge of tomato and looked at her, raising his brows in inquiry. "What?"

"Nothing." Kate shrugged. "Yeah, I'm staying at Jack's. For a while."

Jerry nodded and appeared to dismiss the subject.

As they set their loaded trays down in the dining room,

Jerry's beeper went off. Jerry swore. As if on cue, the gravelly voice spoke over the loudspeaker. "Jerry McIsaac, call the operator. Jerry McIsaac, call the operator immediately."

When Jerry came back from the telephone, he said, "Some dumb-ass roughneck out at Rig 21 fell off the platform and managed to break his leg. If these friggin' Slopers had their way I'd never finish a meal." He looked at her hopefully. "Want to come?"

Kate's plate was barely visible beneath a crisp New York steak and a pile of golden brown steak fries. She sighed deeply. "Okay."

"Try not to overwhelm me with your enthusiasm, Shugak."

"Try not to underwhelm me with yours, McIsaac."

They grinned at each other.

She was just slipping to sleep that night when she realized that almost every waking moment of her day had been spent with either Toni or Jerry. The realization brought her fully awake and she shifted beneath the covers. Her assignment to Toni's tour bus, plus her volunteer work with Jerry, were beginning to make her feel restive. Both jobs offered the freedom of the field, and at the same time saddled her with anywhere from one to forty companions, and ferreting out dope dealers was a job best undertaken alone. And especially not in the company of your prime suspects.

She shifted again. The Slope was as crowded as town, more so. On her homestead in the Park, her nearest neighbor was ten miles away. Here, her neighbors were on all sides, around the table at every meal, in the halls, next door, for two floors above. She had to smile. She had to make polite conversation. The week-on, week-off schedule made her feel schizophrenic, a person of multiple personalities, one for home, one for town, one for Prudhoe. There was little privacy; the only time she was alone was when she was in her room, and at that she could hear the person overhead walking back and forth and her suitemate playing his television. She had come to hate the constant sound of the television. She could hear it now, a distant buzz.

The only television Kate normally saw was the screen Bernie had at the Roadhouse, eternally tuned in to a basketball game, and Bobby's television, which existed solely to be hooked up to a VCR. "The world is too much with us already," he had said once, explaining his steadfast refusal to get a satellite dish.

Kate missed Bobby. Not twelve hours apart and she already missed Mutt. She missed the feel of her home ground beneath the soles of her feet. And here it was March, and—or was it April? No, it was still March. It was odd how difficult it was to keep track of time north of the Arctic Circle. Almost as hard as it was keeping track of marriage certificates.

On top of everything else, her jeans were beginning to get uncomfortably tight around the waist. In her life, Kate had never had problems with her weight. She didn't like the feeling.

The television in the next room increased in volume. Kate gave her pillow a savage punch and pulled it down over her ears, and amused herself until she fell asleep by mentally arming a helicopter gunship and taking out every repeater on every mountain peak next to every village in the state of Alaska. Let 'em read books.

She thumped her pillow again. Tomorrow she would get some of those foam earplugs Dale Triplett issued visitors at the Production Center.

• • •

The next morning Toni and Kate picked up a group of AT & T engineers and took them out to a drill rig, Milepost Zero, a Production Center, and, holiest of holies because they got to visit their equipment in action, the communications center. When asked if AT & T switchboards were not the most powerful, the most reliable, the most efficient, the best built switchboards in the known world, Toni dimpled, accessed a line and held the receiver up so all could hear. "The dial tone's on." The engineers thought that was the greatest thing they'd heard said since the words "Mr. Watson, come here, I need you" entered the ether, and for a moment Kate was afraid RPetCo was going to lose Toni to Ma Bell.

They were done by noon, handing the executives off to the Amerex tour guide at Checkpoint Charlie. Back in camp, Toni told Kate, "Go ask Harris what you should do for the rest of the afternoon. But tell him I'll need you again tomorrow."

CHAPTER 8

INSTEAD, KATE CAJOLED GIDEON out of a box of assorted pastries, liberated Frank Jensen's truck off the bull rail and drove out to the dig on Tode Point. The road paralleled the coast and the clouds held off long enough for her to get her first good look at the Arctic Ocean. It was a crazy quilt of cracked ice and overlapped edges and broken bergs, extending across the northern horizon as far as she could see. Kate stopped the truck once where the bank dipped low and climbed down it. There was no lead in the ice, no open water of any kind for her to dip her toe into so she could say she had. She found an oddly shaped piece of driftwood instead, put it in her pocket and, feeling like a tourist, drove on.

The doughnuts, crullers and sugar cookies were received with rapture and Kate herself made royally welcome, or as royally welcome as a person could be made in a trailer perched on cement blocks that left itself open to the chill draft of every passing breeze, and that seemed to have only one light, a twenty-five-watt bulb hanging from a cord in the middle of the ceiling. It was enough to make out the dim outlines of the six bunks fastened to the walls, all of which were piled high with tools and packs and rolled sleeping bags and other equipment of less recognizable provenance. The bathroom was shoved into one tiny corner behind a door that refused to latch, and the rest of the floor space crowded with tables jammed in edge to edge. The place smelled like a zoo, Kate thought, and said so.

"*Eau d'ages*, Kate," Chris Heller said cheerfully. "We love the smell of hundred-year-old muktuk in the morning, don't we, troops?"

"You bet!" they chorused on cue.

Kate laughed. "Okay, okay. Show me what you got."

"Whampftifoozeeuvefundestedee," Karen said.

"I beg your pardon?"

Karen swallowed the rest of the cruller and, licking chocolate off her fingers, repeated, "Wait till you see what we found yesterday."

An expectant hush fell as they huddled around a table with a cloth draped over it. Conscious of an audience, Karen whipped the cloth back with all the panache of Harry Houdini.

Kate regarded the object on the table in silence. Karen, impatient, said, "Well? What do you think?"

Kate looked up. "What is it?"

All four faces registered first incredulity, then disappointment. Too late, Kate realized she wasn't keeping up her end as honorary resident descendant of the Tode Point hunters.

"You mean you don't know?" Rebecca said, her voice forlorn.

"Nope," Kate said, trying not to sound defensive. "I'm an Aleut, remember, not an Eskimo."

They brightened at this. "That's true," Kevin said with a forgiving smile. "Well, go ahead, pick it up, take a closer look. See if you can guess what it's for."

Kate picked the object up and held it closer to the one window and the pale arctic sun. "It looks like a bone, maybe even a human bone. Bones, I should say. Maybe the radius

153

and ulna from the forearm?" There were smothered titterings and covert nudgings around the circle. "Or maybe the bones from the foreleg of a caribou." An approving nod from Chris told her her second guess was right. "The claws are bird claws. Not eagle. Raven? And they're bound on the end here with some kind of sinew. Caribou? Walrus?" She grasped the bone handle in one hand, claws on the end of it poised to scratch. "Tell me this isn't a back scratcher."

There were wide grins. "Close, but no cigar," Chris said. "It is a scratcher, but not for your back."

"What for, then?"

"For the ice." Kate looked blank and Chris took the scratcher and demonstrated on the tabletop. The claws made a squeaky ripping sound. "The Eskimo hunter would be out on the ice, see? Hunting seal. He'd find an open lead and take the scratcher and scratch a couple times on the ice next to it. Turns out the seal is a real curious animal; like a cat, it lives in fear that something might happen somewhere and it might miss it. So, when the seal heard the scratcher he'd poke his head up for a look, and wham!" Chris beamed at her. "Supper time."

"I'll be damned." Kate raised a finger and touched it to one of the claws. "You've got to hand it to the old ones. They really did know how to affect their environment, didn't they?"

"That's nothing," Chris said, "wait'll you see this." They dragged her outside and fifty feet beyond the trailer to the dig, the outside of which resembled the dugout shelter Kate and Jack had found on Anua. Chris held out a cautionary hand in front of Kate. "No, don't go in, we've got everything sectioned off. You might step on Karen's latest potsherd and then we'd have to kill you."

Karen made a rude reply. Stooping to peer in the doorway,

Kate saw square sections of earthen floor at varying stages of excavation neatly cordoned off with staked lengths of string.

"Around here, Kate," Chris called from beyond the dugout. He indicated what looked to Kate like a pile of rocks as tall as she was. She stared from it to him and back again. "So? It's just a pile of rocks." Ten feet beyond, an upthrusting pipe and valve assembly reared its unsuitable head out of a small, square patch of snow. It was enclosed by a small square fence built of what looked like plumbing pipe, each corner fitted with elbows, T-connectors joining the two railings every foot or so.

"Yes, it is, but not just any pile of rocks," Karen said. Kate figured she probably couldn't even see the wellhead for the cairn.

"Yeah," Rebecca chimed in, "the Eskimos built them all over the Slope to help them drive the caribou herds." She probably couldn't, either.

Kate looked from the wellhead back to the stone cairn. "What?"

"It's true," Kevin said, grinning. "The caribou would mistake the cairns for men and shy off in the other direction, which happened to be the direction the Eskimos wanted them to go."

Kate couldn't stop the marveling smile that broke over her face. "You're kidding me."

Chris shook his head, as proud as if he had invented the caribou-herding cairn personally. "Nope. Pretty clever, huh?"

"No lie. I like it. It's almost as neat as the scratcher. Or a storyknife."

"Storyknife!" "Have you got a storyknife?" "Where?" "What's it look like?" "How old is it?" "Where's it from; what's its history?"

Kate patted the air, laughing again. "It wasn't mine, in Unalaska, it's made of ivory, I don't know how old it is, and I think it came originally from the Yukon-Kuskokwim Delta but I don't know for sure." She told them of Sasha's storyknife, and of the stories Sasha and her storyknife drew together in the sand, and saw that she was regaining some stature in her listeners' eyes, even if it was only by association. They hung on her words, a few taking notes, avid for every scrap of anthropological and/or archaeological information to come their way.

She interrupted herself and said, "You know, there's a lady working at the Base Camp you might want to talk to, maybe even bring over here. She's an Eskimo, name of Cindy Sovalik. She makes beds for the catering department."

"Really? Where's she from?"

Kate searched her memory. "It's a village east of here— Ichelik, that's it."

"Have you met her?"

Kate grinned. "Almost."

"What's she like?"

"All I know is she's a room steward at the Base Camp. And that she makes kuspuks for cash customers on the side," Kate added.

The prospect of getting their hands on a real live Eskimo was almost more than the self-styled grave robbers could bear. They were all so very young, so very earnest, so single-minded in their pursuit of the historical example. They reminded her of Andy Pence, her roomie and fellow deckhand on board the *Avilda*. What they lacked in experience they more than made up for in enthusiasm. They made Kate feel her age.

She reached in her pocket. "I brought something to show you, too." Untying the cord on the little velveteen sack Jack had given her, she shook it over her palm and held out her hand.

"Wow," Chris breathed.

"Go ahead," Kate said. "Pick it up. Look at it. Tell me everything you know about it."

It was a challenge they couldn't resist. "Either Aleutian Aleut or Bering Sea Eskimo," Rebecca said, eyes narrowed on the little carving.

"Bering Sea Eskimo," Kevin said positively.

"St. Lawrence Island," Karen said, narrowing it down.

Chris took charge. "Gambell?" He looked at Kate. "No, not Gambell. Savoonga. Probably from the Kukulek sites."

In spite of herself Kate was awed. "You guys are good."

The four exchanged slightly sheepish glances. "Actually," Rebecca said apologetically, "we're not that good. There's been a rash of stuff from St. Lawrence through the U lately. The St. Lawrence islanders are digging up every square foot of ground that'll take a shovel, looking for artifacts to sell."

"Yeah," Chris said in disgust, "I spent last summer on St. Lawrence. You ought to see it. People been digging up so many graves, the place looks like it's been carpet-bombed."

"The reverence one is likely to have for their ancestors decreases in direct proportion to how hungry their children are at the time," Karen said, her voice tart. "St. Lawrence Island doesn't have exactly what you'd call a booming economy."

"Yeah," Kevin agreed, "and it's the same story in a lot of the villages all over the state. These folks used to make a pretty good living off the land and the sea. Now they've got the Fish and Game breathing down their necks, and the processors screaming discrimination, and they're lucky if they can get their nets wet twice a week. Not that there's anything in the water worth catching anymore, since the long-liners started dragging up the bottom of the ocean out in the Doughnut Hole and selling it off to Japan."

"I know, I know," Chris said impatiently, "I don't mean to judge. But they're destroying their own heritage. What are we, if we're not the product of thousands of years of evolution, and if we don't know how we got where we are—"

"How are we supposed to know where we're going?" the other three said in chorus.

Chris flushed and laughed. "Nice to know you've been paying attention."

"You're right, though," Rebecca said, sobering. "It is nothing more than cultural cannibalism."

She looked accusingly at Kate. The other three followed suit, and for a moment Kate felt like she'd been caught robbing a grave. "It isn't mine," she said, her voice rising a little. "It belongs to a friend." They didn't say anything. "Honest. I didn't dig it up out of my grandmother's grave, in fact, she's still living, so I couldn't have. It's not for sale."

"Wait till somebody makes an offer," Chris said cynically.

Kate looked down at the little seal. "How much would something like this go for?"

"The Detroit Institute of Arts paid fifty-five thousand dollars for an ivory figure from Point Hope, no questions asked."

Kate was incredulous. "How much?"

"Fifty-five thousand individual United States greenback dollar bills."

"Bullshit," she said involuntarily.

"It's true," Chris insisted.

Kevin nodded glum agreement. "Sotheby's auctioned off a stone lamp from Kodiak for fifteen grand a while back."

Shaken, Kate said, "It's no wonder there's a black market in the stuff if it's going for prices like that." She thought. "But wait a minute, didn't I read somewhere that they passed a federal act making that illegal?"

"The Archaeological Resources Protection Act," Karen said, nodding. "Actually, it was passed in 1979, but they beefed up the penalties recently." She looked at Rebecca. "You're our resident legal expert, Becky. What is it now, twenty grand maximum in fines and two years in jail for a first offense?"

"And up to a hundred grand for a second," Rebecca confirmed, nodding. "But it doesn't apply to buying and selling, only to the pot hunting itself, and only on sites located on public lands."

"Shit," Kevin said, disgusted, "most of the state of Alaska is public land. How are you supposed to police 591,000 square miles, most of it wilderness, with eleven park rangers equipped with nothing but a writ?"

"The worst part of it is, the diggers move things," Chris said.

"Move things?"

"Yeah." He pointed at the seal Kate held. "That alone doesn't interest us much. It's a beautiful example of the carver's art, it'd probably sell for a hell of a lot of money in Detroit or New York, but our interest would be in where it was found." He saw Kate's uncomprehending look and elaborated. "Where it was found geographically, of course, like where in Alaska, but especially where in relation to the rest of the dig. This"—he held up the seal—"this was probably an amulet, a charm for a seal hunter, to bring him good luck on a hunting trip, to honor the animal he was hunting. Maybe he wore it around his neck, maybe it was attached to his visor, maybe it was fixed to his kayak. We'd have a better way of knowing for sure if we could see where it was found."

"Like if it was found near the remains of a kayak, you'd be pretty sure it was a kayak charm," Kate said, "whereas if it was found in a grave around a skeleton's neck, you'd know it was a personal charm. And *that* would tell you something about who and what the guy in the grave was."

He gave her an approving smile and Kate was proud she'd said a smart thing, but his smile didn't last long. "The way it stands now, it's a charmer of a charm but it doesn't tell us anything we didn't already know. Like this little bear we found. Come on, I'll show you." He led the way back to the trailer and pulled a drop cloth from the corner of one table, revealing three ulu blades, fragments of various wooden bowls and a thread spool shaped from ivory, but no bear. "Where is it?" He looked around, pulling sheets back from the other tables, one after another, revealing an extensive collection of objects made from rock, bone, wood, ivory and skin, but still no bear. "Doggone it, you guys, where's the bear we found week before last? The little ivory one? The polar bear?"

Kevin pointed. "It was on that table, on the corner there, right next to the lamp with the walrus head, yesterday."

Chris straightened, frowning. "Well, it's not there now. Neither is the lamp."

"What?"

The four of them turned the trailer upside down, but they couldn't find either the bear or the lamp. The team was deeply upset at the discovery. "Those were two of our best pieces," Rebecca said, near tears.

Chris put a comforting arm around her. "Cheer up, Becky. Look, I know I locked the door last night when we left. They were good pieces, the best. Otto probably took them for safekeeping. Try not to worry about it until we talk to him."

"Where is Otto?" Kate asked.

"He stayed behind at the Base Camp this morning," Chris told her. "Said he had to make some phone calls, do some paperwork."

Wake up slow with Toni, Kate thought.

Chris walked her to her truck. She climbed in and rolled down the window. "Chris," she said. "What do you think really happened to them? To the missing artifacts?"

"I don't know." He kicked at a lump of snow. "I'd hate to think—I just don't know."

She asked a question she knew he didn't want to answer. "Has anything else gone missing lately?" He met her eyes, his own troubled, but she was right, he didn't reply. "You think they might have been stolen?"

He shrugged, saving himself the need to say it out loud.

"You trust your people?"

"Of course," he said, "of course I trust them," but his indignation sounded forced and he contradicted himself with his next breath. "They auctioned off a wooden Tlingit bowl at Christie's last week for five thousand dollars. Our staff archaeologists barely make minimum wage. How can we compete with that?"

"Appeal to people's finer feelings," Kate suggested, only half facetiously.

"People don't have any finer feelings when it comes to cold hard cash," Chris said morosely.

Kate's inconvenient memory kicked in with Ekaterina's enraged expression, and the words that went with it, *Shame on you, Katya*. "No," she agreed, "I guess we don't."

A mile or so from the dugout she stopped the truck and looked back. At that distance the mound of the roof blended

161

into the horizon, indistinguishable but for the scurrying figures around it. At that distance the mound might be a landed whale, and the figures the crew that had landed it, yesterday or a thousand years ago.

Behind the mound the stone cairn was barely discernible. The wellhead stood out in clear relief, and ten miles beyond it the gas flares at the Central Compression Plant burned without ceasing.

• • •

She was corralled by Harris Perry at the door of the Base Camp and, along with the other three B Shift roustabouts, detailed to help clean up a crude spill on Z Pad. A wellhead valve had malfunctioned and Z Pad was right on the Kuparuk River, so the cleanup was a matter of some urgency. Black gook stretched out in a pool twenty feet across and the smell of sulfur made Kate's eyes water. The in-house environmentalist was there with a response list attached to a clipboard, and succeeded so well in getting in everyone's way that one of Kate's fellow roustabouts, a burly, taciturn man in his fifties, shouldered her into an open lead in the otherwise frozen river. The environmentalist emerged bawling, sloshed to her Suburban, slammed inside and kicked gravel fifty yards peeling out. The other two roustabouts promised the burly man a night out on the town their next week in. Kate was careful to add her congratulations to those of her coworkers. The Kuparuk River looked cold and Kate had always had an innate aversion to getting her feet wet.

"Greenies," the burly man said with loathing. "For a thousand years it was a frozen wasteland. Now all of a sudden it's the goddam delicate tundra."

The rest of the afternoon was spent laying out absorbent pads, with Kate doing most of the work under the disinterested gaze of three self-appointed supervisors, who all made a lot of money that afternoon sitting in a truck chewing toothpicks.

She recounted the afternoon's activities to Dale and Toni over dinner, not forgetting what had happened the last time she had brought a grievance to this table. Dale said instantly, "Prudhoe Bay, Where Conservation and Corporation Meet."

"Oil Field or Wildlife Refuge?" Toni retaliated. "Only Your Stockbroker Knows for Sure." She sipped her coffee reflectively and added, "I don't know why we don't just quit the Slope and go into advertising. We're wasted here."

"Speaking of wasted," Dale said, "how was that Seattle SWAT team you toured last month? I forgot to ask."

"Actually, not a bad bunch of guys. For hired killers."

After dinner Toni carried Kate off to a pinochle game with Warren Rice and Sue Jordan. Kate lost twenty bucks, partly because she never failed in her belief that her partner had everything she needed to make a run, mostly because she'd always been more interested in the players than in the cards.

Halfway through the third game Otto Leckerd materialized and Hartzler abandoned shooting the moon for going there. "Otto," Kate called after the lovers.

He turned to look at her, hand brushing but not quite holding Toni's. "What?"

"You find those missing artifacts out at the dig?"

"What missing artifacts?"

"You know, the ivory bear, the stone lamp? Chris and the others told me about losing them. Have you found them yet?"

She watched with interest as the color left his face, leaving it a pasty white, and kept watching as the color flooded back in, turning him a tomato-red. Her gaze shifted to Toni, who was looking at her with a considering expression, brows slightly puckered. As soon as Toni noticed Kate looking, her forehead resumed its usual porcelain-smooth perfection. She hooked her arm through Otto's and pressed it to her side. "What's all this? Have your little spirits been walking off with artifacts?"

Otto met Toni's eyes and his flush began to fade. "Not that I know of," he said, trying on a smile for size. It was a good attempt but it fit tight across the chest. He looked back at Kate. "No, we haven't found them," he told her. "We think they got mixed in with another shipment to the university by mistake. I put a call into the department. I'm sure it's only a matter of time before they turn up."

He smiled at Kate again, a better effort this time. She smiled back, thinking, I'm sure it will be. She wasn't as sure precisely where they would turn up.

Ann McCord wandered through as the pinochle game broke up and invited Kate to a party in Gideon's room. Kate was tired and all she wanted was bed, but she was on the Slope to find a drug dealer and a late-night party seemed a likely lead. When she stepped in the door to see a bag of cocaine being cut on the counter by one of the kitchen helpers, she was sure of it. Half a dozen other people crowded into the room cheered him on. He finished drawing lines with a razor blade and held the now nearly empty bag up and inspected it. "Actually, I'm getting a little low. Going to have to resupply pretty soon."

He looked at Ann, who grinned and shrugged. "No problem. Plenty more where that came from."

Gideon grinned and made room for Kate in front of the counter. He gestured to the mirror. "Special guests first."

Kate shook her head. "No, thanks."

He looked surprised. "Oh. You sure?"

Kate nodded. "Yeah."

"Well." Gideon turned to a small refrigerator mounted on the wall above his bed, a site most Base Camp residents reserved for televisions. "A beer, then. Or wine, I've got some great chardonnay."

"There hasn't been a good chardonnay made since 1981," Ann told him.

Gideon made a face at her. "Some cabernet, then. Joe Heitz. I don't offer Joe to just anybody."

Kate shook her head. "I'd take some juice, if you've got any."

Gideon looked askance, and turned to rummage in the refrigerator. "I don't know, I—oh. Here. Some cranapple okay?"

"Fine."

"I could dress it up a little for you." Gideon hefted a bottle of vodka from the shelf at the opposite end of the bed.

Kate, tired of shaking her head, said baldly, "No."

He looked at her. "You don't want a line, wine or a shot. What's the matter with you, you some kind of narc?"

It was a remark made too close for comfort. Kate forced a laugh. "Yeah, you're all under arrest. Up against the wall."

On the phone a young man in kitchen whites was saying blearily, "That's right, Warren, I want to talk to Australia." Conversation quite naturally ground to a halt around him and Kate took an unobtrusive breath of relief. "Who? I don't care, just somebody with a sink."

With gentle fingers Gideon pried the phone out of his hands. "Wade? Wade?" Wade had a hard time focusing. "Wade? Why do you want to talk to Australia?"

Wade blinked a few times. "Because?"

"Why?" Gideon repeated.

"Because," Wade said, "I want to find out why the water goes clockwise down the drain up here and counter clockwise down there." He flung out a thumb that nearly impaled the woman next to him. "Martha just got back and she says it does and I want to know why, is all."

Another man offered to call his sister in Uruguay and see if she knew, and an argument immediately erupted over whether Uruguay was enough "down there" to qualify.

Kate eventually got her cranapple juice, straight, but things were never quite as friendly out after that, and she left as soon as the glass was empty.

She went back to her room, getting madder with every step.

No matter how many times she'd been through the same reaction it never failed to annoy her. First surprise, then suspicion, lastly hostility. So she didn't want a drink. So what was the almighty goddam big deal? She didn't drink at all, ever. Her mother and her father had both been alcoholics. Her cousin Martin was a living, breathing object lesson in substance abuse. Alcohol and all its attendant problems had been the ruination of village life in Alaska and was decimating her race, and it was her choice to stay away from it. It was also her right, but it was almost impossible to convince some people of that.

It had been the same in college, at parties with people passing joints around. Kate had always refused, and her classmates had regarded her if not with suspicion, then as something more than a prude and something less than a self-made saint. It was just another way she was different, along with the color of her skin and the smarts that kept her on the dean's list for four years in a row. When she wouldn't go out on a toot with the boys at Quantico, she got the same reaction. She was tired of it.

Slamming the door of her room behind her, she pulled her clothes off and flounced into bed. As she stretched up an arm to turn off the light, she remembered the boy in the Fourth Avenue bar, and her anger evaporated.

At least she had a choice. At least she could say no.

• • •

The next morning she rose early, hooked three doughnuts over the fingers of one hand and filled the largest paper cup she could find full of coffee, half and half and two packets of sugar, and retired to the library with yesterday's Anchorage Daily News she had scrounged from the front desk clerk. Arranging herself on one of the easy chairs in front of the window overlooking the parking lot, she found The New York Times crossword puzzle, unlimbered her pen and began not filling in answers to clues like "medieval goblet" and "Jewish month." The coffee and the doughnuts (one chocolate, one old-fashioned, one glazed) went a long way toward easing her feeling of ignorance.

Persian money? She wondered how big the ivory bear was that had been lost. She wondered how big the stone lamp was, too. She wondered how many security guards were versed in the Archaeological Resources Protection Act. She wondered how many of them would recognize a bona fide Native Alaskan American Indian artifact if it bit them on the seat of the pants.

Latvian citizen? She thought of her otter, and how perfect it was, and how tiny. She thought of the old man's carvings, and how perfect they were, and how tiny. Small in Oban, she read, and filled in w-e-e. Yes, they certainly were wee. Wee, sma' creatures. Wee, sma' and easy to smuggle. She remembered the story Chris had told her about the $55,000 ivory figure and bit the end of her pen. Pound for pound, Alaskan Indian artifacts were as lucrative as drugs. Maybe more so.

"N.Y.C. transit system" blocked every attempt to be solved. Kate threw down the puzzle in disgust, invoking a curse on that rampantly geographical chauvinist Eugene T. Maleska and all his progeny. A movement outside caught her eye and she looked up.

There was, for a change, no fog and no falling snow and no great amount of wind to blow the snow lying on the ground, and the view in the early morning light was perfectly clear. The public relations van, used for tours when a tour group consisted of ten members or less, was plugged into the end of the bull rail closest to the Base Camp's front door. Next to it stood Otto Leckerd and Toni Hartzler. At first Kate assumed they were taking a fond farewell after a romantic evening and almost averted her eyes. Then she saw the box. It was a small, battered cardboard box, and Otto was trying to take it away from Toni. Toni held it out of reach, talking rapidly.

Without thinking, Kate rose to her feet and went to stand in front of the window. Otto made another grab for the box, and it looked as if he was yelling. They both hung on to it, both talking at once.

Kate was watching Otto's face over Toni's shoulder when his expression changed. He had seen her. She made an elaborate show of drinking coffee, looking up and catching sight of them for the first time and giving a friendly wave. She left the window in a leisurely manner and went to examine the books locked behind glass on the library shelf. A handwritten card announced that the key was available from the clerk at the front desk. The biography of MacArthur by William Manchester looked interesting. Author and subject had both spent a lot of time in the South Pacific, as soldiers in the same theater of the same war, so it might even be accurate. She tried to see Otto's and Toni's reflection in the glass but the angle was wrong and there wasn't enough light anyway.

When she looked around again, very casually, Toni was alone and closing the passenger door of the van. Kate caught a glimpse of the box sitting in the front seat. Her eyes narrowed, trying to make out the writing on the side, but it was too far and all she got an impression of was a logo in red and white. She watched from the corner of her eye as Toni unplugged the headbolt heater, climbed in the driver's side and drove around the Base Camp module and out of sight.

Kate wheeled and moved rapidly through the lounge and down the hallway that led to a service entrance in back of the kitchen. The Base Camp buildings were assembled from smaller modules, all of which had fire doors at every corner with stairways leading down the exterior walls. Kate hit the door bar on the run and took the stairs outside two at a time. She was at the northwest corner of the main module; around the northwest corner of the fire/safety module she caught the red gleam of taillights before the pilings holding everything off the gravel pad blocked them out. The building was so large, and required so many pilings to hold it up, that it was impossible to see through to the gravel pad on the other side of the building.

Breath coming out in frosty puffs, shivering a little in the cold air, she trotted forward, beneath the fire/safety module, to thread her way through the pilings. According to Toni the architects, in recognition of the unrelenting force of the

169

omnipresent onshore wind, had aerodynamically designed the Base Camp modules to minimize snowdrifts and, accordingly, snow removal. They had done a superb job, transforming housing for 474 workers into a series of what were essentially huge, cubic airfoils; there were no drifts beneath the copper-colored module, only a dry, hard crust upon which the rubber soles of her safety boots squeaked, tread as lightly as she might. Surrounded as she was by the metal siding of the building overhead and the metal sheaths of the concrete pilings, every squeak bounced back at her, multiplied ten times, so that at first she missed the low mutter of the van ahead.

It came again and this time she heard it. She went up on tiptoe, sneaked up on a piling and peered around.

The van was in park with the engine idling, stopped in front of the fire/safety garage. There was no traffic on the Backbone beyond and no sight or sound of anyone but the three of them. Through the open window came Toni's voice, not loud enough for Kate to make out the words. She could hear Jerry clearly. "No, I won't do it," he said, and there was as much fear as there was anger in his tone. Toni's voice came again, a soft, soothing murmur. "No," Jerry repeated, this time with less force. "Dammit, Toni, it's getting too dangerous." Toni said something and he mumbled something more, all of which was lost to Kate except for the words "—good, the best, I'm telling you, we can't take any more chances—"

A drift of wind caught the rumble of the engine and wafted it toward Kate, muffling the rest of his words. Toni spoke again; Jerry's head drooped in a clear sign of defeat. Toni handed him the box through the window and he accepted it without looking up.

The sole of Kate's boot slipped on the hard-packed snow,

her body shifted and hit the metal of the piling with a dull thud. A white fox exploded out of the snow directly in front of her, running flat out, tail streaming behind it, right beneath the van and out the other side. There was a kind of combination clop-crunch and on Kate's right a caribou cow with two of last year's calves shot from beneath the module, trotted in front of the van and across the pad.

At the van both heads turned as one to look at what had startled the animals, and Jerry took a step in her direction. Kate broke and ran, dodging back and forth between pilings in the hope she wouldn't be seen, or at the very least recognized. She hammered up the stairwell only to find the fire door didn't open from the outside. Taking the steps two at a time on the way back down, she ducked beneath the main Base Camp module and headed through the pilings for the front entrance. Rounding the corner, she remembered the security guard stationed at the door and bypassed it for the garages. She was in luck; Cale Yarborough was just backing out. She gave the field manager a cheery wave as he looked askance at her plaid shirt, jeans and no coat. A quick trot through the administration offices, up the back stairs, and she was in the library with her feet up on the table, coffee cup in hand, hard at work on the crossword puzzle when Toni walked in.

The brunette as usual looked perfectly groomed and composed, but Kate noticed her breath was coming a little fast. She smiled widely and tried by sheer force of will to slow her own rapid heartbeat. "Morning. You don't happen to know a three-letter word for the New York City transit system, do you?"

"Good morning. MTA, maybe? Like Charlie on the?"

Kate frowned. "I think that was Boston. 'Now you citizens of Boston, don't you think it's a scandal—' "

171

"'How the people have to pay and pay,'" Toni chanted. Together they sang, "'Fight the fare increase, vote for George O'Brien, and get Charlie off the MTA!'" They both laughed and Kate thought what a pity it was how much she liked this woman. "I thought I saw you up here," Toni said, nodding toward the bull rail.

"Oh, was that you down there? I saw somebody wave and just to be on the safe side I waved back."

She smiled again. Toni returned it, eyes flickering down Kate's relaxed body. "You look comfortable."

Kate folded the newspaper and gave her a suspicious look. "Do I detect a warning in that observation? As in not to get too comfortable?"

Toni looked wounded. She was very good at it. "Who, me?" She grinned, and for the first time Kate noticed what a practiced grin it was, all flash and sharp upper incisors. "Just be at the office at ten. We have to be out at the airport by ten forty-five."

"Who's coming?"

"A bunch of state supreme court justices and their wives and their court administrators." She paused. "Sixty-three of them."

On that superb exit line she departed.

Kate blew out a deep, relieved breath, letting the paper fall to her lap, and looked down at her feet, propped on the table and crossed at the ankles.

Snow was melting from the toe of one safety boot to form a tiny puddle on the tabletop.

• • •

The room to Toni's door was locked. Kate slid the master key she had filched from the pegboard in Ann McCord's office into the keyhole. The door resisted. There was a footstep down the hall, and Kate grasped the knob and twisted it with all her strength. It gave and she slipped inside Toni's room just as the outer door to the suite began to open. Soundlessly, she closed the door without releasing the knob. The outer door closed, followed by the door to the bathroom. She released the knob.

The toilet flushed. The bathroom door opened and steps went into the next room. Some rustling movements were followed by steps coming out again. Kate heard a shower turn on full force, relaxed, and turned to survey the room.

It was exactly like any other room in the RPetCo Hilton: a built-in captain's bed with drawers beneath, a built-in bookshelf over the head of the bed, and two closets. A counter ran from the bookshelves to the opposite wall, where there were a row of drawers stacked beneath it and a shelf and a mirror above. Between bookshelf and mirror was a window, this one facing west.

Kate tossed the drawers first and didn't find anything beyond some dirty underwear that probably belonged to Toni's alternate, since they were BVDs. The closets were next; same result, a lot of neatly hung blazers and slacks, a pair of Birkenstock sandals and a box of Tide.

There was a selection of books on the shelf above the head of the bed. Like Jerry McIsaac, Kate had her own set of laws and the first one was, "You Are What You Read." On Toni's shelf there was a first edition of *Crossroads of Continents*. A trade paperback edition of *Russia-America, the Forgotten Frontier.* An old edition of *Inuit,* which Kate opened to find many of the pages dog-eared and much of the text underlined. "Eskimo carvers rarely began with a specific object in mind," she read. "Instead, they studied the blank, turning it over and over in their hands, until they saw one or more images. They then released them by shaping the blank into these forms."

The same way Michelangelo sculpted "David" and the "Pieta," Kate thought, half a world and a millennium away. She shut the book and replaced it on the shelf. An object on the shelf above caught her eye, and she stood on tiptoe to see.

It was a length of baleen, the long, black, tapered gill of a whale. This one was old, with drawings inscribed on its side that looked like a group of motion dancers, some hunched down with arms outstretched, others beating drums. It was amazing how much life and movement had been captured by the artist. Kate turned the piece over to see if he'd signed it. He hadn't, which made her think this sample must be very old indeed.

She debated taking the baleen out to the archaeological dig and having Chris look at it, then rejected the notion as too risky. Kate replaced the baleen, wondering again how much Jerry had told Toni of her previous life.

The shower shut off and she slid from the room and the suite. She stood a moment, holding the knob of the suite door, listening. The person in the shower was whistling softly to himself. The shower door opened, the door to the second bedroom closed. She relaxed.

"Hey."

She turned to see Ann McCord watching her with a frown on her face, clipboard and pencil in hand. Next to her was a cart filled with folded towels and squirt bottles of cleaning products.

"Oh," Kate said. "Hello."

Ann's eyes flickered from the number on the suite's door and back to Kate. "I thought your room was 786."

Kate summoned up a smile and stepped closer. "It is. Toni wanted me to get her something out of her room."

Ann looked at Kate's empty hands. "Oh?"

Kate shrugged. "It wasn't there." She tried another smile. "She probably left it in the van. You know Toni."

Ann regarded her without replying. "Well," Kate said, "gotta go. I'm driving the bus for Toni today. Bunch of judges coming up."

She walked down the hall, her spine itching from Ann's hard stare all the way around the corner. Detouring on her way to Ann's office to drop off the master key, she went out to the bull rail. When she reached the PR van she stopped, turned and looked up. The library alcove was clearly visible through the windows; table, chairs, shelves and books. She could almost make out the title of the Manchester book on MacArthur.

● ● ●

The judges, wives and administrators were a delightful surprise; intelligent, articulate and appreciative of every attention. The day passed quickly, and when Kate pulled up at the Base Camp to drop Toni off, the brunette gave her an affable smile, thanked her for her help and vanished in the front door without further ado. Kate, relieved, pulled the bus around to the bull rail and swept it out and washed all the windows in gratitude.

When she finished she had mud up to her eyebrows and no feeling left in any of four alternate extremities, so she knocked off work early, went to her room to grab a towel and her swimsuit and headed for the pool room. She showered quickly, donned her suit and went through to the sauna. The thermostat next to the door indicated that it was on and already occupied by someone who liked it hot. She opened the door and went in.

In the dim light of the single, shaded bulb she saw a woman, short and solid without being in the least bit fat. She had a large flat face with prominent cheekbones and a pronounced version of Kate's own hint of epicanthic eye fold. She was seated at the end of the bench, and looked up as Kate entered.

"Hello," Kate said.

"Hello."

Something held Kate where she stood, looking at the lines drawn by time and experience in that marvelous old face, the clear steadiness of the unflinching brown eyes. "You're Cindy Sovalik."

"And you are Kate Shugak." Her English had an Inupiat accent, thick through the vowels and hard on the consonants.

"Yes." Kate sat down at the opposite end of the bench. "I've heard of you, auntie."

"I've heard of you, too," Cindy said, and called her a word Kate didn't understand but, given Cindy's age, did not question. It didn't sound uncomplimentary. In English, Cindy said, "Ekaterina Shugak is your grandmother."

Kate ladled water on the fake coals. Steam hissed up and enveloped them both. She sighed and leaned back against the wall. "Yes, auntie."

"I see her every year at AFN. A strong woman."

"Yes, auntie." Kate ladled more water on the coals.

"And a wise one. She has much to teach."

Cindy's voice was calm but stern, with just a hint of—what? Warning? Reproof? Kate paused, ladle outstretched. Brown eyes met hers unflinchingly. What did this old woman know about her, about her relationship with her grandmother?

Kate tore her eyes away and emptied the ladle, setting it aside and leaning back against the wooden wall. The heat and moisture seeped in through her skin to flesh and bone, opening her pores, unknotting her muscles, soothing her nerves. All that bouncing over rough gravel roads, the constant growl of the engine, the incessant chatter in the seats behind her, the high-pitched scream of gas through pipes, the clank of thrown chain and the ubiquitous mutter of the television, all these irritants melted, dissolved in and dissipated by the hot, rising steam. Kate closed her eyes. Her shoulders relaxed. She breathed deeply, emptying her mind of thought, and let herself float.

"What do you do here, Kate Shugak?" Cindy's voice did not startle her, as it seemed to coalesce out of the steam and heat to form a third presence in the room.

"I work for the oil company, auntie," Kate said, opening her eyes and turning her head lazily to look at the other woman. "Like you."

"No." Wise old eyes looked back at her. Kate met them steadily. "You do not do the work I do. You do not do the work others do."

The steam appeared to have fogged up her reflexes. Kate didn't even twitch. "No."

The other woman was silent for a moment. "There is danger."

"Perhaps."

"There is danger," the older woman repeated, the flat certainty in her voice causing Kate a ripple of alarm.

She frowned. "What do you know, auntie? What kind of danger? Who from?"

The old woman rose to her feet, her brown skin gleaming in the dim light, and looked down at Kate gravely. "There is

177

danger," she said for the third time. "Take care."

The door closed behind her and Kate was left alone to contemplate the tongue-in-groove paneling on the walls.

Quoth the raven, nevermore, she thought. And then she said it out loud. "Quoth the raven, nevermore."

It didn't help as much as she thought it would.

CHAPTER 9

SHE HAD DINNER THAT evening with Dale Triplett and Billy Bob Nielsen. *The Rocky Horror Picture Show* was playing in the Base Camp theater that night and Dale had half convinced Kate and Billy Bob to join her. "We'll need some toast, though. I'll have to ask Gideon."

"Toast?" Kate and Billy Bob exchanged puzzled glances.

"And rice, of course, but I'm sure I can get some of that from Gideon, too. And toilet paper, and newspaper and a squirt bottle filled with water. What else? Oh, yeah, a lighter. You don't smoke, do you?"

"No," Kate said, "and I think I'm busy this evening after all."

"You certainly are," Toni said over her shoulder in a cheerful voice. "Or did you forget there's a war on around the pinochle table? You have to give Sue and Warren a chance for revenge."

Kate twisted in her seat. "What revenge? I lost twenty bucks last night."

"Details, details," Toni said airily, pulling Kate's chair out and perforce bringing Kate to her feet. She slid a hand beneath Kate's elbow and tugged. "Night all," she told Dale, "and have fun doing the Time Warp again."

"Time Warp?" Billy Bob said apprehensively.

In the lounge Kate sat down across from Toni while Warren

179

dealt the cards, Sue keeping up a running speculation on the rumored rif. Toni ran the bid up to thirty-nine in spite of Kate's anguished expression. Kate had nothing but tens and kings to pass her and Toni swore roundly and proceeded to run them firmly into the hole the first hand. "May I hold the back door open for you, ladies?" Warren inquired, and Sue snickered.

Jerry showed up halfway through the second game, and at Toni's request fetched a round of drinks for the table, coffee for Toni and Warren and juice for Sue and Kate. Kate looked up as he placed the glass in front of her, smiling her thanks. His returning smile didn't reach his eyes. She opened her mouth to ask who died, but before she could get the words out Toni jumped in with a bid so outrageously at odds with what Kate had in her hand that she turned to remonstrate, and by the time she looked around again Jerry was walking away. "Hey, McIsaac, where you going?"

"Can't stay," he said without looking around, "I'm on call tonight."

"Oh. Well, thanks for the juice. Thirsty work, being cheated out of a life's wages." She sipped her juice and studied her cards.

In the middle of the third game she began to yawn, and by its end she could barely keep her eyes open. "Sorry, guys," she mumbled, shoving herself to her feet. "I'm wasted. See you in the morning."

"Seven A.M. sharp," Toni called. "Don't forget we've got the House Interior Committee landing at eight."

Kate gave a vague wave and walked away. She'd never noticed before how much concentration it took to put one foot in front of the other.

"Hey, Kate." Dale's voice seemed to echo down the hall.

With a tremendous effort Kate turned. Dale's blond hair was plastered wetly to her scalp. Kate squinted. It looked like it had little white worms in it. "What wrong with your hair?" she said. Her voice sounded thick and far away.

Dale laughed and reached up to brush at it, dislodging what turned out to Kate's immense relief to be grains of rice. Billy Bob was standing next to Dale, the same grains of rice in his hair and the same silly grin on his face. They were holding hands. "You're holding hands," Kate pointed out, in case they'd missed it.

Dale blushed and Billy Bob gave Kate a valedictory squirt with his water bottle.

For some reason Kate thought that was hilarious. She giggled, a very odd sound coming from her torn throat.

"Kate?" Dale said, her blush fading. "Kate? Are you all right?"

"I am perfect," Kate said precisely, and continued her unsteady progress down the hall.

"She's bombed," she heard Billy Bob say, and wondered who he was talking about.

Her surroundings looked unfamiliar. She knew she was in the right building; she recognized the basketball court and of course there was no mistaking the sound of a dribbled ball. She altered course for the court, thinking she might find a worthy opponent for a game of one-on-one. A table leapt out in her path and hit her across the thighs. "Ouch," she said in surprise.

"Hey, Kate," one of the players yelled. She refocused her eyes. It was Frank Jensen, the horny mechanic, and in automatic alarm she shifted her feet prefatory to making a shuffled escape. He came puffing and sweating off the court. "I went looking for my truck yesterday afternoon. Somebody

181

said they saw you drive off in it." He smiled but it was more of a leer. "Paybacks are hell. Better lock your door."

"Always," she said, "always."

He watched as she headed toward the double doors leading to the corridor. The second time she careened off a wall, he gave a snort of disgust and returned to the court.

It wasn't Kate's fault she kept running into things. The walls kept shifting position, trying to trick her and trip her up. She'd never before realized how malicious a wall could be. She turned into the corridor she prayed her room was located on and strained to read the number painted on the wall at the end of the hall.

"One," she said aloud. A wave of relief swept over her. It was definitely the number one, painted on the wall in bright red, a figure as tall as she was. There was no mistake. First floor. Shoes, scarves, ladies' lingerie. She giggled again and shuffled forward. "One," she said, counting doorways. "Two, three, four, five, six. Right. One step. Left. One step." She peered at the number on the door. Maybe, maybe not. She opened it and went in. It took thirty seconds to decide which was the correct door, right or left. She made a wild guess and chose right.

The wall switch was located after prolonged fumbling. There was a flight bag beneath the counter she might have used in a former life. She snapped the light back off and, without bothering to remove any clothes, tumbled onto the bed.

Her eyes closed as if operated by weights but she retained a kind of around-the-edges consciousness. She'd never been so tired. She obviously wasn't cut out for Slope work, all this to-ing and fro-ing between town and tundra was causing her to hallucinate. For example, she could swear she could hear her father laughing. Her eyes snapped open at the sound, but there was no one there.

Or wait. In the corner, in the shadows? "Abel?" she said, her voice high, quavering.

Not Abel, but her mother, no, her mother's body as she had found her, cold and stiff, surrounded by snow, a thin film of frost over her skin, an October frost, a frost that killed.

The room vanished, to be replaced by the summit of Big Bump and the world falling away from her feet. She fell, too, fell, fell, fell, half flying, half gliding, to slide with no splash into the icy green waters of Prince William Sound. Down she dived, deeper and deeper, caught in something that bore her inexorably and ever downward. Wire cut her hands as she clawed for escape. "Please stop," she sobbed, "please stop, please stop, please stop."

"Oh, God," someone groaned, "I can't do this, I really can't do this."

"Shut up," another voice hissed, "you want somebody to hear us?"

Kate recognized those voices with immense relief. She opened her eyes and smiled at Jerry and Toni. They were real, they were solid. No ghosties, ghoulies or long-legged beasties or things that go bump in the night. She'd never been so glad to see anyone in her life. "Hey, guys. What's going on?" Jerry started and let go her arm. She watched her body flop limply back on her bed and giggled.

"Grab her," Toni said, lips compressed. Jerry hesitated, his eyes huge and panicked. "Goddammit, I can't do this all by myself, grab her arm!"

Spurred by Toni's ferocity, Jerry took hold of Kate's left arm, pulled it across his shoulder and heaved. "Get the door," Toni whispered. When Jerry shifted to do so Kate slipped back toward the bed. "Don't let go of her you idiot!" Kate started to giggle again, the sound muffled when Toni clapped a hand over her mouth. Kate snorted and snot oozed out of her nose and onto Toni's fingers. Toni cursed and Kate mumbled apologetically beneath her hand, "Sorry."

Jerry finally got the door open and they muscled Kate through it. Kate felt like she was back on the *Avilda*, the floor heaving beneath her feet, the walls slanting first one way and then another. She watched, quite detached, as Jerry tried to hold her up with one hand and with the other shove open the heavy metal fire door at the head of the emergency stairs. When his fingers caught in the crack he hissed a curse and stuck them in his mouth, removing Kate's support for the second time and leaving Kate to go down for the third.

Instead, Kate flung her free arm around Toni's neck and hung on, smiling affectionately into Toni's grim face. "I liked you right from the start," she said muzzily. "You're so smart, and you're so funny." Her face puckered, and she rested her forehead against Toni's. "How come you had to go and ruin it?" A tear slid down her cheek.

"Here," Toni said, shoving Kate away roughly, "hold her. I'll get the damn door."

"Whee!" Kate was in free-fall; Jerry barely had time to catch her. She thumped against his chest. "Jer ol' buddy," she said confidentially, "I feel kinda funny. In fact, I feel real funny." She started to giggle again. "*Real* funny. I feel *real* funny and I need a *real* pill."

"Come on," Toni whispered, beckoning, her back braced against the open door. Jerry got his hands underneath Kate's arms and hauled her outside by main force. Toni let the door go too soon and it caught one of Jerry's shoulders. He swore at her.

"Don't be mad at Toni," Kate said imploringly. "She can't

help it if men come on to her. She's a honey trap. Like Kathy the dispatcher. 'Member?" She wrapped her arms around Jerry's waist and snuggled into his chest. "Besides, Otto doesn't stand a chance. You're—" She craned her head back to look up. "You're *taller*."

She let her head fall again and over it Jerry snarled, "Otto? You've been fucking *Otto Leckerd?* That square-headed rock picker who can't be bothered to take a shower two days in a row?"

"Oops." Overwhelmed with guilt, Kate peeped at Toni. "I'm sorry, Toni," she said in a tiny voice. "I thought Jerry knew."

"Never mind that now," Toni said harshly. "Just get her down these goddam stairs and into the fucking truck."

"Oh, are we going for a ride?" Kate said, raising her head. "Oh, boy." She gave Jerry a cheerful grin, and watched with a detached, almost critical interest as the two of them managed to maneuver her body down the metal stairs and into the passenger side of the truck idling at the foot of the stairs.

Kate collapsed on the seat, narrowly missing the steering wheel with her head. "Whoops." That sobered her mood of hilarity for a moment and she eyed the wheel from her prone position. It looked promising. Discovering hitherto unknown powers of locomotion, she levered herself into an upright position, grasped the wheel in one hand, by a miracle found the clutch and shifted into first. The truck jerked forward, catching Toni with one leg in and one leg out on the passenger side and Jerry in the act of opening the driver's side door. Toni's outraged shriek of pain almost but not quite drowned out Jerry's yelp of alarm.

The forward jerk caused Kate's foot to slip off the clutch and the truck continued to jerk forward in abrupt movements.

"Whoa"—jerk—"boy"—jerk—"whoa"—jerk —"now," Kate said, and found the gas. The tires caught on a patch of glare ice and the truck spun into a brodie. "Whooppee!" Kate yelled, pulling the wheel and stepping on the gas. "Ride 'em, cowgirl! Belle ol' buddy, if you could see me now!"

The truck spun in dizzying circles. She caught a glimpse of Jerry, running next to the driver's side door, his mouth open, his arms flapping. She spun the wheel in the other direction and just missed clipping Toni, legs pumping furiously in retreat. A stacked pile of drill pipe materialized in front of the truck; Kate swerved to avoid it only to scrape up against another pile of seven-inch production tubing.

In the end, despite much earnest concentration, Kate was unable to find second gear, and stalled the truck on her sixth attempt. "Rats," she said. Both doors were flung open and Toni and Jerry hurled themselves inside. Kate greeted them rapturously. "Whee! That was fun! Let's do it again!"

Toni yanked her from beneath the wheel and when Kate resisted, hit her in the face, hard.

"Hey," Jerry said, "there's no need for that."

Kate's face puckered again, and she stared at Toni accusingly, one hand nursing her bruised face. "Ouch. That hurt. What'd you have to do that for?"

Toni hit her again, more savagely this time. Kate heard the popping sound of skin breaking and felt a warm wet substance seep down her cheek.

"Toni, dammit, cut that out!"

"We can kill her but we can't hit her, is that it?" Toni said in a hard, cold voice unlike Kate had ever heard her use. "It's not like we haven't done it before, McIsaac."

"Done what before?" Kate inquired.

"Shut the fuck up about that!" Jerry gripped the wheel

tightly. "Look, she's obviously under the influence and she's behind the wheel of a vehicle. She damn near took out the entire Stores pipe yard. Why don't we just call Security? She'll be fired and off the Slope on the morning charter."

"No. She knows too much, about too many things. We stick to the plan. Just drive the goddam truck, okay?"

"Okay," Kate said brightly, expectantly. "Where we going?"

They didn't answer, and Kate passed out with her head on Toni's shoulder as they drove down the Backbone into the dark arctic night.

Rough hands woke her what could have been minutes or days or years later. Her mouth tasted like the inside of a litter box and her head felt roughly the size of Seattle. Something struck her shoulder hard enough to penetrate the fog and she gave a low cry of pain. "Shut up," someone snarled, and pulled on her hurt arm. Her feet dragged over snow too quickly to get the soles down and in working order, and her shins banged into something sharp. "Ouch," she said indignantly, and fought to raise her head and open her eyes.

Toni on her right, Jerry on her left, they were dragging her up a flight of metal stairs. Her head fell back and she saw stars, and wondered for a moment if they were a product of her head wound.

Head wound. How had she hurt her head? Why did she feel so cold? Why were Toni and Jerry dragging her up these stairs? Where did these stairs lead? "Where are we?" she tried to say, but her tongue was so swollen she couldn't get the words out.

A door opened and light streamed out into the night along with a wall of sound. Kate greeted it with positive relief. Only one place on the noisy Slope was this noisy. "Skid 14," she said, proud she could get the words out. "We're at Number

Three. How come?"

The scream of natural gas at six hundred pounds psi drowned out her words, and she watched, brow furrowing, as Jerry and Toni dumped her limp body in one corner and stood erect to yell at each other. Again, Kate could hear nothing but the gas moving through the overhead pipes. She blinked, watching the argument with a sort of divine detachment. There was a problem here, she could acknowledge that much, but she wasn't absolutely certain it was her problem, and she was willing to wait for further data before doing any serious theorizing.

Jerry yelled again, his expression desperate. Kate, watching dispassionately, thought he might start to cry. Toni yelled back, her usually serene face twisted into such an ugly mask that even Kate in her disengaged state found it disturbing. Toni screamed out a final word, took Jerry in both hands and pushed. With the momentum of the shove he almost ran out the door, right past Kate, his face turned away from her. Kate watched Toni reach over a pipe and give a small valve two twists before following Jerry.

The door closed behind them and Kate was left alone. "Me and Skid 14," she said. "A match made in heaven." The gas screamed overhead. Something clanked. Something else started a rapid knocking sound. Her eyes wandered until they encountered a sign, a sign she had seen before. "Caution," it read, "SO2O4 may be present." Or no, it read, "Caution! SO2O4 may be present!" Odd how much more urgent the message seemed when she added the exclamation points.

An alarm went off somewhere. Kate turned her head to locate the source of the new noise and banged her head against the yellow plastic casing of a Scott Air Pak. "Ouch," she said reproachfully. "Stop that."

Another alarm went off, a third, and lights began to flash. It triggered something in the back of Kate's mind, sent a shot of adrenaline through her nervous system, woke Sleeping Beauty to a kiss of death. Automatically, without stopping to think of why or how, with swift, unfumbling movements as if she'd done it every day of her life instead of once during orientation, she opened the Scott Air Pak, pulled out the self-contained breathing apparatus and donned it.

With her first breath her head began to clear, but her body was still being fought over by one self that wanted to drink hard, drive fast, chase men and shoot the pope, and another, more fuddled self that stubbornly insisted she listen to it, that something was wrong, that she had something important to do. She inhaled again, because it seemed like a good idea and because it was something she was capable of doing. The Air Pak was an escape unit. She had five minutes, that was all. The second voice gained in volume and urgency. Kate fumbled for a handhold, sent stern, specific mental commands to feet, ankles and knees, and by dint of strenuous effort, intense willpower and a minor miracle found herself on her feet.

She paused in momentary self-congratulations until her eye caught sight of the valve Toni had turned. Valve. Toni. Had. Turned. Valve. Turned. Alarms. Flashing. Lights. Her scattered consciousness coalesced into three separate pictures, one after the other, the first of the alarm board in the Communications Center, the second of the alarm board in Skid 7, the third of the alarm board in Skid 18. But no, Skid 18 was gas only. Or was it?

The voice raised itself to a shriek of warning that spurred Kate to stumble out the door, catching the tank of the air pak on the door frame, tripping on the top step and plunging headlong down the flight of stairs, catching herself on the railing at the last minute before she plowed up a foot of snow with her nose. Or rather her face mask. She felt rather than heard the door swing shut behind her.

Shielded by the modules from most of the exterior lighting around the center, Kate slumped down on the bottom step and pulled the mask free. She was in shirt and jeans and safety boots and nothing else, it was late March on the Slope, which meant spring was weeks and even months away, and yet she didn't feel cold. The little voice whispered to her, warning her that this wasn't right, she should get inside now, that even if she didn't feel cold she was anyway, that people had died of hypothermia with more on. People like her mother. Also someone might come through the door at the head of the stairs at any minute, and if she didn't want to be swept into the role of sabotage suspect she should get the hell out of there.

The little voice was growing more articulate by the moment, and was accompanied by a return of physical function, so the process of getting to her feet was less laborious than before. Walking, too, seemed less of an effort, and she moved, one halting step at a time, one piling at a time, under the module and out the other side. She peered around, squinting as if that might bring her eyes into better focus, trying to find a landmark. There it was, the glow of the most brightly lit and tiniest building on the pad, the guard shack. Fixing that glow with a stare, because if she blinked it might disappear, she plodded slowly toward it, now that she was out from under the module foundering over the odd drift, but always moving steadily and inexorably toward that glowing spot of bright promise.

It was a toss-up who was more surprised when she fell in the door, the guard or Kate. He sat on his stool, gaping, as she picked herself up off the floor. She opened her mouth and paused, afraid her tongue might not have caught up with the rest of her body. "Childress," she managed finally to gasp. She was beginning to feel the cold, or rather the tingling that invaded her body that told her she had been very cold and in the warmth of the guard shack was now starting to thaw. "Call him."

His mouth closed with something of a snap and an expression of disgust crossed his face, one she remembered from the mop girl at McDonald's. "You're drunk. Who are you? Who's your supervisor?"

With a spurt of anger she lunged for the phone. "Goddammit," she snarled, as out of patience as she was out of strength. She grasped the receiver and enunciated each word with great care. "I'm an undercover investigator for the Anchorage District Attorney. This is an emergency. Call your security chief."

"You *are* drunk," he said, his eyes running over her contemptuously. "You people will find it, won't you, even on the Slope." He gave a snort of disgust and reached a hand out to dial.

Rage, Kate discovered, was a great restorative.

She knocked him off his stool, picked him up by his shirt front and slammed him against the wall. "Stay put, don't move, or I will hurt you," she said through her teeth. The combination of the torn, husky growl of voice and his first sight of the ugly, twisted scar on her throat froze him momentarily, long enough for her to punch up an access line to Anchorage and dial Childress's home number.

It picked up on the second ring. "Childress? This is Kate Shugak."

"Shugak! What the hell is going on, it's three o'clock in the fucking morning! What—"

"Shut up. I need you on the Slope. As soon as you can get here. And tell this kid to do what I say."

His voice sharpened. "Have you found the dealer? Who is it? What—"

"Childress!" Kate bellowed. "Somebody just tried to kill me and I don't have time for explanations! Just tell this kid to do what I say and get your ass up here!" She thrust the receiver at the guard, whose eyes were huge and his face paper-white and Kate only hoped he wasn't going to faint.

"Mr. Childress? This is the security guard at Production Center Three. I—" He listened, his eyes going wider. "Yessir. Yessir. Yessir. Nossir. Yessir. Yessir." He hung up and turned to her, an expression of awe on his face. He put out his hand and deepened his voice. "My name's Poss. Dave Poss."

Oh, fuck, Kate thought, I've just acquired me a British Secret Service wannabe. The pounding in her head increased. Her mouth was bone-dry. "Have you got something to drink?"

Mute, he held out a cup of cold coffee. Grateful, she drank it down without a whimper. He watched her, the rudimentary beginnings of a pencil-thin mustache, the Boston Blackie kind, twitching with excitement.

She put the cup down. "Thanks. Okay." With the heels of her hands pressed to her eyes she tried to think. "Okay," she said again. "Do you know, has there been anything out of the ordinary happen inside the center this morning?"

"Has there ever," he said, "there was a leak in Skid 14 thirty minutes ago. We had enough bells and lights and sirens go off to make you think it was the Fourth of July."

"Is anybody likely to check up on you for a while?"

"No." He sounded faintly disgruntled. "Everyone else is in Skid 14. I have to stay here, make sure no one gets on the pad

192

who isn't supposed to."

She frowned. "Is this the first time you've seen me tonight?"

He looked taken aback. "It's the first time I've seen you ever."

Kate painfully followed this statement to its logical solution. "So there is another way to get on this pad?"

He looked wary. Kate looked at the phone. He sighed. "Sure. There's the access road to A Pad, that leads to the spur road that runs between Checkpoint Charlie and CPS."

"Okay," Kate said for the third time. "Can you get me back to the Base Camp without going through any checkpoints, without anybody seeing either of us?"

His eyes fired. "I can try."

"Okay," Kate said. She felt like a parrot, repeating the same words over and over again. "Okay. Get me back to the Base Camp without being seen."

It took them an hour to get back to the Base Camp, a trip that yesterday had taken Kate twenty minutes in the bus. Most of the time she spent crouched beneath the dash on the passenger's side of the security Suburban. Dave Poss by way of a disguise had donned a Raiders cap with the brim pulled low, with the result that every time Kate looked up from her cramped position she thought she was hallucinating again, this time entertaining visions of Daffy Duck. Daffy Duck at the wheel of a green Suburban with the words "RPetCo Security" painted two feet high in bright yellow paint on the doors was almost more than Kate's rubbed-raw senses could handle.

But not quite. Poss crept up on the Base Camp like the Japanese crept up on Pearl Harbor; secretively, stealthily, almost hitting a Stores forklift whose night shift driver gave a cheery wave and yelled an even cheerier, considering Dave had nearly sideswiped him into a pile of well casing, "Hi, Dave!"

"Hi, Mike!" Dave yelled back. He caught his breath, and looked down at Kate guiltily. "Sorry."

"Drive by the safety module," Kate growled in response. Poss did so. "See anything?" Kate said in a low voice.

"No," Poss whispered. "All quiet on the northern front."

"Keep going around to the front. Drive by the bull rail. Do you know what the PR van looks like?"

Poss was hurt. "Of course."

"Is it there?"

The Suburban lurched into a hole and out of it again, banging Kate's head against the dash. "Yup. Plugged in right where it's supposed to be."

I'm on call tonight, Jerry had said as he walked away from the pinochle table. Kate's head throbbed with the effort to think. "Okay," she said finally, "take me around to the administration annex. The outside door."

"The cleaning crew might be in there."

"I'll have to chance it."

A few moments later Poss drew up in the shadow of the building, the passenger side door a baby step from the bottom stair. Painfully, Kate uncurled herself from beneath the dash. "Okay, here's where I get out. You"—a finger stabbed for emphasis—"you get back to Three and stay put and keep quiet until the day shift shows. After that, go back to your room and wait there until either I call or Childress does. What's the extension in the guard shack?"

"Four-three-three-three."

"Four-three-three-three. Good. Okay, you got it?"

He hesitated. "What if someone finds out I was gone?"

"Refer them to Childress."

He looked at her, all youth and gung ho and sap rising. "Shouldn't I come with you? You don't look so good, maybe I—"

"No!" The last thing Kate needed was an underfoot puppy. He would have protested. She held up one hand. "What did Childress tell you?" He looked mutinous. "What did he say?" Kate repeated, feeling like his mother.

"To do what you said," Poss said sulkily, feeling like her son.

"All right. Go. And for chrissake go back the short way this time in case I need to call you."

Kate heard the Suburban's wheels spin as she mounted the stairs. This door was not a safety door and did open from the outside; Kate opened it and stepped in, halting as the door closed silently behind her on its hydraulic catch. She held her breath, straining to hear movement inside the building.

There was none. She must have missed the cleaning crew. Good. Moving swiftly, with almost all her agility and grace restored and spurred by an ever-increasing sense of rage, she made her way through the annex and into the garage. The garage gave on to the front entrance and the security desk, but she kept her back turned and her head averted as she climbed the stairs. When she reached the first landing she risked a glance back. The guard had his feet propped on the desk, his head resting against the back of his chair, his eyes closed and his mouth open. If he wasn't sleeping he was dead. Good again, either way. She padded silently up the rest of the stairs.

Luck, a fickle bastard who so far that evening had made himself conspicuous by his absence, was finally with her. The camp clerk was gone and the front desk deserted. She who hesitates is lost, and Kate nipped around behind the counter. The computer was on, the cursor blinking greenly at her from the screen. She sat down, typed "McIsaac, Jerry" and hit Return. Instantly the name appeared on the screen, followed by, Safety, North Slope Assigned, B Shift, Tuesday, and, glory of glories, a room number, OCX II 109. She typed in "Rogstad, Lillian," and the darling little byte box informed her that Diamond Lil was in Anchorage on a medevac. Her room number was listed as OCX II 107.

"All *right*," she muttered. "So Jerry's on call alone *and* alone in his suite. Everything you ever wanted to know about the Prudhoe Hilton but were afraid to ask." She exited and sat thinking for a moment. OCX II was the second operations center extension, the module between the main Base Camp module and the fire/safety module. One-oh-nine meant the room was on the first floor, and the low number meant it was probably off the left corridor, which sounded right since the left corridor led to the arctic walkway that led to the safety module. It made sense to locate the fire and safety teams close to the fire and safety module to cut down on response time.

She looked up at the clock on the wall. Ten minutes had passed since she had left Dave. All things being equal, she had as good a chance of the front desk clerk coming back and discovering her as she did of being nailed anywhere else in the building. The safest place to be was probably her room, Toni would never think of looking for her there, but she didn't care to test the distance between.

She waited, abandoning the chair for the floor in case anyone walked by, folding her legs and hands. The minutes plodded by with excruciatingly agonizing slowness. Sitting there, she vowed never to buy a digital clock as long as she lived. An old-fashioned clock with a second hand counted the time down much faster.

She forced herself to wait twenty minutes, and then five

minutes more, before dialing four-three-three-three. It picked up on the third ring. Dave Poss's voice was breathless but blessedly there. "Production Center Three, guard shack. Poss speaking."

"It's Shugak, Dave." An indrawn breath of pure joy greeted her. "Shut up and listen. I want you to call 911 and report a medical emergency at Three."

"What kind of emergency?"

"I don't care what kind of emergency, use your imagination!" Kate's head hurt when she yelled and she lowered her voice. "Just do it, and make it bad enough that they'll need to call out the medic."

"What'll I say when they find out it's a fake?" his panicked voice demanded.

"Turn yourself in to the FCC for abuse of public airwaves," she snapped and hung up.

She waited, eyes fixed on the clock. Five very long minutes from the time she hung up the phone a distant siren began to wail. Jerry's response time was up. "Attaboy, Dave," she muttered, and vaulted the counter to hit the hallway running. A moment later she heard voices and ducked into the doorway that opened onto to Toni's office. She stepped inside and closed the door after her, holding on to the knob with her ear pressed to the door.

The voices grew louder, along with the clank of a cart and the creak of its wheels. "Did you hear about those two women who got thrown out of Coldfoot last night?"

"No, what about them?"

"They were selling magazine subscriptions."

"So?"

"So they sold twenty-five thousand dollars' worth of magazine subscriptions. In four days."

"Oh? Oh. Oh!" The two voices erupted with laughter, which carried on well past Hartzler's door. From a distance Kate heard the second one, sober now, say thoughtfully. "Twenty-five thousand? In four days? Are we in the wrong business?"

Good question. Kate waited another minute for the voices to fade completely, and tossed the office on general principles, although she expected to find nothing. Aside from a bottom drawer filled with a set of jacks, a rubber slingshot, a little sandalwood box that if you slid back the lid too quickly a little wooden dragon jumped out and bit you on the thumb, and a box of Kix, there wasn't much of interest. She closed the drawer, unsurprised. Toni was smarter than that. She opened the door and applied her eye to the crack.

This time the coast was clear and she ran lightly down the corridor, turning to cross the main module, pass by the serving line and dining hall and into the OCX II. Room 109 was an outside room at the end of the corridor on the left. Kate opened the outer door and went in.

It took her thirty seconds to find it. Jerry wasn't half as smart as Toni was.

CHAPTER 10

SHE WAS WAITING FOR him when he walked in the room an hour later, sitting in the straight chair with her feet crossed on his counter, the box sitting next to them. He stopped in the doorway, his face going white. "Kate?" His voice was high, unnaturally so. "Kate? Is that you?"

The shock in his eyes dissipated some of her anger. "Surprise."

"Kate?"

"Why, Jerry?" she said. "You're making more money than God for working twenty-six weeks a year. Just tell me why."

He didn't move. "Kate? Is it really you?" His face crumbled and he tumbled to his knees, buried his face in his hands and began to sob. "Kate. Oh, God, Kate, when I got the call I thought it'd be you." His shoulders heaved. "I thought it'd be you and I couldn't bear it."

"No thanks to you it wasn't." He sobbed harder, and she was disgusted. "Stop it, Jerry. Stop it!" She manhandled him onto his bed and shut the door. He was still sobbing when she turned back, and she slapped him, hard, across the cheek. The sharp crack of flesh on flesh resounded in the little room. The sobbing stopped abruptly and he stared at her out of wide, startled eyes. "That's better." Kate sat down again, knee to knee with him.

"I'm sorry," he whispered.

"You mickeyed my drink, didn't you?"

He nodded, unable to meet her eyes. "I'm sorry, Kate."

The rage was back then, suffusing her entire body in a red, hot flush. With an effort she subdued it, tamped it back, screwed the lid down, with an effort she remained seated, with an effort she didn't rise up out of her chair and come down on Jerry like the wrath of Shugak. But entirely against her will she heard herself say, "You know about my parents. You know what life is like in the bush. You know why I don't drink. You know why I don't do dope. And you mickeyed my drink. You son of a *bitch*."

"I'm sorry, Kate."

When she could trust herself to speak she said, "Sorry doesn't quite cut it."

He didn't answer because there was no answer to that and they both knew it.

"Tell me about it, Jerry," Kate said more calmly. "Tell me all about it. From the beginning." She folded her hands in her lap and regarded him with a steady, dispassionate gaze in which he could find no hint of past affection or friendship, and no trace whatever of sympathy. He shivered, sniffling and wiping the back of his hand across his face in a gesture more suited to a ten-year-old, and surprised them both with a half smile. "You look like somebody carved you out of stone."

"Tell me about it," she repeated. "From the beginning."

He rubbed nervous hands down his thighs. "The beginning? The beginning was a year ago, the first time I came up and sat next to Toni on the charter. I fell for her." His eyes met Kate's, shamed but defiant. "I fell hard. She's— she's—oh, the hell with it, it's none of your goddam business anyway."

"It isn't when she doesn't fuck you into breaking seventeen different laws," Kate agreed. "Keep talking."

He kept talking. As much as he tried to shield her, a picture of Hartzler emerged that was less than flattering. Jerry may have thought he'd fallen for Toni, but Toni had made sure of it, zeroing in on the poor jerk the way the B-17s had on Berlin. It was a pity, Kate thought, how even the best of men thought with their cocks. Toni had certainly led Jerry by his, down a garden path that may have looked winding en route but that in hindsight showed a straight line straight down. "At first it was just a favor; would I take a package down for her that she didn't want to go through security. Of course I said yes. I figured it was something out of the kitchen, Gideon's always making angel bars for people to take home, or maybe a package of T-bones or lobster tails. I remember Sally and Sandy and Hugh hiked the Chilkoot Trail once with nothing but RPetCo raisins and nuts and peanut butter in their packs."

At first, Jerry said, such favors were requested once every six or seven weeks. After a while it became routine to take a package down for Toni on every medevac. "Security never looked at anything I took out on a medevac. It was easy just to stuff it into a box with a red cross on it and toss it in with the rest of the gear."

She closed her eyes briefly, thinking of the small, heavy box she had helped load onto the Lear during Martin's medevac. She wondered if the stone lamp and the ivory bear were what had made it so heavy. "Jerry. Did you never, ever, even one time, stop to think about what you were doing? Did you never, ever, even one time, think it might end with you in jail? Did you never, ever, even one time, Jerry, just one time, call yourself a grave-robbing son of a bitch!"

He stared at her, mouth agape. "Grave robber?"

"What else would you call it?" she demanded.

"What grave? I thought we were talking about the money."

It was Kate's turn to stare. "Money?"

"Yes, money," he said, faltering at her expression. "The cash from selling the cocaine."

"Cocaine?" Kate said.

They stared at each other in silence, Jerry surprised, Kate confused.

It was sad but true, and a fact Kate would later blush to remember, but she hadn't thought seriously of the original reason for her presence on the North Slope since the morning she spent at the dig. The scratcher, the stone cairn, the idealistic enthusiasm of the young archaeologists and their dismay at the disappearance of the artifacts had displaced her concentration until all she had been able to think of was the missing ivory bear and the missing stone bowl, and whatever else it was that was missing but that Chris Heller would not tell her about. Her suspicions had inevitably zeroed in on Otto, and after the scene at the bull rail on Toni and Jerry, but for grave robbing, not for dealing. She had figured Ann McCord for the dealing. McCord could have smuggled it up somehow with Catering's food orders, and run it around camp in her steward's cart. The pieces fit together, but they weren't all of the puzzle.

It's not like we haven't done it before, McIsaac. Unbidden, the memory of Toni's comment in the truck earlier that evening surfaced in Kate's mind, and the last wisps of the drug-induced fog in her brain were swept away, leaving nothing but a razor-edged awareness behind. "Of course," she said. "You wouldn't kill me over a little thing like grave robbing." A wave of tiredness swept up and over her and she felt it seep all the way down deep into her bones. "Toni's been dealing the coke in camp."

"Yes."

"And you've been her bag man." His eyes fell and he nodded. She said only one word and she said it softly, but his face went scarlet. "Jerry."

Another silence fell, one she had to sum up all her resources to break. "What about Chuck Cass?"

"What about him?" Jerry said woodenly.

"I heard what Toni said in the truck tonight, Jerry."

He met her stare defiantly for a moment, then his shoulders slumped and he muttered, "He was using big time, and he wanted a way to help pay for his action. He said he'd turn us in if we didn't cut him in."

Kate didn't ask him who had pushed Cass into the pool. She didn't want to hear the answer. "When did you start smuggling out the artifacts?"

Involuntarily his eyes darted to the box on the counter. His voice was dull. "Right after Leckerd opened the dig on Tode Point. I thought, what the hell? It was just junk, a bunch of old rocks and bones and walrus teeth. She used some of what we made dealing to buy it from Leckerd." As he spoke the name, Jerry's face darkened.

"A piece of that junk auctioned for fifty-five thousand dollars," Kate said.

Jerry gaped at her. "What? Fifty-five grand?"

"Fifty-five thousand."

Disbelieving, he said, "For a piece of bone that looked like it was hacked by a seven-year-old with a butter knife?"

Suddenly Kate felt sorry for him. "Afraid so."

"She didn't tell me," he said numbly.

"No," Kate said, "she didn't, did she? Who else?"

"What?"

"Who else was dealing the dope, besides you and Hartzler?"

He looked at her. "I know most of it, Jerry, you might as well tell me the rest. It'll be a lot better for you in the long run."

He slumped against the wall, all the energy gone out of him. "Ann McCord. I left it in my office, Ann picked it up that night and put it on her cart. She's head steward; she rolled that cart all over the BOC doing rooms that weren't on regular change-out. Buyers would leave the money in their rooms, she'd take it and leave the dope."

As she had been doing a room off Hartzler's hallway the previous morning, Kate remembered. "Anybody else?" She thought of the report Jack had dug up on Childress's finances. "Anybody in town?"

Jerry shook his head. "Toni wanted it kept small. She said the smaller the operation, the less chance of attracting attention."

"Whose idea was it to kill me?"

His eyes slid away. "Mine."

Kate remembered the dispatch with which Toni had sent the fox pup off to that Great Den in the Sky, and was disgusted. "Jesus Christ, Jerry, I might as well hand you the noose right now. You're going to take the fall for her, aren't you? You're going to waltz right in and lay your head on the chopping block and wham." She leaned forward. "We're not talking about the love of your life here. We're talking about a woman who will spread her legs for any man she thinks she can use to make a buck. She's screwing Leckerd. I saw her halfway into the sack the night of the turtle races with a production supervisor who, for all you know, is running hits out to the production centers for her. Hell, I saw her all over Gideon Trocchiano, who's probably sprinkling it on the cereal in the mornings."

"It was my idea to kill you," he said clearly, and Kate wanted to hit him, hard. He saw it and couldn't help shrinking back out of reach, but he said, "She said it was a shame, that she really liked you, but after you saw her get the box from Leckerd and give it to me, we didn't have a choice."

Tight-lipped, Kate said, "Yeah, a real shame. I liked her, too, and I'm real sorry I have to bust her ass."

She looked at her watch. Incredibly, it was five-fifteen. Through the window she saw that it was still dark out. It shouldn't still be dark at that hour at that time of year, but the fact didn't register with her. She picked up the phone and dialed the extension for the guard shack at Three. "Dave? Shugak again. When do you get off shift?"

The young voice at the other end of the line held a guarded excitement. "My relief will be here at six."

"Do you come straight back to the Base Camp then?"

"Yes."

"All right, I want you to come to room 109 in the OCX II. I've got someone I want you to baby-sit until Childress gets here."

Kate hung up and Jerry regarded her with wry exhaustion. "What, you don't trust me to stay put?"

"Why should I?" Kate's tone wasn't accusatory, merely matter-of-fact, but he winced. "How did she get the dope up on the Slope?"

"At first? I don't know. For the last six months I've been bringing it up for her." He saw her expression and actually smiled. "I've been through Anchorage International so many times I know most of those security guards by their first names. Most of the time they just wave me through. Even if they looked, all they'd find in my bag is instruments and bandages and medicine. When you're cutting it ten times before you sell it, it doesn't take much to turn a profit."

He said it so casually, so entirely without guilt, that Kate stared at him, half in disgust, half in wonder. "I thought I knew you."

His shoulders moved in a barely perceptible shrug. "I don't guess anybody knows anybody. Not really."

"I don't guess," she agreed.

She didn't make the mistake of asking him why again, and they sat in silence until six-twenty, when Dave Poss hammered at the door. "Hi, Dave," Jerry said.

"Hi," Dave said. "Jerry?"

"Watch him," Kate said, hooking a thumb over her shoulder.

He stared from her to Jerry and back again. "Watch Jerry? Why?"

"Because I say so. He doesn't leave this suite, he doesn't make any phone calls and if he has to use the John he does it with the door open and you watching. Is that clear?"

"Yeah, but—"

Kate's voice cracked like a whip. "Is that clear?"

His shoulders braced. "Yes." He wanted to add "sir" so badly his teeth clenched with the effort it took to hold it back.

"When does the airport tower open, do you know?"

"Six, I think."

"Do you know the number?"

"Yes."

Kate sighed inwardly. "Dial it, please?"

"All right." Dave stepped to the phone and punched nine to exit the Base Camp and seven more digits. It was picked up on the first ring. "Hey, hi, Clint. This is Dave Poss, RPetCo Security. I've got someone here who wants to talk to you. Her name's Kate Shugak and she's cleared all the way through to Childress." He handed the receiver to Kate.

The voice was stiff and a little suspicious. "Ms. Shugak?"

"Hello. Do you have a flight inbound with Childress on board?"

"Yes."

"ETA?"

Silence.

"Do you have an arrival time?" Kate asked.

Reluctantly, the voice said, "Yes."

Kate looked at Dave Poss and wondered if obstructionism was hereditary or just plain infectious. "And what might be that arrival time?"

Even more reluctantly, the voice said, "They departed from Anchorage at six, they should be on the ground here by seven-twenty."

"Thank you so much for all your help," Kate said sweetly, and hung up. "Childress is due in at seven-twenty. If I'm not back before then, you can turn Jerry over to him."

The guard looked down at Jerry, who looked at Kate with a half smile. "I don't guess I have to ask who's next."

"Cheer up," Kate said, "maybe they'll give you adjoining cells. Then you could be sure of having her all to yourself."

And with that singularly low blow, Kate turned on her heel and left the room.

• • •

Toni wasn't in her room. She'd been there, the bed was rumpled and the towels used. The suite door banged open behind her and she turned. "Hello, Ann," she said.

Something in her calm expression made the other woman hesitate. "Hello. What are you doing here?"

"I'm looking for Toni. You know where she is?" "No," Ann said automatically, but Kate was watching her closely.

Kate looked back down at the empty bed. "She's with Otto," she said. "At the dig." She raised her eyes. "Isn't she?"

Ann took a step back. Kate shook her head. "Too late. Jerry told me everything. Go to your room and wait for Security."

Ann swung her head from side to side, still backing up. "Forget it."

Kate gave a short, unamused laugh. "Run, then." She brushed by the other woman and stopped in the hall to look over her shoulder. "But ask yourself. Where?"

Toni's van was missing from the bull rail and Kate headed for the garage. It seemed her fate to intercept Cale Yarborough each time he backed his truck out and Kate waved to get his attention. He halted, a displeased expression on his face as he rolled down his window. "What d'you want?"

"Your truck," Kate said, opening his door. It seemed colder now than it had been at any time all night and she had to work on not letting her teeth chatter. "Get out."

He stared at her incredulously. "Get out of the goddam truck, Yarborough. I'm Kate Shugak, in case you don't remember."

"I remember," he said furiously, "and I also remember you ain't nothing but a goddam roustabout. Who the hell do you think you are, telling me to get out of my own goddam truck?"

"I think I'm a special investigator personally hired by John King to find out who's running drugs into your side of the field," Kate said bluntly. "I have found them, and I'd like to catch one of them before she heads for Rio on the next available plane."

Yarborough stared at her, stunned into immobility. She caught his elbow and yanked him out of the driver's seat.

"Childress is on his way up, he'll be on the ground at

Prudhoe at seven-twenty. Pick him up and meet me at Tode Point." She climbed behind the wheel.

"Pick him up? How'm I supposed to pick him up when you've got my truck?" he yelled after her.

"You're the field manager, you figure it out!" she yelled back.

As she fishtailed off the pad onto the Backbone she noticed that it seemed to be getting darker instead of lighter, as if the sun were setting instead of rising. A shiver of fear chased down her spine as she wondered if she was reacting to Jerry's mickey again, and then realized the darkness came from a weather front rolling down off the Arctic ice pack, a great boiling mass of fog and snow that engulfed everything in its path: rigs, modules, flow lines, roads. Her first reaction was a wave of relief that she was in her right mind. Her second was to swear and thump the wheel, before flooring the gas pedal, trying to outrun the menacing wall of weather.

No one could have. It was the grandmother of all spring storms and it hit her windshield at exactly and precisely the moment she turned off the Backbone onto the Tode Point access road.

Instantly it was whiteout conditions. She couldn't see a foot in front of the windshield, much less the milepost markers lining the sides of the roads. The temperature in the cab dropped thirty degrees in as many seconds. The wind struck the truck like a blow, rattling her inside it like the last nut in a can of cocktail mix. She had to slow to a crawl, feeling her way with the front tires, praying the next gust of wind wouldn't roll the truck and her with it right off the road. If that happened, she thought with a touch of hysteria, it might be best if she just kept on going east until she wound up in Canada. The longevity of the average Sloper after she had wrecked the field manager's truck was problematic at best.

The drive, fifteen minutes from the access road the last time she'd traveled it, this morning took nearly an hour. Her feet were blocks of ice, cold sweat beaded her forehead and her hands felt permanently attached to the wheel when finally the blowing snow in front of the hood took on a more substantial quality. She slammed on the brakes with both feet. The truck skidded and stalled, fetching up with a light bump against the thin metal of the trailer wall.

It took all her strength to get the truck's door open against the push of the wind, and it caught her once, painfully, across the shins, right in the same spot she'd nicked them on the stairs to Skid 14.

Once outside, the truck door slammed shut behind her and she knew she'd never get it open again. It was the trailer or death from exposure. A fitting end, some would say, for her mother's daughter. She fought to keep her balance against the force of the wind, against the voice that said, "But I'm so tired, can't we just sit down and rest for a while, just a little while?"

There is danger, Cindy Sovalik's voice said clearly. *There is danger.*

Kate peered around, eyes slitted against the snow that stung her cheeks, half expecting to see the old woman materialize out of the storm. She didn't, but the certainty in that voice spurred her to action. Head down, she struggled through the drift rapidly piling up around the truck and felt her way down the wall of the trailer to the door. She banged on it with her fist. After a moment it opened, and an incredulous voice exclaimed, "Kate! Jesus, what are you doing out in this?"

Hands pulled her inside and she collapsed on the floor, panting and blinking ice out of her eyes. When she could see, she found four concerned faces staring back. "Chris," she wheezed.

"Kate, what are you doing here? You could have been killed in this storm. Karen, where's the thermos? Pour her some cocoa."

A steaming mug was thrust into her hands. She almost dropped it. "Here, I've got it," someone said, and the mug was held to her lips. She gulped the liquid gratefully.

"Want more?" Rebecca said. "No? Okay. Here, Kevin, take this. Come on, Kate, let's get you up into a chair."

When she was seated, she reached up a hand to feel her cheek. She had to press hard to register the touch of her fingers. She looked around. "Where is he? Where's Otto? Is Toni Hartzler with him?"

Mention of Hartzler's name brought an instant, if temporary, silence. "How did you know?" Chris said, eyes wary.

"Where are they, at the dig?"

Chris looked at his colleagues, back to Kate, and nodded slowly. "We found a burial chamber yesterday afternoon. The rest of us've been here all night, but Otto left at about ten. When he came back this morning, he had Toni with him. They went out to the dig ahead of us and we were just about to join them when the storm hit."

"You still missing those artifacts?"

Chris stilled, a sick look coming into his eyes. "Yes."

"Otto took them." She interrupted the exclamations of shock and dismay by getting to her feet.

Chris knew instantly where she was going and didn't like it. "Kate, you don't have to go look for them, they can't go anywhere in this."

It had been a very long night and was beginning to look

211

like it was going to be an even longer day. Kate was operating on instinct and adrenaline. She'd come out to Tode Point to find Toni Hartzler and she wasn't going to stop until she had her right in front of her. She shook her head doggedly and pushed past him to the door. Behind her she heard him say, "Kevin, give me your mitts. Karen, toss me your balaclava."

"Chris, are you nuts? If she wants to kill herself, fine, you don't have to—"

"Just hand me the frigging mitts, will you?"

Kate, unheeding, shoved the door open, stumbled down the two steps and struck blindly off into the gale. Chris came up behind her and grabbed her arm. "Not that way!" he shouted over the roar of the wind. "This way! We got a safety line rigged just before the storm hit!"

Bent over, eyes almost shut, she blundered after him, clutching the hem of his coat. She tripped and almost fell half a dozen times. Each time he waited patiently for her to find her feet again. Finally he shouted, "Here!"

She peered around him and saw a bulge in the snow that might have been the roof of the dugout. He pulled her down to the door and beat on it. "Otto! Otto, it's Chris! Let us in!"

Without warning the door fell open and Chris fell through it and Kate fell through it on top of him.

From a sprawling position on the floor, Kate looked up and met Toni Hartzler's astonished gaze. The brunette was crouched over a jumbled pile of dirt and bones and artifacts. The jumble looked as if it had been spaded up and dumped haphazardly, with no relationship to the neat, sectioned areas Kate had seen on her first visit. Toni held the scratcher in one hand, as if she had been using it to comb through the dirt.

"Otto!" Chris yelled. "What the hell are you doing? You can't—"

Toni leapt to her feet and cleared the tumble of bodies on the doorstep in a single bound, to vanish into the storm.

Kate went after her.

"Kate!" she heard Chris yell. "Kate! Don't! *Kate*!"

Toni was struggling through the drifts, grunting with the effort, when Kate took three giant steps and came down on her with all talons extended.

"Fucking bitch," Toni growled, trying to throw her off. She was bigger than Kate and she hadn't been drugged in the last twenty-four hours and she might have even had a few hours sleep, so she was fresher than Kate.

But Kate was angrier. Toni tried to pull free and Kate rolled with her, over and over in the snow, until something hard struck her in the spine and halted their progress. She looked up, blinking, and recognized the stone cairn. They had dislodged some of the rocks. Toni grabbed for one and brought it down hard on Kate's head.

Kate rolled and then had to duck away from the scratcher in Toni's other hand, the raven claws missing her face by inches. Toni jumped to her feet and took off, and Kate followed, taking half a dozen giant steps before tackling her again. The scratcher went flying. "Fucking bitch!" Toni jerked an elbow into Kate's ribs and, when Kate gasped and paused, turned and hit out at her face, connecting with the black eye she had previously given her.

"Ouch!" Kate tried to get a hand around Toni's arm, difficult to do as it was clad in a thick parka. Toni kneed her in the gut. "Oooff!"

Snow blew into Kate's eyes and down the neck of her shirt. Her jeans were wet through all the way up to her knees, her feet numb in her safety boots. She gathered all her strength and, just as Toni managed to free herself to scramble away, brought clenched fists down on the back of Toni's head. The other woman groaned and went limp for a moment, and Kate, who felt the reverberation of that blow all the way up her spine, let herself fall forward, a dead weight, across Toni's body. Another groan, another moment of blessed stillness beneath the roar of wind and whip of snow.

And then damned if the bitch didn't start to fight again. Kate couldn't believe there was that much fight beneath that sleek, pampered exterior. "Shit!"

They rolled together in the snow, each struggling to find a choke hold on the other, until Kate's back fetched up hard against something else. She thought it must be the cairn again and was surprised to look up and see the pipe and valve assembly of the abandoned wellhead.

While she was distracted Toni slugged her in her right breast and pain radiated over her body in waves. Someone screamed. When she opened her eyes again Toni was scrabbling to her knees.

A hot, visceral fury caught her up by the scruff of the neck and launched her at the other woman like a ball out of a cannon. They went over the fence surrounding the wellhead and down together at the foot of the wellhead, hard, Toni harder because she was underneath. Somehow in the middle of all that red rage Kate got her hands inside the neck of Toni's parka and began to squeeze. At first Toni fought, but as Kate's hands tightened she ran out of air.

Still lost in that red mist, Kate squeezed harder. Toni choked and cawed, her clawing hands unable now to grab with any strength.

"Kate!" Chris Heller's voice came from behind. "Kate! Stop it! Let go!" A new pair of hands reached around her to pull at her own. "Let go!"

There is danger. Once again, Cindy Sovalik's voice rang in Kate's ears. *There is danger.*

Shuddering, her grip loosened, falling away from Toni's throat, and with a great, hawking cough Toni sucked air into her lungs.

"Jesus, Kate!" Chris Heller looked out at her from a terrified face.

Kate crawled to her feet, to stand on unsteady legs.

Toni looked up and saw her. "Fucking bitch," she croaked, and kicked out, connected with Kate's right knee.

A sharp shooting pain shot up Kate's right leg and it almost buckled. At once the rage was back. Without stopping to think, she swooped down on the other woman and forced her to her knees in front of the wellhead. "Lick it," she shouted over the roar of the wind, shoving Toni's face close to the pipe.

"Kate! Are you crazy?" Chris said, trying ineffectually to separate the two women.

"No," Kate yelled, shrugging him off. "Lick it."

The wind howled. The snow swirled around their heads and slipped beneath their knees. "No," Toni croaked.

"Kate!" Chris said. "No!"

"Lick it," Kate growled for the third time. She caught both Toni's hands in a grip that made the brunette cry out and with the other hand pinched Toni's nose between a thumb and forefinger. The tour guide thrashed about wearily, trying to free herself.

Kate's gulping breaths scorched her lungs, her thundering pulse battered her eardrums, the muscles in her legs quivered in bewildered exhaustion, but her hands and her voice remained relentless. "Lick that pipe!"

"Damn you," Toni gasped, at the end of her endurance. almost weeping. "God *damn* you. You're supposed to be dead.

215

You're supposed to be fucking *dead*."

"Do it! Now!"

Toni gave another halfhearted heave but Kate's grip was relentless. Her breath exploded out of her chest into a white cloud, instantly dissipated on the wind. A moment later Kate smelled the acrid odor of warm piss and knew she had won. Toni opened her mouth and stuck her tongue out. It flattened out against the pipe and in the freezing temperature instantly froze to the metal. She moaned in impotent protest.

Kate rose and staggered back a step. Toni made as if to move but she was held more securely than if she had been bound hand and foot.

Chris was driven to his knees by a gust of wind. "Jesus, Kate," he shouted, "we can't leave her out here. She'll freeze to death."

"Good," Kate said.

"Kate!"

"It's a spring blizzard," Kate said. Her fury had been replaced by fatigue, leaving her limp and trembling. "It'll probably stop as soon as it started. It'll warm up then."

She staggered back to the cairn and sifted through the snow until she found the stone Toni had thrown. She replaced the stone on the top of the pile. As she looked, the cairn seemed to grow clearer in color and shape, more solid in outlook, and she realized that she had been right, the wind wasn't blowing as hard as it had been.

Toni's sobs were audible from where she stood. "Am ee-eeng! El! El! Uh-uhee el ee!"

"You're crazy, you know that, Shugak?" Chris said, his voice shaken. "You are fucking insane."

There is danger, Cindy Sovalik had said.

Turning, Kate tripped over the scratcher. Picking it up, she

216

cradled it in her arms against the blowing snow, all the way back to the dugout.

CHAPTER 11

"WHY DIDN'T THEY LOCK the door on you?"

"Skid doors don't lock, from either side. Besides, they'd have had to lock all three, the one to Skid 7, the one back to the control skid, and the emergency exit. They didn't think they had to. For all they knew I was still seriously out of it, and ess-oh-two works pretty fast, or so they told me in orientation."

"Usually you don't even have time to smell it before it kills you," John King agreed, his face tight and his voice grim. "You were lucky."

Jack looked out of his living-room window, an elaborately casual set to his shoulders.

"So it was Hartzler and McIsaac, with help from McCord," Childress said. He gave Kate a sharp look. "That it?"

"Plus whoever sold the stuff to Hartzler in the first place in town, but finding them's your job. You wanted the stuff off the Slope. It's off." For now, she thought.

He gave a curt nod, probably thinking the same thing.

"About the thefts from the archaeological dig," Kate said.

"What about them?" King said.

"Otto started talking the minute I got back inside the dugout and didn't shut up until Childress showed. Jerry McIsaac tucked the southbound artifacts in the stretcher next to the medevac patients. As you know, those patients are forklifted up onto the plane."

"No security check," Childress said, making a note.

"Exactly. There's no telling how much went south since the dig opened."

"Hartzler's playing it cute right to the end," Childress said. "She's not talking, and so far the police haven't found any records."

Kate nodded. "I didn't find anything on the Slope, either. I'd bet she ran everything on a cash basis. The best hope you have of finding either connection is to have someone sit on her phone and pray they call before the story hits the news. Right now Chris Heller's checking the inventory they've been keeping on artifacts received. He's a bright boy, that Heller," Kate added. "He caught on to the fact that things were disappearing his first week up. He's trying to contact the members of Leckerd's first dig team now, to find out if any of them saw anything suspicious."

"I don't give a shit about a bunch of stone knives and bear claws," John King barked.

"I do," Kate barked back. He glared at her and she met it with one of her own. "One of the archaeologists was telling me there's a law, the Archaeological Resources Protection Act. It was passed in 1979. A couple of years ago they added on to it, making damage to an archaeological dig a felony."

"So?"

"A federal felony," Kate said.

"So?"

"So," Childress said, eyeing Kate, "if they skate on the drug charges, as has been known to happen a time or two, the U.S. attorney nails them on the—what was it? The Archaeological Resources Protection Act. Not a bad idea, Shugak." Childress said it grudgingly, but he did say it.

Of course he immediately dissipated any goodwill generated by the remark by adding, "I still say RPetCo Security could have handled this problem."

"Yes," Kate agreed, "you could have, just as well as I did and, simply by virtue of the fact your people know the Slope and I didn't, probably better." Childress was taken aback and showed it. "But not as fast. I got lucky. I knew one of the players, and he knew me and knew what I did for a living. If I wasn't suspicious of Jerry McIsaac at first, he was of me. When he passed those suspicions on to Toni Hartzler. . ." Kate shrugged. "All I had to do was sit back and let things happen."

And nearly get killed two or three times in the process, Jack agreed silently.

John King rose to his feet and held out an envelope. "Your last paycheck."

She took it. "King?"

"What?"

"Mind telling me what that Christmas tree's doing on Tode Point?"

"None of your goddam business," Childress said.

King silenced him with an upraised hand. The light reflected off the lenses of his glasses and hid his expression. "It was an exploration well back in the sixties. A duster."

"That's not what I asked you. I asked you what it's doing on Tode Point."

"It was a duster," he growled, irritated. "It was plugged and abandoned years ago."

Kate nodded. "King, the most important stipulation in a state oil and gas lease requires that all structures be removed and the site returned to its original state."

King's face went brick-red. "The fucker's been out there for twenty years!"

Kate's voice remained calm, even pleasant. "Tode Point is a national archaeological site as well as an Alaska Native cultural heritage site. There shouldn't be a wellhead there. There shouldn't even be a well there. I'd bet every dime you paid me there never was a lease for it."

He met her calm, even speech with blustering sarcasm. "And just what do you expect me to do about it?"

"I expect you to move it. Now. I expect you to tear down that fence, dismantle that wellhead and pick up every stone of gravel you laid down within a mile of that dugout. I expect you to reseed the area, and then I expect you to pray the grass grows fast and the geese come back even faster." She smiled in the teeth of his snarl and Childress's furious curse. "Those archaeologists found a burial site last week, King. If you prefer, I could try talking them into believing it was the grave of a legendary shaman, the dugout a shrine and the whole area sacred ground." Still smiling, she added, "It shouldn't be too hard. They're very grateful to me for catching Otto in the act."

John King opened his mouth to blast her ears back and Jack spoke from the window. "King. May I remind you, Kate is Ekaterina Shugak's granddaughter."

King's mouth shut with an audible snap. As hydrocarbon-centric as he was, even John King had heard of Ekaterina Shugak. There was a short, fulminating silence. Finally he growled, "Okay. We'll move the fucking Christmas tree."

"And the fence, and the gravel, and reseed the area."

"I said we'd do it!" he bellowed, and stamped outside, followed by Childress, who slammed the door so hard the house shook.

• • •

"Well." Jack stood to thrust his hands in his pockets and roam restlessly about the living room. "Once again I do my best to get you killed, and once again fail miserably."

"Don't."

"Okay," he said. "Ever again." He'd been avoiding looking at her, avoiding looking at the spectacular shiner covering most of the right side of her face in a gorgeous medley of royal purple and mustard yellow.

"Cut it out," Kate said, with more force this time.

He took a deep breath, exhaled. "Sorry. Didn't mean to go all Neanderthal on you."

She had to smile. "Sure you did. Jack?"

"What?"

"No more narcotics cases, okay? Drugs have a way of making the smartest people stupid, stupid and greedy. I don't want to have to witness it firsthand."

"No more narcotics cases," he agreed.

"No more Slope cases, either."

He was startled and showed it. "Why not? Hell, you don't even have to make your own bed when you work on the Slope."

"Because you don't even have to make your own bed when you work on the Slope. It's not real. And it's dangerous." She paused, and he waited. "It scared me."

"Scared you how?"

She thought about it for a moment. "I liked it," she said at last, frowning a little. "The place is unreal and the people are out of control and I liked it. I liked steak on Tuesday and Thursday and prime rib on Sunday. I liked not having to make my own bed or cook my own meals or wash my own dishes.

I liked being six hundred air miles from any responsibility of any kind except for doing my job. I liked the money. I liked the gang-beeping and the turtle races and Belle's little cowboy outfit and the Japanese guy looking for the bangoon. I liked it a lot."

"Get thee behind me, Satan," he suggested. "Why, Kate, you may be human after all." Quickly, before she could snap a reply, he said, "About that lease language you quoted to King? I thought you said restoration of the site was at the discretion of the commissioner?"

She shrugged. "If he can't be bothered to look up the original language himself, too bad."

Jack's grin was involuntary and quickly hidden. There was a brief pause. "You were a little hard on Hartzler, weren't you?"

"She got most of her tongue back, what do you want?"

"She got frostbite in both hands and both feet, too," Jack pointed out dryly.

"Them's the breaks. A good thing she's going where she won't have to worry about turning up the heat."

He shook his head. "You are one hard-nosed bitch, Shugak."

"You do say the sweetest things." She ran a hand through her hair. "I guess I'd better call the railroad, see what time the train leaves tomorrow."

Jack stared out the window, hands in his pockets. "You could stay."

Kate's voice was surprisingly gentle. "No. No, I couldn't."

"Not even for Costco? The Book Cache?" Me? he thought, but didn't say out loud.

She heard him anyway. "No."

Even though he was expecting it the word fell like a blow.

"Mind telling me why?"

"Jack," Kate said. His jaw stayed stubbornly outthrust, and she sighed. "I like my homestead."

"It's lonely."

"Yes," she said. "That's one of the reasons I like it. I like living alone. I like turning Don Henley up to nine and cleaning the house at one A.M. if I feel like it. I like farting whenever I want." She sighed again. "I don't like television. I don't like 747s on a short final into Anchorage International roaring down my chimney. I don't like the bass on a car stereo playing Ice-T threatening to break my windows."

"Watch your mouth, my son the rapper's upstairs."

She looked at the back of his head as he stood, staring out the window, and said softly, "And I'm no mommy."

"I love you," Jack said. It was the first time he'd said it out loud. It was the first time in five years he'd been sure she wouldn't run if he did.

Kate slid her arms around his waist and pressed her cheek against his back. "I know." He tried to turn in the circle of her arms and she wouldn't let him. "I know."

His hands came out of his pockets and locked over hers. "Well, at least I made you solvent for a while. As long as I can keep Johnny from helping you spend the rest of it on more games for that damn Game Boy you bought him." He waited. "What's wrong? Talk to me."

She shook her head. "I don't know. I don't know if I can explain it." Her voice turned halting, hesitant, as if the words were finding their own way out. "You remember that cairn I told you about?" He nodded, and she said, "It was the damnedest feeling, standing there, looking at that pile of rocks some ancestor of mine built a thousand years ago to make the caribou migrate in the direction he wanted them to. And then

I looked over and saw that Christmas tree, and I wanted to rip and tear."

"Why?"

"At first I didn't know why. The human race has always managed the earth, since the race stood up on two legs, the cairn proves that. The wellhead just showed that our management techniques have become a little more sophisticated. Although not that much more sophisticated," she added. "Jack, did you know they don't even pump the oil out of the ground up there? The formation's just one big pressure cooker. They punch holes in it and stand back quick before the oil jumps out and squirts them in the eye."

"Somehow I don't think it's quite as simple as all that."

"Well, maybe not quite," she admitted.

Jack rubbed her hands. "So why were you mad?"

She thought, rubbing her cheek against his spine. "I guess," she said slowly, "I guess because the difference is how much damage the managers do in the process, or leave behind afterward. I was taught to give back. In the village, the old way, the right way, the one way is to give back, always somehow, in some way to give back. At Prudhoe, we're taking something and we're not giving back. We're robbing the biggest grave of all. Oh, hell," she said, disgusted with how inadequate the words were, "I can't explain it. Forget it."

For a moment Jack was silent. "Let me ask you something. How did you get here?"

She snorted. "I know all the arguments, Jack. Snowmobile, train, Blazer, I know, all those vehicles run on products made from oil."

"So? What should we do?"

"I don't know. Something else. Soon."

It was time. He turned and she met his eyes and her own

widened. "What? Jack, what is it?"

• • •

The drawer slid out from the wall. The plastic bag was unzipped. Kate stared down at the brown, seamed face, the rheumy eyes closed. "That's him."

Jack nodded to the morgue attendant. The bag was zipped up, the drawer closed.

In the hallway she said, the sound of her torn voice made worse by its complete lack of emotion, "How did he die?"

He squeezed her shoulder. "This'll be tough, Kate."

She looked at him, and her patient, unwavering stare reminded him of a line of poetry, drummed into his head long ago by some forgotten high school English teacher. *This is the way the gods ordained the destiny of men, to bear such burdens in our lives, while they feel no affliction. . . . Endure it, then.* Priam to Achilles, wasn't it? No, Achilles to Priam. It was Hector who had died, and Achilles who had killed him.

Kate waited. Enduring. Jack said, "They found him in the doorway of a downtown store Sunday morning."

Kate's expression didn't change. "Exposure?" Jack nodded. "Drunk?"

"Two-point-one."

A muscle twitched next to Kate's mouth. "Nobody saw him?"

Jack said deliberately, "If they did, they figured he was just another drunk in a doorway."

"Of course they did." She paused. "What was his name?"

"Emil Johannson."

She was silent for a moment, and then surprised him with the ghost of a laugh. "Emil Johannson. A good Yupik name."

Outside on the street, she pulled the little otter from her

226

pocket. Jack stood next to her, waiting patiently, watching her fingers gently caress the little paws, the thick curve of the tail. "You want to hear something funny, Jack? When Jerry started telling me how they got the stuff off the Slope, I assumed he was talking about the artifacts. I wasn't even thinking about the dope, I could have cared less if every Sloper snorted a pound of cocaine a day and two pounds on Sunday. All I could see was that old man and his box of ivory, ready to trade it in on a fifth of Windsor Canadian."

"What are you going to do with it?"

"The ivory?"

"Yes."

The little otter looked up at her from behind inquisitive whiskers. "I don't know yet."

His coal-black eyes gleamed brightly in the sun. The spring breeze ruffled through his ivory fur.

And then she did.

● ● ●

Two days later she was in her grandmother's kitchen in Niniltna. Afternoon sun poured through the windows in a steady, unceasing stream, gilding the worn linoleum, turning the bulk of the squat oil stove into a brooding graven image, backlighting Ekaterina's head so that Kate couldn't read her features. "I've come for a favor, emaa," she said, and named it.

The old woman was silent for a long time. "How did he die?" she asked finally.

"It doesn't matter now," Kate said wearily. "He's dead."

Another pause. "What was his name?"

"Emil Johannson. Do you know any Johannsons from St. Lawrence?"

"I might."

Kate gave the box a little shove. "This belongs to them, then. Will you return it?"

The silence stretched out between them. Kate counted dust motes shimmering in the air. At last the old woman stirred. "Why did you do it, Katya?"

Kate made no pretense of misunderstanding. She gave a faint shrug. "I wanted to see the Slope."

With some acerbity Ekaterina said, "I've been trying to get you up to the kivgiq in Barrow for three years."

The corners of Kate's mouth creased. "Maybe I'll go now." She paused, thinking of Cindy Sovalik. She would like to see the old woman again, to talk with her. There was much to learn, there. "I wanted to see Prudhoe. I wanted to see what all the shouting was about. Oil pays for our electricity, hell, it paid for the town's generating plant, for the school." She paused. "I wanted to see the monster up close and personal."

"And now that you have?"

"It has a human face, emaa," Kate said. "And the project itself is impressive as hell. Not as impressive as the Kanuyaq Copper Mine, I grant you, they humped their equipment in over mountains and rivers and glaciers on their backs. No haul road, no airport for them. But Prudhoe is impressive. And they have done a good job. I don't know that they would have done as good a job if the government and the environmentalists hadn't been breathing down their necks every step of the way, but for whatever reason, they did do a good job."

"And now?"

"And now? The job is done. I am home." Kate looked across the kitchen table at her grandmother, age and wisdom and authority carved into her face with every line. She had to make Ekaterina understand. "This isn't an apology, emaa. I'm not sorry I went." Kate took a deep breath. "I am sorry I hurt you." She had to struggle to get the next words out. "Please forgive me."

When it came, the old woman's voice was low and soft, as soft and vulnerable as ever Kate had heard it in her life. "Do you know how much it hurt me, Katya. after your father died, when you chose to live with Abel, instead of me?"

"I do now," Kate said gently. "Emaa. Who was it who told me, you don't own the land, the land owns you? I couldn't leave it. I couldn't." To her horror, Kate felt her breath catch on a sob. She fought for control.

"You were all I had left of them."

"When they died, the land was all I had left of me," Kate said. "It still is."

Ekaterina raised her head and looked at Kate. "I'm not sure I understand that."

"Oh, emaa," Kate said, her ruined voice caught on a shaken laugh, "you don't have to. You just have to accept it."

Unable to hold her grandmother's gaze, Kate looked beyond the sunlight to the dozens of framed family pictures lining the wall. She and her father and her mother were there somewhere, a picture she knew so well she didn't have to get up and look for it, a picture she had memorized and knew every shape and shadow of by heart. Her mother seated on the floor of the cabin, laughing, fighting off the eager advances of a large gray husky mix that bore a distinct resemblance to Mutt. The husky ridden by a baby girl in diapers with dark tangled hair. Her father leaning on one elbow to one side, his face split wide in a huge grin.

Yes, she knew the picture, and yes, she knew it was there. Hung to the right of one of Martin at his naming potlatch. To the left of Axenia's graduation picture. Above Luba and Barney's wedding portrait. Below the one of Niniltna High School's 1990 varsity basketball team, four of the starting five of which were Ekaterina's direct descendants, grinning around their Class C state championship trophy.

"I'll make cocoa," her grandmother said, the words startling Kate out of her absorption.

The two women stared at each other across the table. Her voice husky, Kate said, "Remember, I like it lumpy."

A smile whispered across Ekaterina's brown, seamed face. "I remember."

Ponderously, she rose to her feet and put the teakettle on the stove.

● ● ●

The truck pulled into the clearing and Kate let the engine die. "Home," she said with a sigh, and relaxed against the seat. Mutt indicated a wish to exit the truck in no uncertain terms and Kate opened her door. Mutt flattened her ears, gathered her muscles together and took Kate and the steering wheel in a single, smooth graceful leap, disappearing into the bushes with barely a rustle.

Kate looked closer. Those bushes were budding. Tomorrow she would go down by the creek and look for pussy willows. And maybe the next day she would get out needle and twine and mend her dip net. The ice was almost gone from the Kanuyaq River in front of her grandmother's house. Who knew? The day after she might be eating one of those reckless and impetuous salmon that never did get the time of year to swim upstream quite right in their genes.

A lump of snow dissolved and coalesced with other drops

and ran to the end of a branch. With a soft plop it dropped to the ground. It had snowed while they had been gone, but it had thawed again, too, and the shallow drifts were melting like powdered sugar in the spring sun. The smell of wet earth filled her nostrils. The air was soft on her cheek. In the distance she heard the anticipatory chuckle of water over stone. An eagle screamed a taunting challenge far away, receiving only the low, roguish croak of a raven in reply.

Peace.

AUTHOR'S NOTE

This book is a work of fiction. There's no such man as John King. There is no RPetCo. There were never any drugs at Prudhoe Bay. There wasn't any booze, either. Nobody ever wrapped duct tape around the TransAlaska Pipeline; turtles never raced at the Base Camp; two women never sold $20,000 worth of magazine subscriptions in two days at Crazyhorse; nobody's ever sold Native American artifacts to the Detroit Institute of Arts for $55,000; no oil company ever spilled ten million gallons of oil into Prince William Sound; and I've got some land for sale in Wasilla, guaranteed swamp-free, beneath which Arco's about to find a natural gas field the size of the Sadlerochit.

AFTERWORD

Did I see a pipeliner pull a grizzly bear's tail in Prudhoe Bay?
No.

I saw a pipeliner pull a grizzly bear's tail at Galbraith Lake
Pipeline Camp.

Seriously. I couldn't make that up, my imagination isn't
that good. Nearly all the events described herein really did
happen, including the turtle races. I was there. I saw them.

I spend four months in 1975 working on the TransAlaska
Pipeline for Alyeska at Galbraith, and the following year went
to work for BP at Prudhoe Bay. I went because it was where
all the best stories were coming from, not to mention the best
paychecks. Alaskans of my generation had never seen money
like that in our lives and we were all filling out applications at
Arco and BP and Veco and paying Dobie dues down at the
Teamster's Union. Yes, I saw guys playing check poker with
twelve-hundred dollar checks. What the hell, there'd be
another one just like it next week.

I only meant to stay a year, but BP kept promoting me to
better jobs at higher pay, so I stayed for six. I had Toni
Hartzler's job in the end, tour guide for the Western Operating
Area, aka the BP side. I picked up state supreme court justices
and Exxon boards of directors and engineers and architects
and shareholders and spouses and ferried them around the

Slope by the van- and busload. Most of the ignorant questions I was asked are immortalized in *A Cold-Blooded Business*. Like I said, I couldn't make this stuff up.

A few years back an Anchorage bookseller told me a story about a guy coming into her store, looking for more of my books. He was a Sloper and he'd just read *A Cold-Blooded Business*. "She even knows where the lights switches are!" he said.

Bet your ass I do.

MAP OF NINILTNA

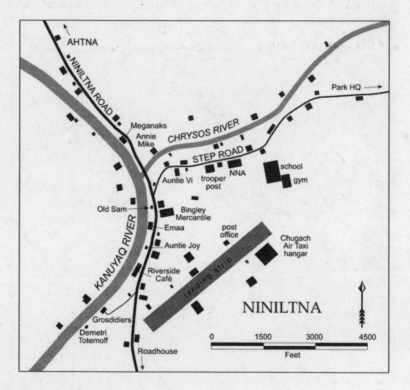

MAP OF NINILTNA

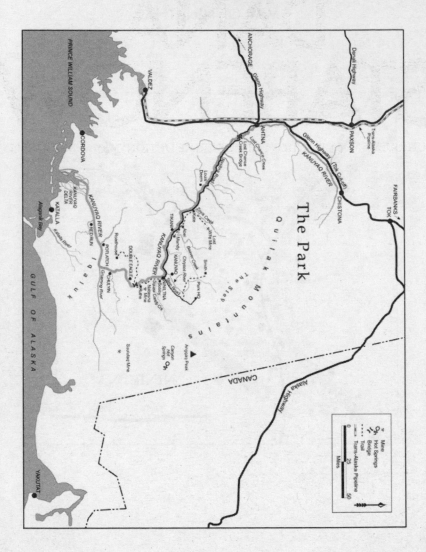

MAPS BY DR CHERIE NORTHON
WWW.MAPMAKERS.COM

DANA STABENOW

'UNIQUE IN THE CROWDED FIELD OF CRIME FICTION' MICHAEL CONNELLY

PLAY WITH FIRE

A ten-year-old girl asks Kate to find her
missing father and when Kate stumbles
across a body in the woods she fears she
may have found him...

A KATE SHUGAK INVESTIGATION

5

ONE

The origin of mushrooms is the slime and souring juices of moist earth, or frequently the root of acorn-bearing trees; at first it is flimsier than froth, then it grows substantial like parchment, and then the mushroom is born.

—Pliny

"KATE. LOOK UP."

Kate kept her head down, in part out of a natural obstinacy, in part because she lacked the energy to do otherwise.

The young woman with the blonde ponytail lowered her video camera and huffed out an impatient breath. "Kate, how am I supposed to make my Academy Award-winning documentary film on the Mad Mushroom Pickers of Musk Ox Mountain if you won't cooperate?" She slapped down a persistent mosquito. "Come on," she said in a coaxing voice and raised the camera again. "One teensy-weensy, insignificant little smile. What could it hurt?"

With the paring knife she held in her right hand, Kate cut half a dozen more mushrooms and tossed them into the overflowing five-gallon plastic bucket next to her. Suppressing a groan, she straightened a back that screamed in protest and bared her teeth in the blonde's direction. Spread across a face covered equally with soot and sweat, the fake grin echoed the

1

whitened, roped scar pulling at the otherwise smooth brown skin of the throat below. All in all, it was a fearsome sight.

"Great! Fantastic! Beautiful! You look like a woman who runs with the wolves!" The blonde's face scrunched into an expression of ferocious concentration behind the eyepiece. The camera lingered long enough for the grin to fade to a grimace as Kate stretched again, then panned down and left, to rest on the quizzical yellow stare of the gray wolf-husky hybrid sprawled on a rise of ground. "Get up, Mutt," the blonde pleaded. "Give me a little action. A grin, a snarl, anything! Look like the wolf Kate runs with!"

Mutt, chin resting on crossed paws, closed her eyes. It was too hot to do anything else.

The blonde grumbled. "You people are just not cooperating with me." The camera panned up and left, to linger on a sign nailed to a blackened tree trunk. The plywood base was painted white. Its message was lettered in neat block print, by hand, and was brief and to the point:

1 JOHN 2:22

The blonde lowered the camera and delved into the capacious left-hand pocket of her coat, a voluminous gray duster that swept behind her like a train, snapping twigs from blueberry bushes, trailing through narrow streams of peaty water, picking up the odd bear scat. It was wet to a foot above the hem. Her jeans were wet to the knee.

A paperback edition of The Holy Bible materialized from the duster pocket like the voice of God from the burning bush. A few seconds later she found it. "'Who is a liar but he that denieth that Jesus is the Christ? He is antichrist, that denieth the Father and the Son.'" She looked up. "Only the third one today and we're almost to the end of the New Testament." She pondered a moment. "Let me pose you an existential question."

"Dinah."

"Oh quit, it'll be good for you." She didn't say why, only squared her shoulders, raised one arm in the obligatory oratorical stance and declaimed, "If scripture is posted in the forest and there's no one around to read it, does it make any sense?"

"Almost as much as if someone were," Kate couldn't resist replying.

"I was afraid of that," the blonde said gloomily, and slapped at another mosquito. "Damn these bugs! I feel like I'm running a blood blank for anything with three pairs of legs and two pairs of wings!" She slapped again. "Jesus! How do you stand it?"

Kate's jeans were wet to the thigh. Sweat was pooling at the base of her spine. It felt like eighty degrees on this Thursday afternoon in late June. The sun wasn't setting until it got good and ready— at this time of year not until midnight—and she'd had enough of existentialism two pages into *No Exit* and three weeks into English 211 at the University of Alaska in Fairbanks fourteen years before. She pushed back a strand of black hair, leaving another streak of soot on her cheek, and hoisted the bucket. Ten feet away sat a second white plastic bucket, similarly full, and she headed toward it with grim determination.

"You can't!" Dinah wailed. "Kate! Dammit, I've been waiting for this light all day! Ouch!" She smacked another mosquito.

Kate picked up the second bucket, balancing the load, and paused for a moment to wonder if, after all, she should have taken Billy Mike up on his crew share offer. Hands, arms and

back, she now knew from bitter experience, ached just as badly after a week of picking fish out of a skiff as they did from a week of picking mushrooms off the forest floor. She hitched the buckets and followed Mutt up the hill.

Dinah scrambled after her. "Okay, okay, I'll get up with you tomorrow, we'll catch the morning light, it'll be all right."

"I'm so pleased for you," Kate said, plodding around a burned-out stump. "My whole life would be blighted if you missed your shot." Another trickle of sweat ran down her back. A mosquito whined past her ear, and behind her she heard another smack of flesh on flesh.

"Hah! Another victory of woman over *Aedes excrucians!*"

Kate didn't want to know, but there was a rustle of cloth as Dinah produced another book, a small paperback entitled *Some Notes on the Arthropod Insecta Diptera in the Alaskan Wilderness.* She dodged a blood-thirsty specimen, waved off another on final approach, slapped at a third and read, " '*Aedes excrucians* is the most abundant and annoying of Alaskan mosquitoes.' "

Kate remained silent, and goaded, the blonde turned up the volume. " 'It differs from other mosquitoes in that it remains active during warm sunny afternoons, especially aggravating to its victims. Its habitat is the marshlands attendant to rivers found from Wrangell to Fort Yukon, from Niniltna to Naknek, and from Kotzebue to Noatak.' " Dinah shut and pocketed the book. "I just hope you're happy, is all."

Kate hadn't called up this particular swarm of *Aedes excrucians,* or any other for that matter, but she held her peace. A buzzing specimen hovered near her right brow, sniffed the air, turned up its proboscis in disdain and whizzed past. From behind Kate a moment later there was a smack of flesh on flesh and a muttered curse.

4

They kept climbing the slope before them, leaving the marsh behind and heading for higher ground, and eventually the bugs began to decrease in number, though they were never entirely absent, not at this time of year, not anywhere in Alaska. When at last the two women reached the top of the rise, Kate paused for breath.

They were hiking through what had once been a pristine primeval forest. The previous summer the worst fire in decades had swept through the area and torn a strip off the Alaskan interior in places as much as five miles wide. When the smokejumpers had at last battled it to a standstill, 125,000 square acres of interior Alaskan scrub spruce, white spruce, paper birch, quaking aspen and balsam poplar had been laid waste, not to mention—and what Kate grudged more—countless lowbush and highbush cranberry, raspberry, salmonberry, lingonberry and nagoonberry stands.

But nature, profligate and extravagant as always, had brought in the following spring wet and mild, and in the ashes of the devastating fire had sprung up a bumper crop of morel mushrooms that had produce buyers flying in en masse from Los Angeles to New York, cash in hand, and had Alaskans flying in en masse from all over the Interior, buckets in hand, in pursuit of that cash.

Kate stretched gingerly. Once upon a time she had liked mushrooms. Now she felt about them the way she did about salmon at the end of the fishing season: that if she never saw another she'd die happy. She raised a hand to scratch her scar, inhaled some soot and sneezed three times in rapid succession. Picking fish was looking better all the time.

At their feet the great loop of the Kanuyaq River gleamed a dull gold. Forty miles to the south of the rise, Mount Sanford rose sixteen thousand feet in the air, flanked by nine-thousand-

foot Tanada and twelve-thousand-foot Drum, blue-white armor glinting in the late afternoon sun. If she squinted south-southeast, Kate made believe she could see Angqaq lording it arrogantly over the Quilaks. The peaks, sharped-edged and stern, looked normal and reassuring; it was the land between, a nightmare drawn in broad slashes of charcoal, that shocked and startled. The scar was a shadow on the land. Ash lay thick on the ground, showered from crisped branches. The trunks of trees had exploded in the heat of the fire and left acres of black splinters behind, looking for all the world like a game of pickup-sticks frozen in an upright position.

It was a charred skeleton of a once-great forest. "What a waste," the blonde said, her voice subdued. "What started it, do you know?"

"Lightning."

"Lightning?" The blonde eyed the cumulus clouds gathering force on the southeastern horizon.

Kate nodded. "It's the main cause of forest fires."

"Oh." The blonde eyed the clouds again. "Even Smokey the Bear might find it a little tough to fight lightning. What a waste," she repeated, raising the camera and surveying the scene through the eyepiece.

Kate heard the low whir of rolling film. "Not really."

The roll of film paused, the blonde raising a skeptical eyebrow.

"It's true. A forest fire is a way for the forest to renew itself and the wildlife in it. In the older forests the big trees get bigger and take over, and new growth doesn't have a chance. New growth is what moose eat. A couple of years after a fire and the moose start multiplying because there's more fodder. It happened on the Kenai after the 1969 fire there. It'll happen here, too."

"Uh-huh." Dinah didn't sound convinced. "It'll take a while, though, to regenerate."

Kate glanced around, and pointed. "What?" the blonde said suspiciously.

Kate stooped to brush at some ash. Something indisputably green peered back at them, an alder by the shape of the leaves.

"I'll be damned," Dinah said, impressed in spite of herself. Mutt sniffed at the shoot of green. Dinah focused on both and the camera whirred. "What a great shot. Death and resurrection. Destruction and regeneration! The green phoenix bursting from the black ashes of devastation!" Lowering the camera she delved once more in her left-hand pocket, producing the tattered Bible. Impatiently, she thumbed through the pages, muttering to herself. "Aha! And 'Death is swallowed up in victory!'" She slapped the book shut and shot Kate a triumphant look. "One Corinthians, 15:54. 'O death, where is thy sting?'" She slapped at a mosquito. "Damn. Did you know there are twenty-seven species of mosquito in the state of Alaska?" She looked back at Kate. "I can't believe there is something already growing here. I would have bet big bucks it'd be years."

Mutt raised a leg over the green shoot. Kate forbore to draw Dinah's attention to the act. "It doesn't take long." She dug a fist into the small of her back. "Of course, twenty-hour days and a good spring rain are a great head start." She picked up the buckets, took one step forward and halted abruptly.

Dinah bumped into her. "Sorry. What?" She followed Kate's gaze and the breath whooshed out of her. "Holy shit."

A brown bear stood to the right of the trail. He was about the biggest creature Dinah had ever seen in all her life outside a zoo, standing six feet at the shoulder and weighing literally half a ton. His brown fur was silver-tipped and his muzzle was

7

sooty, as if he'd been nosing over burned logs.

For once, Dinah forgot she was holding a camera. She almost dropped it. "Holy *shit*" she said again. She knew it was an inadequate assessment of the situation but she didn't really know of anything to say that would be adequate.

"Relax," Kate said.

"What if it charges us?" Dinah hissed.

"Talk in your normal tone of voice," Kate said, and moved forward.

"Kate! What are you doing? You're walking right toward it! Kate!"

"Just follow me, Dinah," Kate said, still in that normal tone of voice.

Dinah swore helplessly and followed, hefting her camera to shoulder height, not sure if she were keeping it out of harm's way or preparing to use it for a weapon. Then she recollected her mission and rolled film. She could see it now. She Died Rolling. Death in the line of duty. The American Documentary Filmmakers Association'd probably name an award after her. She wondered if there was an American Documentary Filmmakers Association. She wondered if they had an award.

The bear looked even bigger through the lens, crowding the edges of the frame. It didn't help that her hands were shaking. She realized that the back of Kate's head was receding and quickened her step.

The bear watched them impassively for the longest minute of Dinah's life. When they had approached within ten yards he dropped his head and melted back into a pocket of alders at the edge of the burn area.

"Just relax," Kate repeated, steps even and unhurried. "There are two of us and we're talking. He wants to come

8

PREVIEW

down this way, though, and bears are kind of inflexible once they've made up their minds to do something. It's best we get out of his way. Lucky he wasn't a sow. They've usually just dropped a cub this time of year. A sow would have been cranky as hell."

She kept talking and kept walking. Dinah was so close behind her now that her toes caught Mutt's heels, and Mutt moved up to point, ears up but silent and unalarmed. The lens of the camera clipped Kate's head once, earning Dinah a hard look from hazel eyes. They passed the thicket into which the bear had retreated without incident and walked on up the hill unmolested.

Dinah was weak with relief, her legs wobbling, her knees barely able to hold her up. "Jesus, Kate. What if he had charged us?"

"You'd have been toast," Kate said serenely without pausing.

Dinah stared at the black braid hanging straight down a very straight spine. "Why me? Why me and not you?"

Kate grinned without turning. "Because I wouldn't have to outrun the bear. I'd only have to outrun you."

There was a moment while Dinah worked this out. When she did, she gave an unconvincing snort.

"Ha ha ha. Very funny." She plodded along in silence for a moment. "I didn't even know there were bears around here."

"You ain't in New York City anymore, Dorothy."

"That's why Bobby hangs everything from that tree every night."

"No bacon or sausage for breakfast, either."

"Bears like bacon?"

"Almost better than anything else." Kate could almost hear Dinah become a vegetarian for the duration in the sound of

her footsteps. "Truthfully, bears will eat anything that'll sit still for it. They don't like to work for their food."

"We'd have been work?"

"Uh-huh. They'll eat anything or anyone that's within reach, whether it's been lying around for a day or a year, as long as it is just lying around." She added, "That's why you don't find any bodies near plane crashes."

Dinah swallowed audibly. "Bears eat them?"

"Uh-huh."

A breeze rose up, keeping the remaining mosquitoes off, and Dinah nosed into it gratefully. Over the top of the next rise the black ash stopped abruptly, as if a line had been drawn beyond which the fire was forbidden to cross. As they approached, an actual line appeared in the form of a six-foot ditch, a fire break dug by the smokejumpers the year before, one of many in an effort to direct the course of the fire away from the Glenn Highway, the main road between Anchorage and the Canadian border, and its sycophant settlements. On the other side of the ditch was a clearing, a small patch of new spring grass encircled by a stand of birch trees. Their white boles stood out against the rising ground of the blackened countryside, slender and strong.

In the center of the clearing was a rock-lined fire pit. Two tents faced each other across it. A square of bright blue plastic tarpaulin was spread to one side, a dozen full five-gallon buckets on it, the rest of the day's harvest. Kate let her two buckets thud down next to them and mopped her brow. Her palm came away smeared with soot.

"Oh Ward, I'm home!" The blonde hastened past her and into the ring of trees.

"In here, June!" replied a deep male voice.

The owner of the voice had installed fat, mountain bike

tires on his wheelchair and it cornered around the rock fireplace like a '69 Corvette. The 350-horsepower engine slammed to a halt at the sight of the blonde. The driver threw back his head and, in a stentorian voice that caused the tops of the trees to sway, bellowed, "BAY-bee!"

"SWEET-heart!" In one movement Dinah shucked out of camera and duster. In a combined hop, skip and jump she leapt into Bobby's lap, flung her arms around his neck and smothered his face with kisses, all of which were returned with interest.

It was enough to make a grown woman vomit. "It's enough to make a grown woman vomit," Kate said, and had to repeat it a second time in a louder voice when the lovers ignored it the first time around.

"Why don't you run away and play, Kate," the blonde suggested around a mouthful of ear.

Bobby sent her a lascivious grin and said nothing at all. Biting the inside of her cheek to hold back an answering smile, Kate got her pack out of her tent and went past them and down the hill to the creek a quarter of a mile beyond.

The rush of spring runoff had carved a pool the size and depth of a tin washtub out of the side of the bank. Smooth, round stones slightly smaller than goose eggs shone up from the stream bed, fiddlehead ferns lined the bank, peat-colored water eddied around the edges of the little pool, and the whole scene looked like something out of Gerard Manley Hopkins. Mutt waded in as far as her ankles, buried her muzzle six inches deep and inhaled the better part of the volume of water. Exhausted from this gargantuan effort, she flopped down beneath a nearby tree and lapsed into a sated stupor. Mutt wasn't accustomed to and didn't approve of heat waves and had decided that the best way to endure this one was asleep.

Kate shucked out of her clothes and waded in. The water was clear and cold and she gasped from the shock of it against her overheated skin. The pool was just big enough to get all of her wet at the same time and she sank beneath the surface, shaking her head so that her hair swirled around her face. She exploded into the air with a tremendous splash and a laugh. On the bank Mutt opened one eye, saw that a rescue was not in her immediate future and relapsed into unconsciousness. Kate couldn't resist. She brought both palms down on the water, hard, and it fountained up over the bank and splashed down on and around Mutt. Mutt leapt to her feet and let out a yip like an outraged dowager pinched on the behind, shook herself vigorously, gave Kate a reproachful look and relocated behind a tree well out of range.

"You're no fun," Kate told her, and reached for the soap. It came in a plastic bottle, bought from REI in Anchorage during her stay with Jack that spring. She'd done a job for an oil company and they'd paid her obscenely well for it. She had done her best to spend every ill-gotten dime before she left town, and one of the places she'd done her best at was at REI. REI was going yuppie in its old age but it still had all kinds of fascinating and useless gadgets for the urban hiker. Kate had found the soap there and bought a bottle at once for the label, which announced that it contained "Dr. Bronner's Almond 18-in-1 Pure-Castile Soap, Always dilute for Shave-Shampoo-Massage-Dental-Soap Bath!... Use Almond Oil Soap for Dispensers-Uniforms-Baby-Beach! Dilute for good After Shave, Body Rub, Foot Bath, Massage! Hot Towel Massage entire body, always toward heart! ... Mildest soap Made! God-made Eggwhite pH9."

It was manufactured by All-One-God-Faith, Inc., and in the small space left over after instructions did its best to save sinners and convert the heathen. "Absolute cleanliness is Godliness! Teach the Moral ABC that unites all mankind free, instantly 6 billion strong & we're All-one." Kate noticed that rhyme was attempted more than once, as in "Our Brother's Teacher of the Moral ABC Hillel taught carpenter Jesus to unite all mankind free!"

Kate wondered who Hillel was. If they ever discovered who was nailing the biblical tracts to the trees, she might get an expert opinion. Uncapping the bottle, she sniffed cautiously. It was almonds, all right. Kate considered herself pretty much beyond redemption by now, but if cleanliness was next to godliness there might be hope for her yet. She washed her clothes first and then herself, soaping her hair twice and scrubbing her body three times, and only reluctantly waded out of the water when her feet began to lose all feeling.

She paused on the bank. The sun was warm on her eyelids, on her breasts and belly. Pine needles prickled the half-numb soles of her feet and she dug in her toes, balancing her weight on spread legs. A wisp of a breeze tiptoed into the little glade and stirred her hair so that the ends tickled her waist. She stood still, palms out, eyes closed, water running down the cleft of her buttocks, the insides of her legs, dripping from the tips of her fingers. Her breasts rose on a deep breath. The faint, acrid smell of charred wood mixed freely with the clean smell of soap, the sweet aroma of running pine sap and the fresh scent of new cottonwood leaves.

The rays of the afternoon sun slanted through leaf and branch to dapple the glade, her skin and the glimmering surface of the tiny pool and the murmuring creek. A bird sang, a clear, joyous, three-note descending scale. "Spring is here," Kate sang with it in a husky rasp, aggravated by the scar on her throat. "Here is spring."

Her arms lifted of their own volition, palms out to the sun, toes digging into grass. The earth's heart beat against her feet, her own kept time with it, and the power of their union seeped up through her soles, flowing into her blood and coursing through her body. Every sense was magnified; she could smell the slight, musty bitterness of the morels, taste the sweetness of the pine sap on her tongue. She heard the exultant scream of an eagle as she plummeted down, talons extended for the kill, the sense of it so vivid Kate felt the stretch of wings across her shoulders, the fan of tail feathers, the coppery taste of blood warm in her mouth. She opened her eyes and could see as far as the Quilaks and the Wrangells and beyond, to Prince William Sound and the rolling blue-green expanse of the mighty Gulf. Never had life seemed so rich with sensual promise. She felt ripe, ready to burst from her skin.

A blade of grass tickled her ankle. The breeze turned cool. She shivered and blinked. A deep, shuddering breath and she was back in her body, senses dazzled by all they had seen. A chuckle escaped her when she realized her nipples were erect. "Lover come back," she said, only half jesting. Mutt opened one eye to give her a quizzical look.

She dug in her pack for a bottle of Lubriderm (another result of the March shopping spree) and smoothed it on; hands, elbows, feet, luxuriating in the feel of it. One thing could be said for picking salmon out of a net: it- was infinitely cleaner work than mushroom picking. She decided that in the future she'd take scales and gurry over soot and ash. "The next time Bobby gets a wild hair to go mushroom hunting," she told Mutt, "he can go by himself. Especially since he's so good at picking up casual labor."

Mutt, by way of agreement, closed her eye.

She strung a line between two trees, hung her wet clothes

and put on clean ones. Sitting cross-legged, she brushed her hair dry, a straight, black, gleaming fall. By then she judged it was safe to go back to camp. Her stomach was growling, so it was too bad if it wasn't.

In the clearing the flap of Bobby's tent was zipped all the way down. Bobby was sitting on a blanket in cutoffs and no shirt, cleaning and sorting mushrooms.

"About time you did some work around here," Kate said.

He reached behind him and tossed her a package of Fig Newtons. "Not just a prince but a god," she said, ripping it open and shoving two in her mouth. He pursed his lips and blew her a kiss and went back to sorting as she rummaged in the cooler for a Diet 7-Up to wash the cookies down with. She popped the top and drank the whole can in one long swallow, submerged it in the melting ice until it refilled with water, and drank that, too. She eyed Bobby over the can, absorbed in his mushrooms.

He was worth watching. Thick through the shoulders like most wheelchair jockeys, his arms were roped with muscle that bunched and flexed beneath smooth skin the color of espresso. His chest was hairless, leaving every rib clearly defined and ridged with muscle. His cutoffs, an inch shorter than his stumps and frayed at the hems, hugged his behind, faithful to every tight, taut curve. The sight was enough to make a grown woman drool.

There was a rasp of a zipper, a rustle of fabric and the squeak of a rubber sole on pine needles. Bobby turned, torso straining, to reach for the bucket. "Yum," said a low voice behind Kate.

"Enough to make a grown woman drool," Kate agreed.

Dinah laughed and sprawled beside her. She was thin to the point of emaciation, had cheekbones to die for and wide,

15

inquiring blue eyes that weren't as innocent as they seemed at first sight. The ponytail had been replaced by a mass of tangled strawberry blonde curls. She was glowing. Kate, years before having been taken up the same mountain and shown the view by the same guide, didn't blame her. She sternly repressed a pang of envy and bit into another Fig Newton. It didn't help much. Sublimation by any other name would taste as tame.

Dinah got a can of pop from the cooler and copped a handful of Fig Newtons and curled up next to Kate, who saw with dismay that she had produced yet another reference work, this one a grimy, dog-eared pamphlet titled *Fun With Fungi, A Mushroom Lover's Guide*. Dinah opened it. And with illustrations, no less. O joy.

"*Morchella elata*" Dinah said, "also known as the black morel. Edible," she added in an aside to Kate.

Bobby threw one at her and she ducked. "The caps are yellowish-brown, spongelike, bell-shaped, and vary in color from cream to brown. They're found in April, May and sometimes June in Alaska. Morels are often particularly abundant in burned-over soil. Why, I wonder?" She turned a page. "Oh. It says here nobody really knows why, but the best guess is it doesn't like competition, from other vegetation, I guess. Hmm. You know why we're picking them?"

Kate took a wild stab. "Two dollars a pound?"

Dinah frowned at her. "Morels don't reproduce in captivity."

"Me, either," Bobby said.

Dinah paged forward and raised her voice. "Morels are perfect partners for sauces because of their ridged caps."

Bobby examined a specimen. "You mean because it grows like something Dr. Frankenstein would transplant inside an empty skull."

"I don't know why I waste my time on these people," Dinah told Mutt.

"Me, either," Bobby said again, and Kate laughed.

Dinah turned to the start of the book. "A Brief History of Fungi," she began the chapter, and had to duck again, this time from half a dozen incoming morels thrown from Bobby's direction, several of which scored direct hits. Deserting righteousness, she said, "Just listen, there's some neat stories in here about mushrooms. For instance"—she ducked again— "did you know that in ancient times the Greeks believed mushrooms were created by lightning bolts? In Scandinavia, though, it was thought that when Wotan ran from the demons, he foamed at the mouth and spit blood, and wherever it struck the ground a mushroom sprang up."

"Yuk. Wotan spit. Jesus." Bobby paused for a moment in his sorting, regarding the mushroom he was holding with knitted brow. "Did you ever stop to wonder who ate the first mushroom?"

"The first King crab?" Kate said, getting into the spirit of things.

"The first oyster?"

" 'He was a bold man that first eat an oyster,' " Kate agreed, with a gravity of which Jonathan Swift would have heartily approved.

"While the Chinese," Dinah said in a slightly louder voice, "considered mushrooms fit only for the poor, the Romans considered them fit only for the rich. They used special utensils to cook them and eat them with." She read further and gave a sudden shout of laughter. "Evidently the special pots for cooking mushrooms, they called them 'boletaria,' anyway, they weren't supposed to be used to cook anything else. But this one pot was, and nearly died of the disgrace. Listen to

what Martial says the pot says: 'Although boleti have given me such a noble name, I am now used, I am ashamed to say, for brussels sprouts.' "

"Poor little pot," Bobby said sadly.

"How humiliating," Kate agreed, just as sadly.

Dinah, reading further, said, "And then there's a kind of fungus that kills grain, and the Romans had a festival each year on the twenty-fifth of April to propitiate the god Robigus, so he would intercede and keep the crops healthy. Everybody dressed up in their best bib and toga and marched out to a sacred grove and anointed the altar with wine and sacrificed a goat and 'buried the entrails of a rust-colored dog.' "

Mutt gave Dinah a wary look. "Oh, don't take everything so personally," Dinah told her, and returned to her book. "In Europe in the seventeen hundreds and eighteen hundreds mushrooms were so popular that kings had to pass laws against setting forest fires to grow more mushrooms." She looked up to quirk an eyebrow at Kate. "Maybe that's what happened here."

"No," Kate said. No one of her acquaintance had ever started a forest fire to grow mushrooms.

Bobby laughed without pausing in his sorting. Dinah gave him a curious look but he didn't explain, and she returned to her book.

"They didn't just eat mushrooms, either, they used them for medicine. Dioscorides prescribed them for colic and sores, bruises, broken bones, asthma, jaundice, dysentery, urinary tract infections, constipation, epilepsy, arthritis, hysteria and acne."

"Acne? You mean like zits?"

"That's what he says. Grind up a mushroom and mix it in with a little water and honey, and presto! B.C. Clearasil."

18

Dinah paused. "Wow."

"What?" In spite of herself, Kate was getting interested.

"The Laplanders used it to cure aches and pains, too. They'd spread bits of dried mushrooms on whatever hurt and set them on fire. The water from the blisters supposedly carried away the pain."

"I think I'd rather have the aches and pains."

"Me, too," Bobby said. He finished sorting, ending with fourteen five-gallon buckets full of clean, dry mushrooms and a big aluminum bowl full of rejects, also clean and dry but deemed by the new mycological expert on the block as unsalable. He regarded the day's harvest with smug satisfaction, and looked over at the two of them, one cocky eyebrow raised. "You two gonna get these shrooms over to the buyer anytime today? I heard a rumor yesterday that the price might go up to three bucks a pound."

"From the same guy who told you the day before that a buyer was flying in from New York and would pay two-fifty?" Kate inquired sweetly.

"Git!" he said.

"A little Hitler, with littler charm," Dinah murmured.

"What was that?" Bobby said suspiciously, ears pricking up.

Dinah gave him a sweet smile. "Stephen Sondheim," she replied, and left him certain he'd been insulted but not quite sure how.

Dinah took a quick bath, finishing just in time to help Kate hump the last of the buckets down to Kate's truck, a red-and-white Isuzu diesel with a plywood tool chest riveted to the bed behind the cab. It was a half mile walk between campsite and the narrow turnaround on the gravel road, and on her last trip Kate said to Bobby, wheezing a little, "Next time you think of

me to go mushroom hunting with?"

"Yeah?"

"Don't."

He hid a grin. "But Kate, I'm disabled." He looked down at his stumps with mournful eyes, and said wistfully, "Don't you think I'd help if I could?"

She just looked at him, and he could only hold the mournful expression for about three seconds before breaking into a roar of laughter Dinah could hear all the way down the hill. "What's so funny?" she said as Kate heaved the last two buckets up into the bed of the truck.

"Bobby thinks he is," Kate grunted, and leaned up against the side of the truck to catch her breath. Parked next to the truck was Dinah's 1967 Ford Econoline van; its pale blue color was barely visible beneath a thousand miles of AlCan Highway mud. Through the streaked windows Kate could see that all the seats except for the driver's had been removed, to be replaced with a camp stove, jugs of what she assumed was water, and boxes of supplies. She leaned forward, eyes narrowing. "Are those books?"

Dinah came over to peer in next to her. "Uh-huh."

"Reading books?"

Dinah shook her head. "Looking-up books."

Kate stared at her. "Such as?"

Dinah shrugged. "*The Riverside Shakespeare*. Edith Hamilton's *Mythology. Chamber's Etymological Dictionary. The World Almanac*. The King James Bible. Or no, I've got that here somewhere." She patted vaguely at one of the many pockets in her long, gray duster, which she had donned for the excursion into town. "And, oh, I don't know, an Alaskan atlas, an Alaskan almanac, an Alaskan bird book. The *Cambridge Encyclopedia of Astronomy*. The *Devil's Dictionary*."

20

"The *Devil's Dictionary?*"

"Yeah. By Ambrose Bierce?" When Kate looked blank, Dinah said, "His definition of monkey is 'an arboreal animal which makes itself at home in genealogical trees.'" Kate laughed and Dinah said, "I'll dig it out on the way home."

"What have you got against fiction?"

"I don't know." Dinah thought it over, and said finally, "It's not real."

Kate looked at her, one brow raised. "I've always liked that about fiction, myself. Get in."

In first gear they bounced and jounced and bumped and thumped along the gravel road for the thirty minutes it took to navigate the two miles to another road. This one was gravel, too, but it was wide enough to take two cars at the same time, an Alaskan interstate, and Dinah said, "Slow traffic keep right."

Kate turned right, shifted into second and the truck purred along the road, the occasional frost heave and runoff ditch nothing to compare with the game trail they'd left behind. A quarter of a mile from the turnoff the forest of scrub spruce, alder and birch changed abruptly from the exuberantly lush, leafy green of a normal Alaskan spring to blasted heath black, the trees no more than splintered stumps, branches charred and unbudded. Dinah's breath drew in sharply, and when Kate looked at her she said sheepishly, "I know, I've seen it every day for a week now. It just gets to me. Every time, it gets to me."

Two more miles of this and the road widened briefly. A sprawling building with a U.S. flag flying out front and a sign that read U.S. POST OFFICE, CHISTONA, ALASKA hung next to another sign that read CHISTONA MERCANTILE, which hung above a third sign that read, AMMUNITION,

BAIT AND GROCERIES. The road narrowed again and then widened to accommodate the turnoff for a white clapboard church with a small spire. Past it, the road narrowed yet again and stayed that way for another ten miles, until they came to the gravel road's junction with the Glenn Highway. Tanada consisted of a sprawling log cabin set well back from the road. Poppies, daisies and forget-me-nots grew from the roof and a Miller sign blinked from the window. A gas pump occupied center stage of the large parking lot, which was otherwise filled with a dozen trucks and cars parked in haphazard fashion around a flatbed truck. The flatbed bore license plates from Washington State. Kate pulled in between a dusty gray International pickup with the right front fender missing and Wyoming plates and a blue Bronco with Minnesota plates packed so high with cardboard boxes and wadded-up clothes that she couldn't see through the windows.

"Look at that," Dinah said, pointing. A Subaru Brat with the gate down and boxes stacked in the bed was parked to one side of the lot with a sign advertising Avon's Skin-So-Soft for sale. Dinah looked at Kate. "Avon's Skin-So-Soft?"

Kate shrugged. "It's the best mosquito repellent around, according to some people. You get in line, I'll pack the buckets over."

"Okay." Dinah headed for the flatbed, camera in hand, and when Kate came up with two buckets there were already three people behind her. There were six in front of her. There was a scale on the back of the flatbed and a man standing next to it; behind him, a steadily rising pile of boxes attested that they had arrived just in time. Tall and thin with tired eyes, the man had a pencil behind one ear, a notepad in one hand and a wad of cash big enough to choke an elephant in the other. He was explaining, in a patient tone that told Kate that it was for the twenty-third time that day, that he was paying two dollars and two dollars only, a pound; that if he paid any more he wouldn't see any profit himself; that he'd been buying mushrooms in Tok for the last two days and didn't know who had started the three-dollar-a-pound rumor, and that the nearest ladies' room was in the Tanada Tavern but they weren't letting the pickers use it and he had a roll of toilet paper in the cab of the flatbed if the ladies wanted to use the bushes.

The door to the Tanada Tavern slammed back against the wall and two men staggered out in a drunken embrace that turned out to be a fight, although neither one was sober enough to connect a blow. Grunting and swearing, they stumbled into the line waiting in back of the flatbed, nearly trampling Kate and causing her to spill half of one of her buckets. She set the buckets down out of the way before she spilled any more. In the meantime the two pugilists had reeled off in a new direction. They didn't see the little boy standing in their way, staring at them with his mouth half open.

"Hey!" Kate took six giant steps, reaching the site of the collision at impact. The little boy went down and the two drunks went down on top of him. Kate grabbed one of them by the hair and yanked his head back and he howled and rolled off the pile. She put an ungentle foot in the other's belly and he rolled in the other direction. She picked the boy up and stood him on his feet. He swayed a little. "Are you okay?" she said. She ran her hands over him. He was covered with dust but everything felt intact and she didn't see any blood. "Kid? Are you all right? Say something."

His blue eyes were enormous and she expected them to fill with tears at any moment. His face was soft and round and she judged him to be seven or eight and tall for his age.

He didn't cry, although his indrawn breath was shaky and his voice thin. "I—no. I'm okay."

"Kate!" Dinah's voice was loud and alarmed. "Look out!"

Kate looked around in time to see one of the drunks make a clumsy rush for her, arms outspread and fists clenched. She shoved the boy backward and took a step back herself and, unable to either change his trajectory or abort his launch the drunk rushed right between them, or he would have if Kate hadn't tripped him. He sprawled in the dirt, cursing, and when he tried to get back to his feet she kicked him in the ass hard enough to send him sprawling again. He kept trying to get to his feet and she kept kicking him, all the way over to a Chevy pickup parked in front of the bar, half orange, half rust, University of Alaska plates. Ah. A scholar. She let him open the door. When he fumbled his keys out she took them away from him, assisted him into the cab of his truck with her foot and closed the door behind him. He toppled over on his right side and very wisely passed out.

She looked around for his friend, who had been terrified by the ungentle manner in which she assisted the first drunk into his truck and who was headed back to the bar for a little liquid courage.

Kate was right behind him. Inside the door, he scuttled out of her way and she walked up to the bar, behind which a big burly man stood mixing drinks. She tossed the keys on the bar and the buzz of conversation died. "It's illegal in this state to serve a drunk," she said into the silence, eyes and voice equally hard.

Somebody laughed. The bartender regarded Kate without expression for a moment, and then added a maraschino cherry to one drink and straws to all. He uncapped a bottle of beer, loaded everything on a tray and carried it away. The conversation came back up.

Kate closed her eyes, shook her head and went back outside. To her credit, Dinah had held on to their place in line. A few people gave Kate curious looks. Most were studiously examining the sky, the trees, the ground, their fingernails. The boy was gone. Kate went back to the truck for the next two buckets.

She had the truck half unloaded when the sound of her name halted her. "Katya."

She looked around. A massive figure, square-shouldered and big-bellied, clad in a dark blue house dress Kate would have sworn she'd seen her wearing when Kate was in kindergarten, stood planted in front of her as if she'd grown there. "Emaa." She hadn't seen her grandmother since April. She smiled. It was less of an effort than it used to be.

Ekaterina Moonin Shugak regarded her out of calm brown eyes, her brown face seamed with wrinkles, her black hair pulled back into a neat bun at the nape of her neck. "You are picking the mushrooms."

"Yes." Kate nodded toward the road. "I'm here with Bobby. We're camped a couple miles past Chistona. Just above the Kanuyaq."

"The fourth turnoff?"

"The fifth."

Ekaterina nodded. "Cat's Creek."

Kate, surprised, said, "I didn't know it had a name."

Not by so much as the lifting of an eyebrow did Ekaterina betray that she lived to show up her grandchildren, but Kate knew, and with difficulty repressed a smile. If it hadn't been named Cat's Creek before, it was now.

Kate nodded at the mushroom buyer standing on the back of the flatbed. "You cut a deal with him?"

Ekaterina said nothing.

"How much are we getting off the top of every pound? A dime?"

Ekaterina still said nothing, and Kate said, "More?"

Her grandmother said, in a knowledgeable manner that reminded Kate irresistibly of Bobby in all his newfound mycological expertise, "It is known that the mushrooms sell for twenty-five dollars a pound or more in stores and restaurants Outside, and up to forty dollars a pound in Europe and Japan."

"We're getting a piece of the *retail?*" Ekaterina permitted a slight smile to cross her face, equal parts satisfaction and triumph, and Kate said respectfully, "Not bad, Emaa. The last buyer was saying before he left for Tok that he figured he'd shipped thirty thousand pounds in twelve days. Not bad at all."

Ekaterina gave a faint shrug. "They are tribal lands."

"And tribal mushrooms," Kate agreed gravely, and laughed. So that was why Ekaterina was here. She would be on the scene, watching over the tribal investment, ensuring full payment in cash on the barrelhead. It was no more than Kate expected. Ekaterina never did anything for only one reason, especially when it benefited the bank account of the Niniltna Native Association, of which Ekaterina had at one time been chairman of the board, and the direction of which she still guided with an unseen but very firm hand.

Dinah was waving violently to catch Kate's eye, and when she did, she waved just as violently to beckon Kate closer. To her surprise Ekaterina accompanied her, and to her even greater surprise allowed Kate to introduce her. The fleeting thought occurred that they were both feeling their way through this new relationship, and that Ekaterina was trying as hard as she was to slay the ghost of the years of antagonism that lay between them.

"Wow," Dinah said, interrupting Kate's words without apology, swinging the omnipresent video camera to her shoulder, "Kate's granny. I could tell from fifty feet away; there's a strong family resemblance. You have the most fabulous face, Mrs. Shugak. Do you mind if I shoot a few feet? Turn your head a little to your right, that's it, we want the light to fill up those wrinkles. Has anyone ever told you you've got the greatest wrinkles?"

Ekaterina, formal words of welcome on her lips, was stopped in her tracks with her mouth open, and in spite of their new understanding Kate had to struggle against a certain inner glee. "Nope," she said out loud, "I don't think anyone's ever told Emaa that before. This is Dinah Cookman, Emaa. Dinah's a photojournalist," she explained to her grandmother in a kind voice. "She ran out of gas and stopped to pick mushrooms so she could buy enough to get her to Anchorage. Dinah, this is my grandmother, Ekaterina Shugak."

Ekaterina regarded the wide lens of the camera, about all she could see of Dinah except for the mass of strawberry blonde curls billowing out behind it, with a fascination bordering on horror that nearly upset Kate's gravity for the second time.

"It's great to meet you, Mrs. Shugak. Is that right, Mrs. Shugak?"

"Yes, it is," Ekaterina replied with a readiness that surprised Kate.

"Were you born in Alaska?"

"Yes."

"In Chistona?"

"No, Atka."

"Is that another village nearby?"

"No, it is an island in the Aleutian Chain."

"Wow," Dinah said in hushed tones. "The Aleutians. How come you still don't live there?"

"My family moved here when the Japanese invaded Attu and Kiska."

"Wow!" Dinah said. "You mean you were expatriated! I read about that!" She struggled, one-handed, with her duster, eventually producing a book Kate saw was a paperback copy of Brian Garfield's *The Thousand-Mile War*. Someday when Dinah's back was turned Kate was going to inventory the pockets of that duster, just to reassure herself there wasn't an aperture to the fourth dimension secreted in one seam.

"Ah yes," Ekaterina said, nodding, "Mr. Garfield's book. Yes, we were among those people."

"It must have been an awful experience," Dinah said soberly, focusing the lens on Ekaterina's face, "forced out of your homes, moved hundreds of miles away from everything you knew."

"I was only a child," Ekaterina said (she had probably been close to Kate's present age, Kate thought), "and it was war."

"Why didn't you go back, after?"

Ekaterina shook her head. "There was nothing to go back to. Our village had been bombed, either by the Japanese or by the Americans so the Japanese could not use it for shelter. And we had relatives in Cordova and in Chenega. So we stayed."

Kate hadn't heard this many words come out of Ekaterina's mouth all at once in years. "Enough, Dinah," she said. "People are going to think that thing is permanently attached."

"Okay." Dinah lowered the camera. "This tape is almost full, anyway." Her eyes were bright and excited. "There's

stories all over this place just walking around on two legs. See that girl over there? She quit her job waitressing to pick mushrooms. Said she could make more money. And that guy? He builds log homes. He says the rain made them stop, so he's picking mushrooms instead. That guy cuts and sells firewood, but he said he can always cut wood. He says it's been two good years for Chistona, the first year they made money fighting the fire for the BLM, and now they're picking mushrooms for two bucks a pound."

She hesitated, shooting Kate a doubtful glance, and said hesitantly, as if suggesting something she knew to be in dubious taste, "Kate, nobody around here sets fires on purpose, do they?"

"Good heavens, no," Kate said. "Who's that guy?" She nodded at a tall, spare man with a high, smooth forehead and a full head of pure white hair.

Diverted, as Kate had meant her to be, Dinah said, "The guy who looks like an Old Testament prophet? I don't know. Kid next to him looks like a choirboy, though, doesn't he? Say, that's the same kid, isn't it?"

It was. The boy was back, standing at the old man's elbow, his fair, soft curls clustering around rosy cheeks and blue eyes. He looked positively cherubic, and at the same time the family resemblance between the two was evident in the broad brows, in the firm chin, in the expressive blue eyes that in the boy's face were wide and curious and in the man's, stern and curiously grim. Kate wondered how long it would be before the boy's eyes became like the man's.

The boy looked up suddenly and their eyes met. He didn't blush or duck his head or grab his grandfather's leg or do any of the things children do when confronted with the interest of strangers, and Kate revised her estimate of his age upward, to ten, maybe even eleven.

Fortunately the transformation of the boy's eyes from curious to grim was no concern of hers. "Look, it's our turn. Help me lift the buckets up on the flatbed. Emaa? Are you staying with Auntie Joy?" Ekaterina nodded, and Kate said, "Tell her I'll come visit on my way home. Come on, Dinah, tote that barge, lift that bale."

• • •

Bobby cooked lavishly that evening, roasting caribou in a Dutch oven over hot coals, stirring up a raspberry vinegar-white wine sauce in the interim out of the two crates of supplies he had insisted were essential to civilized life as we know it, at home or in the bush. The smell made Kate's mouth water, and was almost enough to make her forgive him for coercing her into hauling the crates up the hill to the campsite. The roast was served with a morel garnish, or rather, as Bobby explained, "We like a little meat with our mushrooms."

Dinah, her mouth full, said indistinctly, "It tastes so good I don't want to swallow. Bobby? Marry me.

"You only want me for my cooking."

"Damn straight. And there's no 'only' about it."

Kate didn't say anything at all. Afterward, the three of them lay around the fire in the setting sun, too stuffed to move, listening to thunder rumble at them from the edge of the horizon. They could see the rain come down from where they were, thin gray sheets of it hanging between the campsite and the Quilaks, turned to silver gilt by the slanting rays of the sun. "Well," Dinah said, burping without excuse, "that beats anything I ever bought out of the produce section at Safeway. *Agaricus bisporus* has nothing on *Morchella elata*"

Nobody asked but she told them anyway. "*Agaricus bisporus* is the cultivated mushroom. The one you get at your local grocery store for two-ninety-eight a pound."

Kate stirred herself enough to say, "Did you bring that desk encyclopedia you said you had in the van?"

Dinah waved a hand in the general direction of her backpack. With a burst of energy that left her exhausted, Kate snagged the pack by one strap and dragged it to her. The *Concise Columbia Encyclopedia* was on top of the pile inside. "Oh God," Bobby moaned, hiding his eyes, "not you, too."

"What you looking up?" Dinah said.

"Hillel," Kate replied absently. "Here he is. Hillel, flourished—I love that word, who knows now if he flourished or he withered on the vine?—from thirty B.C. to ten A.D. Born in Babylonia, he was a Jewish scholar and president of the Sanhedrin, which fostered a systematic, liberal—I wonder what liberal was in thirty B.C.?"

"Probably advocated crucifixion over burning," Bobby said lazily.

"—liberal interpretation of Hebrew Scripture, and was the spiritual and ethical leader of his generation. Shammai opposed his teachings."

"Who the hell was Shammai?"

Kate, taking that as an invitation, turned to the S's. "Shammai was a leader of the Sanhedrin who adopted a style of interpretation of Halakah that opposed the teachings of Hillel."

"So Hillel flourished in spite of Shammai," Dinah suggested.

Unheeding, Kate said, "And what, you ask, was the Halakah? It just so happens—" she turned back to the H's. "Aha. Halakah, or halacha"—she spelled it for their edification—"refers to that part of the Talmud concerned

31

with personal, communal and international activities, as well as with religious observance. Also known as the oral Law, as codified in the Mishna." Kate turned to the M's. "Mishna, Mishna, sounds like a Hari Krishna chant. Here we go. The Mishna's the basic textbook of Jewish life and thought, covers agriculture, marriage and divorce, and all civil and criminal matters."

Dinah said, "So if you wanted to know when to plant your corn, sing a psalm, party hearty, get hitched or hang a thief, you consulted the Mishna and it told you."

"I guess."

"Sort of like the Marine Bible," Bobby said admiringly, and at Dinah's questioning look added, "*The Marine Battle Skills Training Handbook*. You're issued one in boot camp. Covers everything from digging latrines to kissing brass ass. Where'd you hear about this guy Hillel?" he asked Kate.

"I was reading about him on my soap bottle," Kate replied blandly, and Bobby, after one incredulous stare, flopped back with a theatrical groan, but not without grabbing Dinah on his way down.

"May I ask you a personal question, Kate?" Dinah said, snuggling into Bobby's embrace with what Kate considered a disgustingly content expression on her face.

"No," Kate said.

"Where'd you get that scar on your throat?"

There was a brief silence. "A knife fight," Kate said finally. "Three years ago. Almost four, now."

"Tell me about it?"

Another silence. "I caught a child molester in the act. He had a knife."

Dinah winced. "Ouch."

Kate's mouth curled up at one corner, and Bobby, watching

32

curiously, was surprised. "I'll say."

"What happened to him?"

"I took the knife away from him."

"He in jail?"

Kate shook her head. "Dead."

Dinah didn't ask how; she didn't have to.

Kate stared at the fire for a moment, and then raised her eyes, meeting the blonde's with growing awareness. "You're good."

"You sure as hell are," Bobby agreed. He'd heard that story once, the first time he'd seen the scar. Then it had been new and swollen and red and angry, especially angry, but it had paled by comparison to Kate's barely restrained, all-consuming rage. By virtue of their long friendship he had been owed an explanation. She had given one, in short, terse sentences, every word of which cost her more than she could afford to pay, and Bobby had a strong enough sense of self-preservation and a high enough value of Kate's continuing friendship never to raise the subject again.

And now this blonde, from Outside no less, the rawest of cheechakos, the most innocent of Alaskan naifs, a literal babe in the woods, had asked a few simple questions and gotten the whole story, all of it, simply and succinctly and more, gotten it without attitude or resentment. "*Real* good," he said.

She nodded, taking the compliment as simple fact, without a trace of false modesty. "I know. It's what I do." She looked beyond Kate and her face lit up. "Oh! Look!"

Kate turned and beheld a full rainbow, a slender arch of primary colors stretching from the Canadian border to Tonsina. It was a delicate, perfect thing, and the three of them were held captive by the sight. Bobby had a slight smile on his dark face, Dinah looked dazed with delight, and Kate, after a

moment, recognized a feeling of proprietary pride.

The sun, taking its own sweet time, finally intersected the horizon and the rainbow began to dim. Dinah let out a sigh of pure rapture. "A full rainbow at twenty minutes past eleven in the evening. Only in Alaska."

Later, drifting off to sleep in her tent, Kate heard Bobby say in a cranky voice, "Just what the hell was the Sanhedrin, anyway?"

•••

The next day was a repeat of the previous six at slightly lower temperatures. Mutt roused from her state of heat-induced stupor and nipped Kate's behind as she bent over a patch of morels. Kate abandoned a bucket not half full and gave chase. For fifteen minutes they played tag, moving deeper into the blackened forest and becoming totally covered in black soot, until Kate tripped over a branch and went sprawling on her face. Spitting out ash, she raised her head to see Mutt staring down at her with an expression of gathering delight. Kate could just imagine what she looked like, and told the half-breed, "You should talk! You look like you've been hit with a bucket of creosote."

Then she noticed the mushrooms. Morels, hundreds of them, thousands of them, a virtual carpet of them. She jumped to her feet. "Dinah! Bring the buckets! There be fungi here!"

One clump of mushrooms perched on an elongated mound and seemed to grow thicker there than anywhere else. Kate waded toward it and began to pick.

"Kate! Kate, where are you? I found another sign! Amos 5:24!"

"Right here! I—" Kate paused, her hands full of mushrooms.

34

Next to her, the wolf-husky hybrid froze, head lowering between her shoulders, hackles rising, ears flattening, as a low, continuous growl issued from deep in her throat.

"Kate?" Dinah stumbled into the clearing, three empty buckets dangling from each hand. "Wow! Shroom heaven! I found another sign, Kate, Amos 5:24. Kate? What is it? What's wrong?"

"Stay there." Kate rose to her feet, and at the other woman's involuntary step forward repeated sharply, "Stay there."

"What is it?" Dinah said.

"Someone's body."

ABOUT KATE SHUGAK

KATE SHUGAK is a native Aleut working as a private investigator in Alaska. She's 5 foot 1 inch tall, carries a scar that runs from ear to ear across her throat and owns a half-wolf, half-husky dog named Mutt. Resourceful, strong-willed, defiant, Kate is tougher than your average heroine – and she needs to be to survive the worst the Alaskan wilds can throw at her.

To discover more – and some tempting special offers – why not visit our website: www.headofzeus.com

MEET THE AUTHOR

In 1991 Dana Stabenow, born in Alaska and raised on a 75-foot fishing trawler, was offered a three-book deal for the first of her Kate Shugak mysteries. In 1992, the first in the series, *A Cold Day for Murder*, received an Edgar Award from the Crime Writers of America.

You can contact Dana Stabenow via her website: www.stabenow.com